THE DEATH

OF

CASSIE WHITE

A CAITLYN JAMISON MYSTERY

Bobbie Sue —

Enjoy!

M. E. MAKI

Mary E. Maki

This is a work of fiction. Names, characters, places, and incidents are either the product of the author's imagination or are used fictitiously. Any resemblance to actual persons living or dead, events or locales is entirely coincidental.

Visit the author at memaki.com

Published in the United States by Mary E. Maki

ISBN- 9781692753535
Imprint: Independently published

Cover photo: Laura Dent, Northern Neck Images [NorthernNeckImages.com]
Cover photo enhancement: Charles Lawson [Thehighlanderstudios.com]
Cover Design: Six Penny Graphics, Fredericksburg, VA
Author photo: Raymond Maki

Printed in the United States of America

The Caitlyn Jamison Mystery Series

An Unexpected Death

Fatal Dose

The Death of Cassie White

~ ONE ~

A cold wind-driven rain lashed against the mobile home's windows while another storm brewed inside.

Sixty-five-year-old Lilla Higley faced her husband. Her left hand rested on the back of a wooden kitchen chair while her right hand slammed her cane onto the floral-patterned linoleum floor. The cane's tip made an indent in the soft flooring, but she didn't care. She had a point to make. She raised her voice to be heard over the rain that pounded the metal roof.

"Don't go. This job is trouble."

Bud Higley zipped up his overalls in response.

"It's raining. What you clear will wash away. You'll end up doing it again tomorrow. Time and money wasted. Mr. Russell won't pay twice."

Before she could continue, he cut her off.

"I don't have a choice. Besides, tomorrow I have to start work on his marina project."

"We can do without the money. I'll stop treatment," she countered, both hands now on the cane to steady herself.

"That's not an option," he replied, his weathered face turning red. "I'm not angry with you. It's just that . . ."

". . . our state in life," she finished his sentence. After forty-seven years of marriage she knew him well.

Bud kicked at a chair across the table from where his wife stood.

"Nothing's changed. We're still the poor black folks living among the rich white ones. When I think about how our ancestors toiled in those fields," his finger pointing down their long driveway to the fields beyond, "and how they suffered, sometimes . . ."

"Sometimes what?" she asked, stopping him, worried about what he was thinking, what he might do.

Bud hesitated and rubbed his aching leg. Another reason he shouldn't go out in the weather.

"Sometimes I feel we're owed. Instead, I take these jobs, whether I want them or not," Bud said.

Lilla wiped away a tear. She hated fighting with him.

"We've had a good life. We can't stop progress and we shouldn't dwell on the past."

Bud had stopped listening. He bent down to tie his boots.

"Do you remember?" he said.

To appease him, she went along.

"When we considered Ingram Bay as our own town? That was a long time ago," she hesitated, tired of their game. "Get someone else to clear that parcel. Rest today and do the marina job tomorrow."

Her illness had changed their lives. The chemo treatments were expensive and they had no insurance. Bud blamed himself for putting her in harm's way, though it had been her decision to bring him lunch that day.

~

Lilla's warning ran through his head as he drove to the site. Her premonitions were usually right. When he arrived, the rain had let up, but a cool early April wind continued. Spring *should have* arrived by now, but this year winter hadn't eased its grip. He unloaded his bulldozer, got in, closed the windows, and then leaned forward to ponder the property he was to clear. The upscale condominiums planned for this site would destroy land that had been an important part of his life. This virgin forest would be clear-cut and developed into buildings and parking lots.

He'd bought the dozer on credit and paid it off over the years with work he'd gotten from the locals. Then northern developers, like Vince Russell, arrived, purchased land, and started building houses, condominiums and marinas. He'd not questioned the projects. Until now. Local contractors weren't in a position to turn down work. If he declined this job, Vince Russell would hire another contractor and Bud couldn't afford to lose his place in the queue.

State-protected conservation land separated the parcel Vince Russell had bought from the new Forest Green retirement community. Residential growth over the last five years had changed their hometown. Trees and brush had been clear-cut so newcomers could have water views, which resulted in bank erosion that polluted the rivers and the Chesapeake Bay.

He and Lilla could no longer afford to frequent the local hotel's restaurant since its renovation that earned it a five-star rating. Although these projects provided employment for local contractors, where would it end? Would no forests or fields remain? Would he and Lilla be able to afford to live in Ingram Bay?

He brought himself back to the present. He had a job to do, but the plans still concerned him. The driveway would go over into the conservation easement and that was his conundrum.

Bud rubbed his short gray beard while he agonized over what to do. The condo complex should not have been planned so close to the easement. Vince Russell must have known. Bud ran Vince's call through his mind once more.

"Clear a swath to the back of the new condo complex. I'll drop off a set of plans in the lockbox at the site. Get the job done early, got it?"

The phone went dead before Bud questioned the instructions. That's how Vince operated.

Bud studied the plans again as the dozer vibrated beneath him. The driveway would circle out and away from the main unit to the garages *behind* the building. It would violate the easement. He studied the plans once more, then folded them up and put them aside.

He put the dozer in gear and drove ahead, clearing a small section at a time. His anxiety rose when he approached the outer corner. It started to rain. He stopped to let the downpour pass. When it let up, he put the dozer in low gear and angled the swath. When he reached the back of the condo units, he wiped his brow; his heart raced. Another pass and he hoped it'd satisfy Vince.

"Don't go." Lilla's warning went through his head.

On the return he noticed runoff from the recent downpour had flowed into the exposed soil and turned his clean swath into angry rivulets. Was there an underground spring? Either way, he'd have to make another pass to smooth it out.

Lilla was right. I should have waited.

The dozer crawled ahead until it reached the area where his first pass had gone over the property line. He stopped. Colored fabric and what appeared to be a white stick protruded out of the muddy ground.

What the . . . is that?

He checked the time. Vince was waiting to hear about the job, but he needed to satisfy his curiosity and check the damage from the run-off. If there were a spring, it would complicate the project, and he'd have to report it to Vince as soon as possible.

Let's see what this is.

He slipped as he stepped onto the muddy ground. He reached for the dozer handle, righted himself, and walked over to where he'd made the first pass. Some kind of cloth. He walked closer and moved the stick, but it wasn't a stick. He went to the dozer, retrieved a shovel, and gently parted the earth.

What the . . . Dear Lord.

He couldn't believe his eyes. Bones were among the rotted fabric.

Bud froze. His mind swirled with possibilities, but he knew the bones were human.

Who do I call first?

He considered the options and the repercussions of each. He ran back to the dozer and found his phone. His hands shook as he dialed 911. When the operator answered, in a trembling voice, Bud told him where he was and what he'd found. Then he called his boss.

~ TWO ~

Caitlyn Jamison shifted in her seat. She was excited for the opportunity to interview with the SafeGrid board, but also anxious. The interview was taking longer than she expected. A furtive glance at her phone confirmed that fact.

The board was comprised of six area businessmen and John Graves, the CEO. The portfolio open in front of her indicated the one dressed in shirt and tie was Jack Doan, president of the local bank. The others wore appropriate attire for their jobs, construction, marina manager, a drugstore manager, and the owner of the local hardware store. The last member, also in suit and tie, was William Weber, SafeGrid's chief financial officer.

*Aren't there any business*women *in town?*

During the past hour she'd fielded questions on every detail of her education, graphic arts skills, client list, and even her personal life. But they hadn't asked what *she could do* for them.

The company was in Virginia's Northern Neck, a three-hour drive from her home office in Arlington, and in the same town where her parents now lived. When the company's CEO John Graves had set the date of the interview, she'd hesitated. Her biggest client, The Bay Foundation, in Washington, DC, had scheduled its annual meeting in two weeks. The annual report had yet to be finished and sent to the printer. She couldn't finish that job until the foundation provided the latest data from the Chesapeake Bay.

Clients, deadlines, and responsibilities flew through her head. Could she manage her current workload and take on a new client? On the positive side, she'd grow her portfolio *and* achieve financial security. Her hands remained tightly clasped in her lap as she struggled with those thoughts and waited for the questions to end.

Is it a gender issue, age, or both?

At thirty-five, she had the experience *and* an impressive portfolio. To prepare for this meeting, she'd had her lush brown shoulder length hair styled and highlighted and her nails professionally done. She'd agonized over her outfit, finally deciding on black slacks with a matching jacket over a cream colored blouse. She dressed to look like the professional she was.

Before he invited her to interview, John Graves vetted her by phone and email. He seemed genuinely interested in having her awarded the contract, and during those conversations he'd shared his vision for the company's marketing plan. At the end of their conversations she'd assured him she could do the job. It was then he told her the board would make the final decision.

A slight shake of her head showed her impatience. The men got the message; their questions ended.

John Graves turned to her.

"Caitlyn, do you have anything to add?"

"Actually, I do. May I?" she asked, stood and pointed to the screen.

John Graves nodded, looked around the table and received confirmation from the board members.

She placed her tablet on the table and connected it wirelessly to the room's projector.

The men stirred in their seats.

"Gentleman, thank you for inviting me here today. You've reviewed my qualifications and explained the company's vision. I've researched electromagnetic pulses, and learned the average age of the country's high voltage transformers is forty years. Now, I'd like to give you a preview of what *I* can do for you."

She put up the first slide.

"On the left is SafeGrid's current brochure; on the right is a draft of my vision for the company's new brochure."

She put up the next slide.

"The brochure would feature an overview of SafeGrid, and on the next page a graph of the country's power grid and what will happen when a section of that grid fails."

The room was silent. She put up the next slide.

"Moving to the website, this is how I envision it to look. I incorporated information to get your message across, specifically that the country's electrical transformers *have* to be replaced. If they are not," she put up the last slide, "the country will look like this."

The men glanced at each other.

She scrolled her laser pointer across the screen that showed a devastated population.

"Without power, Internet routers would be gone, air traffic control down, there wouldn't be food, fuel, or communication. Chaos. *This* is the reality, and it's why you are here this morning instead of tending to your own businesses. *You* want to stop this unthinkable tragedy before it happens."

Caitlyn let her words and the graphics sink in before putting up the next set of slides featuring examples of marketing materials.

"If you hire me as your marketing consultant, I will work closely with you and focus on the urgency of securing the country's electrical grid by replacing the outdated transformers with your product."

She sat down and tried to gauge how the board received her presentation.

"Thank you, Caitlyn. That was excellent," John Graves said.

The board joined in with nods and thanks.

"Follow me to the sitting area in the front while the board discusses what you presented today. That was a powerful presentation. I'm sure they'll consider you as the top candidate."

"Thank you," Caitlyn responded, though she had no idea how her presentation was received.

"While you wait, can I get you anything?" he asked.

"Water would be great."

He returned with a chilled bottle of water.

"Make yourself comfortable. I'll be back in a few minutes."

She looked around the small room. A desk and chair sat opposite the door that faced the parking lot. Apparently the back door was used as the main entrance. The desk was clear. There didn't seem to be other employees in this building. She'd have to find out where the transformers were produced. She checked her phone and realized the "few minutes" had turned into twenty. She was not used to sitting. John Graves finally came to fetch her and they walked back into the boardroom. Conversation ended as she entered.

The board members were introduced at the start of the interview, but when William Webber stood, he reintroduced himself. The man was tall, over six feet, thin, and his thick jet-black hair streaked with gray was combed back. He had a commanding presence, and his rectangular face featured a stern expression that made him appear formidable.

He didn't intimidate her. She sat straight in her chair and made eye contact.

He turned to face her.

"Thank you for coming," his deep voice in a monotone.

"You're welcome," she replied with a forced smile. Her mind raced. Could she have provided better answers? Should she have put more projects into her portfolio? Were they intimidated by her technology skills? Had she been too forward with the graphic scenes of a transformer and power grid failure?

Her stomach clenched.

"After some discussion . . ." he started and paused.

Spit it out.

"The board voted to offer you a one-year contract."

Relief washed over her, but before she could thank him, he continued.

"Besides signing the contract, you are also required to sign a confidentiality agreement."

The pace of his words came faster now that he was on familiar ground, though his stern expression remained.

"The confidentiality agreement covers all marketing content you develop on our behalf and *all information* you are privy to from the board meetings. You are required to attend board meetings held the first Friday of the month. Will that be a problem?"

She'd not been told about the mandatory meetings. Could she make that time commitment?

Exciting new challenges and financial security went through her mind.

Her hesitation was brief. She'd figure out a way to manage her workload.

"That won't be a problem."

"Good." William Weber pushed the contract and the confidentiality statement across the table.

Warning bells went off in her head and her anxiety heightened.

What are they not telling me?

SafeGrid built specialty-equipped high voltage transformers, nothing that she considered warranted confidentiality.

William Webber let out a frustrated sigh while she studied the contract. Colored tabs showed where she should sign. She ignored the tabs while she glanced through the pages. The document was standard language. The last page listed her duties. She read through the list and noted the confidentiality agreement at the end.

She'd have to work additional hours to keep up with her current clients, but the bottom line was—her bottom line. She signed the contract and the confidentiality agreement and passed the documents back across the table to Mr. Webber who droned on about her responsibilities for developing and managing the promotional and educational component for the company's website and marketing materials.

Then John Graves dropped a bomb.

"Caitlyn will also be our liaison between the government and utility companies."

Silence.

Stunned, she glanced at John Graves and then William Webber. Not only had he not talked with his board about this assignment, he had not cleared it with her. This responsibility was not on the list she'd reviewed in her contract, and not a good sign.

Several awkward seconds passed before the board gave a half-hearted clap.

She nodded and placed her copy of the contract in her briefcase. While she thought about the liaison position, she noticed whispered conversations amongst the men.

They're as confused about this as I am.

John Graves stood and picked up his gavel. The murmuring among the board members ceased. The meeting continued and when it ended she had taken pages of notes.

Each board member stopped by to congratulate her as they left the room. She picked up her briefcase and headed to the front door, her head in a whirl about how she was going to manage her workload. She stopped when John Graves caught up with her.

"Thank you for coming. You did a great job. The board was reluctant to hire a woman, but your presentation and Bill Webber won them over."

"What?" It surprised her that Mr. Webber had anything nice to say.

"Bill puts on a tough act, but he knows talent when he sees it. He was testing you. In the discussion he made it clear you were the top choice, the only choice for our company. As you get to know the community a little better you'll learn that he's involved with several organizations in town."

"Thank you for telling me. I've learned that people play different roles depending on the situation. I'm also curious about where the production plant is located."

"We use this building for meeting clients and file storage. Our production happens in a large warehouse about ten miles south of here."

"I'd like to visit it some day," she said.

"That can be arranged," he replied.

She didn't want to ruin this golden opportunity, but she had to be honest.

"Mr. Graves, I wasn't told that I'd be the company's government and utility liaison. It wasn't mentioned in our conversations and not listed in my contract. I don't have that experience, nor do I have the time."

"I didn't mean to surprise you, or the board, but we need to get the government and utilities to compromise on funding. It shouldn't take too much of your time, but I should have discussed it with you and the board first," he admitted.

Caitlyn nodded though not convinced she could or wanted the additional responsibility.

"I'll get up to speed on the transformer replacement project and then we'll talk about the government liaison position."

"That works," he replied. "Develop the text for the website and get started on the legislators and utilities. I'll be in touch with deadlines and set a date for another meeting. Maybe we can meet in a more comfortable setting."

Another meeting?

She had to get back to Arlington and work on The Bay Foundation's annual report. Meeting in "a more comfortable setting" was not what she wanted. John Graves was attractive, but he was twenty years older, and besides, she kept business and personal relationships separate. She took a deep breath, smiled, and replied, "Thanks again for the opportunity. I'll do my best."

"I'm sure you will," he said with a smile, taking a step closer.

Caitlyn took a step back, smiled, and then headed to her car.

~ THREE ~

Bud Higley stood next to his boss while Ingram Bay's Sheriff Charles Goodall, breathing heavily, cordoned off the area around the remains. The sheriff should have retired five years ago, but he held on because no one challenged him for the job, and he enjoyed his status in the community.

Sheriff Goodall had chastised them for violating the conservation easement, but they were saved from further harangue by the arrival of the county coroner. The coroner slipped and slid down the muddy path complaining about having to be out in these conditions. Bud had no patience for complainers. He'd worked hard all his life and now in his sixties, he still worked hard, in all conditions.

"What's the plan now, Mr. Russell?" Bud asked staring straight ahead as he watched the coroner bag the bones and fabric.

Vince Russell rubbed his chin.

"Start clearing for the new marina. When I get this project figured out, you can finish the driveway."

"I'll go there as soon as the sheriff releases us," Bud replied.

Don't go. Lilla's words returned.

"I'll be in touch as soon as we can get back onto this project. I've got people waiting to move into these condos," Vince said.

Bud, still shaken from finding the remains, didn't understand how it could be back to business as usual. Vince Russell was treating this incidence as a minor inconvenience. He walked to his truck, shaking his head. It seemed that money always came first with not a thought given to who was buried in the shallow grave and how that person got there.

~

Vince Russell stood alone in the wooded area that now had yellow crime scene tape strung from tree to tree and across the path of his proposed driveway. He'd thought this the perfect spot for his condominium complex. Woodlands surrounded the property, and to complete the aesthetic appeal, he'd planned the garage units at the back of the building. When he first walked the property, he noticed a cleared path down to the bay, probably used by ATV enthusiasts. Now that he owned the property that would no longer be allowed. Instead, he'd enlarge the pathway, add docks for residents' boats, and charge for dock privileges.

He hadn't lied about people waiting to move into this prime spot, so he had to figure out a way to save the project. He walked back to his car and headed south into town. He had work to do.

~ FOUR ~

Caitlyn rushed into her parents' house, excited to share her news.

In January they had purchased a home five miles north of the town of Ingram Bay, Virginia in the Forest Green active adult community. The house, on a cul-de-sac with woods to the south and east, had an unobstructed view of the Chesapeake Bay. An open floor plan pulled people in and drew them toward the great room's floor-to-ceiling windows. Two bedrooms were on the main level and one bedroom and bath in the loft. Her father's office was adjacent to the foyer and gave him private space to continue consulting for the oil companies he had worked for his entire career. The kitchen, off to the right of the great room, was light and spacious, which made her mother happy.

As Caitlyn stepped inside the house she heard her father's booming voice exclaim, "that son-of-a-bitch got his due."

She shook her head.

What's he up to now?

A welcome bark from her white Shih Tzu, Summit, greeted her at the door.

"You're a good boy," she said as she scooped him up and nuzzled his soft white fur. Summit had been her cousin's dog, but when her cousin died a year ago, and his parents didn't want the dog, Caitlyn adopted him and he, her. He licked her face in response. She gave him a gentle squeeze, and placed him back on the tile floor. She looked through into the great room and admired the unobstructed view of the Chesapeake Bay.

Breathtaking.

This was only the second time she'd been to her parents' house since they'd moved to Ingram Bay, and although she'd hoped they'd move to Arlington, her father's stubborn streak overruled her objections. He wanted a water view.

"In here," her mother Ann called from the kitchen.

Caitlyn followed the sweet tangy aroma of fresh-baked blueberry muffins. As she entered the kitchen, her mother and another woman, whom she assumed was a neighbor, sat at the kitchen table. Her mother's favorite Wedgewood teapot was within easy reach.

Her father paced from one end of the kitchen to the other.

Caitlyn's mouth watered as she glanced at the muffins on the counter.

"Help yourself," her mother said, taking a sip of tea.

Ann Jamison was the ultimate hostess, though she hadn't let the years entertaining her husband's oil company colleagues define her. She volunteered at various organizations, exercised regularly, and did her best to maintain her health. It showed. Her clear complexion showed few signs of aging. Her dark brown hair was cut to accent her face and her blue eyes. Caitlyn was proud of her mother's accomplishments, and especially her cooking skills.

She chose the largest muffin, placed it on a napkin, took a china teacup from the cupboard, and joined the women.

"Another cup?" Ann asked her guest.

The woman reached for the teapot to refill her cup and then turned to acknowledge Caitlyn.

"Tricia, this is our daughter Caitlyn. Cate, this is Tricia Reilly. She lives three houses down. We've become good friends, and she's filling us in on the news."

Tricia was of medium build and in good physical shape. Her short-cropped reddish blond hair set off her green eyes. Her expression, though, was intense.

Former military, I bet.

"It's nice to meet you, Tricia," Caitlyn said and took a seat next to her mother. "These muffins are delicious, Mom."

"I'm glad you like them," Ann replied with a wink.

Caitlyn leaned towards her mother and whispered, "What's Dad talking about?"

Her mother leaned in and whispered back, "A developer in town. Apparently his construction project went over the conservation easement, and Tricia was telling us about skeletal remains found there this morning."

"What?" Caitlyn said, putting her muffin down.

"Is anyone listening?" Her father demanded. He'd stopped pacing and leaned against the granite counter to catch his breath.

"I am, Dad," Caitlyn said, wiping blueberry juice from around her mouth. Life had been harder on her father. His hair was whiter, his skin more wrinkled. He'd endured years of travel and stress with his job, and that resulted in a less healthy lifestyle. His heart attack last year should have been a warning, but she feared he didn't heed it.

"Tell me about the skeletal remains. Were they found close by?"

"Close by?" her father yelled.

"Herb, settle down," her mother instructed. "Remember your heart."

Ignoring his wife's warning, he continued.

"State-protected conservation land borders our property. That developer, Vince Russell, should know better."

"You're upset about the condos he wants to build there," Ann stated.

"He's also building another marina. And, I wouldn't put it past him to build docks for those condos," Herb countered. "He's clear-cutting the forests down to the shoreline, and that has a negative impact on the waterways."

Caitlyn listened to the verbal volley between her parents.

"Dad, don't you realize when they built this house trees were removed to give you a view of the bay? And besides, you've only been here three months. How do you know the developer's plans?"

"I know because," Herb hesitated, annoyed at her questions, and retorted, "the guys at the coffee shop told me."

Caitlyn rolled her eyes and took another bite of muffin.

Oblivious to the body language, Herb continued. "I checked with the county clerk and he verified the boundaries."

Her father took a breath.

"Recently, one of our neighbors, a retired surveyor, measured and found the construction flags were too close to the easement."

"So what did you do?" Caitlyn asked.

"We went to a town board meeting and voiced our complaint and things got . . . confrontational." Herb paused.

"You didn't," Caitlyn said, putting what remained of her muffin down in disbelief.

"I'm afraid he did," her mother jumped in. "I was at that meeting. In polite society one doesn't stand up in a meeting and threaten to kill someone. But that's exactly what your father did."

"Dad, no," Caitlyn wailed.

"We paid a lot for this house with the caveat nothing would be built near us. Then this developer comes along and clears land for a condo complex, violates the conservation easement—think about the noise, the traffic," Herb said.

Caitlyn shook her head. "I agree that the construction plans should not have violated the easement, but if he owns the adjacent property . . ."

Herb ignored his daughter's rational comments.

"I hope finding those remains will put a stop to the construction."

"How were the remains discovered?" Caitlyn asked, pouring herself a cup of herbal tea.

"Early this morning a guy was clearing for the driveway," her father explained.

Tricia leaned forward and said, "That would be Bud Higley, a local contractor. He's in his mid-sixties, just trying to etch out a living. His wife Lilla isn't well and I suspect it's put a strain on their budget. He does a lot of work for the developer Vince Russell. Bud's a good man."

Herb cleared his throat and took a deep breath.

"When this Higley guy was bulldozing onto the conservation land, he uncovered human remains."

"How awful," Caitlyn gasped.

"Are they certain the remains are human?" Ann asked.

Tricia jumped in. "I heard the coroner declared the remains are human and sent them to the medical examiner's office in Richmond."

"You seem to know the area. Have you lived here long?" Caitlyn asked.

"I've lived in Virginia for forty years. Worked out of Norfolk, but frequently visited here. When I retired I bought a house in this development."

"I'm glad you're helping Mom and Dad get acclimated to the community."

"Have they identified the remains?" Ann asked.

"It's too early to tell, and I suspect the morgue in Richmond is busy. This case will be assigned a number and put in a queue," Tricia replied. She took another sip of tea.

"A body buried in a shallow grave so close gives me the shivers," Ann added.

"Interesting. I wonder how the remains got there," Caitlyn said.

Her father scowled. "I thought you'd learned your lesson about investigating crimes."

"I have, but a cold case is different."

Before her parents could discourage her, she took her cup to the counter.

"I've got work to do," she said, "Let me know what you find out, and it's nice to meet you, Tricia"

"Wait," Herb Jamison instructed.

Caitlyn stopped.

"What?" she asked.

"How did your meeting go? Did you get the job?"

In the excitement of learning about the skeletal remains, she'd neglected to tell them.

"Yes, but it was a grueling interview. The board was hesitant to hire a woman, but I won them over."

"That's great, Cate. We're proud of you," her father said. He gave her a big hug.

Ann and Tricia added their congratulations.

"The job will be a challenge, *and* I had to sign a confidentiality agreement."

"Like government top secret stuff?" her father asked.

"Nothing top secret, and I don't know why I had to sign a confidentiality agreement. SafeGrid is a small company that manufactures replacement transformers strong enough to withstand an electromagnetic pulse. Most of the country's transformers are old and fragile," she explained.

Tricia leaned in.

"It's a start-up?" Herb stated.

"Good question. I did initial research on the company, but it all happened so fast, and I've been preoccupied with another client's annual meeting report."

"I'm glad it's located here," Ann stated. "Small companies are healthy for the local economy."

Herb walked over to the counter, picked up his laptop and brought it to the table. "Let's see what we can find on this company."

Ann moved closer to her husband.

"The site explains what would happen if our country experienced an electromagnetic pulse, either natural or manmade. No information on its history. I wonder who's on the board."

"John Graves is the CEO. He contacted me a month ago. William Webber is the chief financial officer. He's intense, but I guess you have to be when you're in charge of a firm's finances. I don't remember the rest of the names. Here's the company's portfolio. It has photos and short bios of the board members." She slid the portfolio over to her father. He continued to tap the laptop's keys.

"You don't need to do a background check, Dad. It's just a client. I'll do the marketing job they've hired me to do. The pay is good and it'll give me more experience, and besides, I like John Graves. He's personable and dedicated."

She turned to Tricia.

"You've been in the area awhile. Do you know any of the board members?"

Tricia glanced at the portfolio and then pushed it back across the table.

"Can't say I do."

Before Caitlyn asked another question, the ding of an incoming email came into her father's account.

"Answers about the remains," her father announced. "It says 'Items found near the remains indicate those of a young girl. Sheriff Goodall checked a missing person's database, but didn't find a report.'"

"I'm sure the sheriff will investigate, or would this fall under state police jurisdiction?" Caitlyn asked.

"Don't get involved," her father warned.

"I don't intend to," she said, her fingers crossed.

With a nod to her mother and Tricia, Caitlyn headed up the stairs to her room.

~

Caitlyn ushered Summit into the guest bedroom located in the house's loft, plunked down on the bed, picked up her phone and sent her friend Ethan Ewing a text. She'd met Ethan when she learned about her cousin's murder and inserted herself into the investigation. As sheriff of the town, Ethan had allowed her to help, though his motive was to keep an eye on her. She proved to be a valuable asset as she could evaluate the clues and think outside the box. They solved the crime in record time. A bond had formed and they wanted a closer relationship. The obstacle was distance. He worked in Upstate New York; she in Northern Virginia. They'd stayed in close touch by phone and email, and he'd want to know she got the SafeGrid contract. She also wanted to tell him about the skeletal remains found this morning. She leaned back on the big blue and white bed pillows and wished he could come to Ingram Bay and help solve the case. She knew they could do it before the local sheriff or the state police.

She didn't intend to get involved in an investigation, but the fact that a young girl had been buried in a shallow grave bothered her. The girl should be identified and her killer caught. Caitlyn's sense of justice boiled up inside. Her next step would be to talk with the medical examiner.

She typed a text to Ethan. *Got the job; skeletal remains found nearby. Call me.*

She added a heart emoji and then deleted it. She hated walking on eggshells with their relationship—another issue that had to be resolved. Soon.

She opened her laptop and found the phone number for the Richmond Coroner's Office.

"City Morgue," a female voice answered.

"I'd like to talk with someone about the human remains brought there this morning."

"May I ask who's calling?"

She had to come up with a reason. She didn't want to deceive, but she had to know.

"My parents live near the site where the remains were found. I've helped with investigations before and hoped I could assist in the identification."

There was a pause before the woman responded.

"Please hold."

Music played while she waited. What other ways could she get the information?

"I'll connect you now."

Her call went to the voicemail of a Dr. Anderson, and when the opportunity to leave a message came, she was informed the doctor's mailbox was full.

~ FIVE ~

Dr. Chad Owens, Marine Biologist from the State University of New York at Stony Brook, leaned onto the podium and surveyed the young faces. For a mid-week early morning lecture the auditorium of the Northern Neck Community College was near capacity. Laptops were open and the students ready to take notes. They were the future of science. He hoped his talk would convince them to major in marine science. Area high school students had been invited and from the tentative not-sure-I-should-be-here expression on some faces, those students were also in attendance.

He'd agonized over this talk. It had to be in-depth enough to challenge the college students, but not so advanced it would discourage the younger ones.

He was in Ingram Bay, Virginia, as a consultant to The Bay Foundation. The foundation board needed him to verify the latest data on the health of the Chesapeake Bay before submitting it at its annual meeting. When a professor at the community college learned he was in the area, he was asked to give a presentation. Wedged in between his duties with The Bay Foundation, he'd written, edited and re-edited his presentation.

Relieved that this morning's talk was his last commitment, he rapped the gavel. The lecture hall quieted. As he began his opening remarks, his cell phone vibrated. Three calls arrived in rapid succession.

A question-and-answer period followed his presentation, and then everyone proceeded to the foyer to enjoy coffee, tea, and an assortment of pastries. The students talked about the lecture and continued to ask his opinion on various issues. There was no time to check his phone, and it was another half hour before he could get away.

When he got to his car, he threw his laptop and the small gift-in-lieu-of-honorarium on the passenger seat. He pulled out his cell and saw he had several messages. Two were from Charles at the foundation office, the third from his wife, Emma.

"What the hell's going on?" he said. Then panic struck. He had two teenage boys back home.

He accessed his messages and listened to Emma's first. She said that Charles had been trying to reach him. Chad then listened to Charles' messages.

"Chad. It's Charles with the foundation. Call me."

The next message was from Charles again.

"Chad. Just remembered you're at the college. There's a problem in the bay. Our scientists and staff left yesterday afternoon for a conference in California. No one's available to assess the situation. Call as soon as your lecture is over."

There go our plans, Chad thought.

The Bay Foundation's headquarters were in Washington, D.C., but he was working out of their field office in Ingram Bay. He'd put in long hours this week reviewing their procedures and statistics on the health of the Chesapeake Bay and its tributaries. Late yesterday afternoon he'd approved the validity of the data needed for the foundation's annual report. That report would announce that the bay's health was much improved thanks to the foundation's work in educating the population upstream on use of pollutants. The pressure had been intense. Future funding opportunities were contingent on this report.

He was tired, angry, and frustrated. He needed to get back to the university. Classes started next Monday, and he still had prep to do. He also had a responsibility to The Bay Foundation. How did this problem suddenly arise? He'd checked and rechecked all the samples. His analysis of the data was correct.

He called Emma, explained the situation, and then returned the call to Charles.

"Chad. Thanks for calling," Charles answered breathless.

"What's so urgent?" Chad asked, trying to keep frustration out of his voice.

"A Tangier Island waterman reported a dead zone in the bay. Says it's growing fast and emitting a strange odor."

"How can that be?" Chad asked.

"It wasn't there earlier this week when we took samples. You've approved and signed-off on our data."

"When was this discovered?"

"Late yesterday."

"During the storm?"

"Yes. I don't have more details, and you're the only scientist left in the area to investigate the report."

Chad let out a sigh. "I'll come right over to the office, and I'll need to talk to that waterman. Today. Charter a boat."

~

Chad removed his reading glasses and massaged his sinuses. He applied pressure points under his brow, and then at the back of his head to relieve the headache that resulted from intense concentration. He'd gone over the foundation's latest water samples several times. None of them showed evidence of a dead zone ready to bloom. Charles placed a cup of coffee down in front of him.

"Thanks. Any luck with the boat?"

"The marina manager is working on it. He'll call back as soon as he can arrange one. He knows it's urgent."

"I'm going back to the hotel. Call me when the boat is available and I'll meet you at the hotel's marina."

~

Just over an hour later Chad and Charles stepped onto Tangier Island. Joseph Wheeler, the waterman who'd alerted them to the new dead zone, met them at the dock. He was a tall man with a short gray beard, his weathered skin indicated years of hard work on the water. After a quick greeting, Joseph was silent, his gait halting, his posture bent, as they followed him to the nearby Situation Room, a gathering place where watermen discussed the catch of the day and other important issues.

Four men were there when they arrived. Non-islanders were referred to as "strangers," so Chad was not bothered by their curious stares.

Two men occupied a table in the middle of the room and were discussing tide tables. The other two were off to the side busy mending nets. Chad expected it was likely they'd hung around to learn the reason these two strangers were on the island.

Chad chose a table in the back of the room. He turned to Joseph and asked, "Would you like a more private place to talk?"

Joseph looked around the room.

"No. This is okay."

Chad placed a recorder on the table in front of Joseph and explained what it was for.

"There may be details we won't catch here. The recording will allow us to go over your description of the dead zone, how you came upon it, and other observations you might have," Chad explained. "Your insights will be valuable in helping us to figure this out."

Joseph stared at the device, but after a moment he nodded his assent. He wanted to get this over with and go home.

Chad noticed Joseph's hesitation, so he began his questions before the man changed his mind.

"Let's begin. For the record, please state your name and occupation."

Joseph Wheeler regarded the recording device and tentatively began his story.

"My name is Joseph Wheeler. I'm a waterman." He thought a minute and added, "Like my father and grandfather before me. Every day but Sunday I'm on the water, crabbing, fishing, and scouting out new territory."

He glanced at Chad.

"You're doing great. Tell us what happened yesterday," Chad coaxed.

"A storm came up. We didn't go out," Joseph stated.

Chad nodded for Joseph to continue.

"Some of us spent the morning in our shanties tidying up and repairing nets. We spent the afternoon here. Not much gets solved, but it's a way to spend time when we're not out on the water."

"Although there were storms in the area, you left the situation room and went out on the water when you knew it could be dangerous," Chad stated for benefit of the recording.

Joseph hung his head.

"On my way back to the docks the day before I noticed a film. It had an unusual smell."

"What kind of smell?"

"Like garlic."

He halted and glanced at Charlie who was taking notes.

"It sounds strange, but I'm telling ya what it was like," he said, twisting in his chair.

"That's okay, Mr. Wheeler. We understand. We appreciate your being candid with us. It will help identify the substance. Please continue."

"It was near the Virginia shoreline. People on the mainland don't understand the impact of putting chemicals on their lawns and dumping pollutants into the rivers. They think they are far removed from the bay, but in fact the watershed spreads hundreds of miles to the north and west. The film and the smell bothered me all night. My eyes aren't as good as they once were. I had to go back out to confirm what I saw."

The man's expression showed a range of emotions. It wouldn't be easy for a waterman to admit making a mistake when it came to the water, but his actions didn't make sense. Not for an experienced waterman. There was more to this story.

~

Chad handed Joseph a bottle of water and they took a break. The interview was difficult for the seasoned waterman.

What is he not telling us?

Joseph was tense, so Chad took the conversation in another direction.

"Do you have a family?" Chad asked, sitting back and taking a sip from his water bottle.

After some hesitation, Joseph responded, "Yes."

"Tell me about them."

Joseph's face lit up, and he relaxed.

"My wife is Sarah and we have two grown children, a son and daughter. Our daughter Christiana married a waterman and they live on Long Bridge Road. They have one son. Sarah comes from generations of watermen and her parents live near us on King's Street. My folks are gone, and are buried in our yard."

Charles drew his eyebrows together, his head tipped with a questioning look, so Joseph explained.

"Islanders buried their dead in their yards since there isn't a lot of land on Tangier."

"I'm aware of the custom. Is your son a waterman, too?" Chad asked.

The muscles around Joseph's mouth tensed.

"No. Joe works for some government agency. Law enforcement. Bureau something."

"Do you mean the FBI?"

"Maybe. We don't talk about it. He should have come back to the island and been a waterman. He knows these waters. He was a natural. He shouldn't be doing this spy stuff or whatever. He went to college on the mainland and we couldn't convince him to come back."

Young Joe's decision was painful for the family. A whole way of life discarded for a new adventure.

"When he took the job, we knew we'd lost Joe."

"I'm sorry," Chad said, not knowing what else to say.

Joseph continued. "Joe called several days ago to tell us he'd be working in the Northern Neck. We thought we might see him. He said it'd be good to be near home."

"Which meant his assignment was along the coast of Virginia?" Chad asked.

"Or here on the island," Joseph added.

Chad sat back and thought about what Joseph said.

"Did Joe get over for a visit?"

"No," Joseph responded.

"The day you went back out in the storm wasn't just because of the dead zone, was it?"

Joseph's expression turned sad.

"Were you out looking for your son?"

There were holes in this story and Chad was getting impatient playing the waiting game.

"Joe called," Joseph whispered. "His number came up and the connection was scratchy then went dead. We knew something was wrong."

"Why did you think something was wrong?"

"Joe told us we weren't to tell anyone about what he was doing. He made us promise."

Chad took a deep breath. Time was running out just like his patience.

"Is there *anything* you can tell us?"

"He was in munitions training. Sometimes these World War II munitions find their way into the bay from the Atlantic. We had one wash up a few years ago. The military came to disarm it. Caused quite the spectacle. Joe told us some could contain biological weapons. When I noticed the dead zone and the strange odor, I couldn't help but think about what he said. If one of those leaked, what would it do to the bay? The fish?"

The conversation had taken an unexpected turn, but explained why Joseph had ventured out into the storm. He seemed ready to resume their conversation, so Chad started the recorder.

"Tell us what happened next when you went out on the water."

"I thought I'd get to where I had observed the film, confirm it, and then get back. But the storm hit again, much earlier than I expected. It forced me to seek shelter, so I went up the Potomac River. I knew of a cove where I could anchor."

"Were you successful?"

"I found a place close to the shore, but the boat got damaged and needed repair before I dared come across to the island. I fell asleep or was knocked out. I was confused when I woke. Must've hit my head though I don't remember. All I wanted to do was keep the boat upright in that storm."

"Why didn't you call for help?"

"The phone slipped under the netting during the storm, and I couldn't find it right away," Joseph replied, looking down, ashamed at his ineptitude. "I was looking through my tools to see what I had to patch up the boat when a voice yelled and startled me. Some guy said, 'Hey! What're ya doin' here?' And then in an angry tone he said, 'Get the hell away from here.' Two men appeared from a path in the woods. Bad lookin' dudes."

"How old were they?"

"Young. I mean, maybe twenties?" Joseph responded. "I'm not good at guessing age. About the age of my son."

Charles nudged Chad, and pointed to his watch. It was time to go. They had to wrap this up.

Chad pursed his lips. They'd taken the charter on condition they'd only be an hour on the island.

"Mr. Wheeler, we have to leave and get back across the bay."

Joseph stood and shook their hands.

Chad rubbed his forehead. "One more thing. When your son called, could you make out anything he said?"

Joseph nodded.

"All we heard was something that sounded like 'trouble.'"

"Okay. Thanks, Joseph. I'll see if I can find out anything about your son and we'll resolve the issue in the bay."

~ SIX ~

The commuter jet banked on its approach to Dulles International Airport. Passenger Ethan Ewing placed the meeting documents into his briefcase and glanced out the plane's window to admire the landscape.

The ride hadn't been comfortable. Strong winds had buffeted the plane, and the seats were not designed for his six-foot, one hundred seventy-five pound frame.

To block out the uncomfortable conditions, he concentrated on his future. Four months ago a former colleague, Rob Carter, had called and convinced Ethan to apply for a position with the FBI. A position, Rob assured, where he'd be based in Quantico, Virginia. After giving it much thought, Ethan applied and was accepted. Today he'd learn the details. His life was about to change. He'd weighed the pros and cons of leaving a town and townspeople he'd grown to love. Being sheriff of the rural New York town had been a great opportunity, but he was ready for a new challenge.

And then there was Caitlyn. He missed her and wanted them to create a life together. Their long distance relationship wasn't accomplishing that goal. One of them had to relocate. When the FBI opportunity presented itself, he took it as a sign.

Rob had said, "We need agents of your background and experience. I'm sending you an application. Fill it out and mail it back with the required items. I'll make sure it gets to the right folks."

"Why now?" he'd asked, surprised by the call.

"We need agents with investigative skills. I've followed your career, and you have the qualities we need."

"But I'm in my mid-thirties," Ethan reminded Rod. "There must be younger recruits."

"There are, but most are lawyers or accountants; we need *experienced* investigators. Got to go. Call if you have questions."

Ethan applied for the job and went to the FBI's regional office in Manhattan for an interview. Then came physical and psychological exams, and a training program before he was finally accepted.

He glanced out the window and noticed the plane was about to land. He pulled out his phone to check messages. Caitlyn's latest text told him she was in Ingram Bay, Virginia, staying with her parents.

More client meetings. Need to talk about the skeletal remains.

He was pleased she'd gotten the job, but concerned about her excitement over a new investigation. Caitlyn would put caution aside when pursuing justice.

And I'm not there to protect her.

He carefully worded his response. He didn't want to tell her where he was or what he was doing. Not yet. Not until he was sure. He sent a text back.

Congrats on the job. Busy here. More later.

~

Ethan pulled into the FBI Training Facility at Quantico, Virginia, and presented his temporary ID. When assured the description matched, the guard nodded and directed Ethan onto the base.

He found a parking space near the FBI National Academy, put on his suit coat, straightened his tie, and retrieved his briefcase from the back seat. An agent met him at the door, checked his ID, and led him down a hallway to a meeting room. Ten matching armchairs flanked a large rectangular table. The room smelled of lemon polish. Framed photographs of past FBI directors decorated the walls. Before Ethan read the names, someone entered.

"Ethan Ewing, I'm Special Agent Richard Jensen."

"It's nice to meet you, sir," Ethan said as he shook the Special Agent's hand.

Richard Jensen pulled a stack of papers from his briefcase.

"Your credentials are outstanding, and your range of experience and accomplishments impressive. You have urban experience as well as working in a rural community setting. You're the candidate we need. Welcome to the bureau."

"Thank you, sir," Ethan responded, letting out a deep breath.

Special Agent Jensen cleared his throat and looked him in the eye.

Ethan tensed. There was something else.

"We usually give new agents time to acclimate; assign lower-level cases."

Ethan nodded; his insides in turmoil.

Fargo, North Dakota, here I come.

"But we need you in the field. Now."

Special Agent Jensen placed two portfolios in front of him.

"Those have the information you'll need. The blue one has the agents' details; the other one has everything we have about the last time anyone saw kidnap victim Chloe Wright."

Chloe Wright? The name didn't ring a bell.

"I've heard nothing about a recent kidnapping," Ethan responded.

"Let me explain. A few days ago Congressman Herbert Wright of West Virginia received a ransom note about his teenage daughter."

"When exactly did this happen?" Ethan asked, still perplexed he hadn't heard.

"That's the problem. When we started the investigation, the Senator told us in strictest confidence that his daughter and one of her friends left sometime late summer. Since he was up for reelection, Senator Wright didn't want his daughter's disappearance to overshadow his reelection. Instead of alerting law enforcement, he hired a private detective. That person located the girls in Virginia with a group of environmentalists and followed the group to North Carolina. That was when the trail went cold. Then last week the Wrights received the ransom note, postmarked from a small town in the Northern Neck of Virginia."

Finding daughter versus political career. Ethan dared not voice his thoughts.

"What about the other girl?"

"Her parents notified law enforcement and promised the Wrights they wouldn't mention Chloe. That girl is back at school, but when she left the group, Chloe was fine."

"And they received a ransom note *now*?"

"Correct. Two agents were sent to the area from where the note was postmarked."

"Will I report to the agents?" He'd not worked a kidnapping case before. This would be especially stressful since she was the daughter of a powerful congressman.

Special Agent Jensen cleared his throat again.

"That's the other problem. The agents haven't reported in two days. They either uncovered the kidnapping or they've found other illegal activity that got them in trouble."

"Other activity?" Ethan asked, leaning forward, his arms on the table.

"We've been following suspicious activity in the same general location. We consider the Northern Neck a sensitive area because of the proximity of three important waterways that flow into the Atlantic Ocean. We're not labeling it as terrorist yet, but there's that possibility."

Terrorist?

"Who alerted you to this activity?"

"An informant."

"That person is?" he asked, ready to jot down the name in his notes.

"I can't divulge that information. You understand how important it is to protect informants."

Ethan's frustration mounted. It would be helpful to know someone in the area if he needed help. Though if he were captured, it would be one piece of information he couldn't be coerced to share.

"What did that person see?"

"Increased boat activity at the mouth of the Potomac River, and unmarked white panel trucks on the local roads. The agents were briefed on this situation as they tried to locate Miss Wright. They may have gotten too close and been captured or killed. Find Congressman Wright's daughter and the agents."

"Can local law enforcement assist?"

"No. Our agents are missing and kidnapping is a federal offense. As I mentioned, we're not sure if she's a kidnap victim or a runaway. If she was kidnapped and kept for these past few months, it might be a case of human trafficking. The fact they're now asking for ransom money means she's no longer of any use to them except for ransom. We have to act fast before the senator pays off these guys."

"Is it possible she's the one who sent the ransom note?" Ethan asked.

"It's a possibility," Special Agent Jensen stated with a shake of his head.

Ethan tensed as the reality of his assignment began to sink in—kidnapping, human trafficking, missing agents, terrorist activity.

"Questions?" Special Agent Jensen asked before he turned to go.

Millions.

"No, sir. I understand the assignment and I'll do my best to find Miss Wright and the missing agents."

"Special Agent King will prep you on the remaining details of your assignment."

Ethan stood, shook Special Agent Jensen's hand, and returned to his seat. He stared off into space, his stomach in knots.

What have I gotten myself into?

Resolved he had to give it his best shot, he opened the portfolio that had details of the assignment, but before he read the first paragraph, a man entered the room. Younger than Special Agent Jensen, the man was of medium height, crew cut blond hair, brown eyes, and in good physical shape.

Ethan stood.

"Good afternoon. I'm Special Agent King and I'll go over protocols with you and have you fill out the last of the paperwork. I'll then escort you to where you'll be issued a firearm."

"Thank you, sir."

The men sat, and Ethan slid the papers into his briefcase. The briefing materials would have to wait.

For the next two hours he had a crash course on procedures. He filled out the necessary paperwork for the personnel department.

"We'll turn in your rental car and provide you another with a registration to coincide with your new identity. From here on out you'll be 'Cody Blaswell.'"

"Why a new identity?" Ethan asked, surprised.

"If our agents uncovered a sophisticated operation and you infiltrate it, you could be traced," Special Agent King responded.

Undercover. New identity.

He took a deep breath. It was too late to back out. They depended on him to locate Chloe Wright and the missing agents.

"I'm ready," he responded as he replaced his ID cards with the new ones.

"Here's a map of Virginia. You'll head down I-95 to Route 17 south. That'll take you to the town of Ingram Bay. This map will help you navigate the back roads. Virginia's route numbers can be confusing."

Ethan drew a breath.

Ingram Bay. That's where Caitlyn is now. Could things get any worse?

"Something wrong, Agent Ewing?"

Ethan shook his head.

"Everything's fine. Thanks for all the information. I'd better get on the road."

~ SEVEN ~

It was two o'clock and Caitlyn was hungry. She'd researched the status of the country's outdated transformers and had typed up notes to supplement the information for SafeGrid's website. The last line of text read: *After an electromagnetic surge, the country's electrical system would be down. Stores, gas stations, and banks would close. Hospitals would run on generators until their alternative power source ran out. The country would be in chaos.*

"That's a start," she stated aloud, and then emailed the text to John Graves.

She still hadn't received the latest data from The Bay Foundation for the annual report. She sent off another email. If she didn't get the data soon, she wouldn't have time to make the final charts and get the file to the printer.

Exhausted, she closed the laptop and went downstairs to the kitchen wondering why her mother hadn't called her for lunch. Then she remembered. Her parents were running errands.

Summit trotted into the room, sat and stared up at her.

"Okay, boy. You need to go out. Lunch can wait."

They walked towards the side of the property that bordered the conservation land. She thought about the remains and how a young girl could end up buried in that spot.

Caitlyn pushed her hair back, a nervous habit.

Let law enforcement handle it. But would they?

She put Summit back in the house and picked up her purse. She'd get lunch in town.

On her way to the SafeGrid meeting she'd noticed a family restaurant halfway down the town's main street.

When she stepped into the restaurant a mixture of fragrant aromas greeted her. The smaller tables and booths were occupied. She didn't care to sit at counters, so she turned to go.

A waitress dressed in a crisp white blouse over navy blue slacks approached.

"Looking for a seat?"

"Yes, but there aren't any and I'm not a counter person."

"Follow me," the waitress said, as she took Caitlyn to a booth farthest from the door.

A woman occupied the booth. Obviously, the waitress had made a mistake.

"Lilla," the waitress said. "Do you mind a booth mate? This young lady needs a seat."

Lilla smiled and indicated Caitlyn should slide into the opposite side.

"My name's Joan," the waitress said. "I'll be back with some water."

Even though the woman named Lilla didn't seem to mind sharing her booth, it still felt awkward.

Lilla? Isn't that the name Tricia mentioned this morning? Are there two Lillas in this town?

"Thank you," Caitlyn said to Lilla as she slid into the booth.

Joan returned with a glass of water and a menu.

"I'll give you a minute, but Lilla can vouch for the pasta salad."

Caitlyn studied the menu and put it aside. She studied her booth mate, who was intent on finishing her meal. Lilla's blouse and shawl were a swirl of colors. Her silver-gray hair neatly trimmed.

"I'm Caitlyn Jamison. I'm visiting my parents. They've recently moved into Forest Green. That's a community about five miles north of here."

"I know where it is," Lilla responded between bites.

"I hope you don't mind sharing your booth. I have this 'thing' about sitting on stools at a counter."

Lilla pushed the salad aside and toyed with her sandwich.

"Your name's Lilla?" Caitlyn asked, leaning forward, trying to engage the woman.

Is she hesitant because I'm a newcomer?

"Yes."

"Have you lived in this area long?"

"All my life."

"You must have seen a lot of changes."

"Yup and not all of them good."

"Tell me about the town."

"You mean how it was before developers like Vince Russell arrived and started to clear-cut our land, pollute our waters, and bring all these summer folk?"

Vince Russell. The name her father had mentioned.

Caitlyn nodded, but sat in silence, refusing to take sides.

"I remember when the main street was a dirt road. Family run businesses lined the street, and family farms provided most of what we needed. Now, those farms are growing houses, large chain stores have run out the family businesses, and the road through town is busy with vacationers and boaters heading to the hotel and marina."

"You mentioned a developer, Vince Russell. Is he the only developer building houses?"

"Right now he is. My husband does a lot of work for him. Too much, I think, but we need the money."

To be sure she was Bud Higley's wife, Caitlyn asked, "Did you hear about the skeletal remains found this morning?"

Silence. The woman sighed and turned toward the window, her lips pursed.

Joan returned with her pad and pencil, ready to take her order.

"I'd like a cup of coffee and a tuna wrap. I'll have the pasta salad another day," she said with a wink.

"Sure thing. I'll be right back," Joan responded.

Lilla hadn't answered her question and didn't seem interested in continuing the conversation, so Caitlyn pulled her phone out of her purse, checked messages, and was disappointed Ethan hadn't responded to her message about the remains. She slid the phone back into her purse.

"Are you done?" Lilla asked.

"Yes. I guess I am," Caitlyn said, startled, not realizing the woman had been watching her.

"Don't know what the world's coming to. Nobody talks to each other anymore. I sit here and watch families come and go. They sit and don't talk. They pull out their 'things' and peck away. Even the little ones have these 'thingamajigs.'"

"I agree," Caitlyn said, relieved that she and Lilla had found common ground. "I keep hoping things will change and parents will see the damage that's being done. Because of this craze did you know some schools are teaching social skills?"

Lilla didn't have more to say on electronic devices, so Caitlyn brought up the remains again. That *had* to be the hot topic of conversation. Maybe Lilla didn't hear the question.

"Did you hear about the skeletal remains discovered early this morning?" Caitlyn said a little louder.

Lilla sighed, "You don't give up, do ya?"

Before she could respond, Lilla continued. "It was my Bud who came upon 'em. Scared the poor man half to death."

"I'm sorry. That must have been awful for him," but before she could ask another question, Lilla put the rest of her sandwich into a small Styrofoam box. She slid across the faux leather booth bench, stood up, and placed a hand on the table to steady herself. Once sure of her footing, she reached over for her large colorful cloth bag, placed the box inside, and with the help of her cane, started towards the door. She stopped, took a step back and said, "Nice to meet ya."

"You, too, Lilla. Take care."

Lilla ambled towards the door, touching the top of each booth for balance. Caitlyn watched Lilla's progress and was ready to help if she fell.

Two young men came out of the men's room, eyeing her as they walked by. A scent of marijuana emanated from them, and then they intentionally bumped Lilla as they passed.

"Hey old woman, git outta the way," they laughed and left the restaurant.

Caitlyn jumped up, but Lilla recovered her balance and continued on, seeming not to notice the intentional bump.

Furious at this rude and hurtful behavior, Caitlyn stood in the aisle with hands on her hips as she watched the men get into their pick-up truck.

Joan noticed her concern and approached.

"Those are the Brown brothers, Billy Bob and Henry James. They're always in trouble. Their uncle is the sheriff, so they get reprimanded, but never held responsible for their behavior," Joan said.

"It's a shame," Caitlyn stated, controlling her anger. She didn't want to profile them, but she couldn't help it. The truck was so splattered with mud she couldn't distinguish the make or year.

A gun rack hung in the back window, and she recognized the newest alt-right "Rainbow Flag" that flew from the tailgate.

She shuddered.

~ EIGHT ~

Caitlyn left the restaurant a few minutes before three o'clock. If she hurried, she could make it to Richmond by four. So instead of driving back to the house, Caitlyn pulled up maps on her phone and found it wasn't *that long* a drive to Richmond. She put the address of the morgue into the car's GPS, assured she'd be back to her parents' house by dinnertime.

After two wrong turns, annoying one-way streets, and construction blocking other streets, Caitlyn arrived at the Jackson Street morgue. Parking spots were scarce, but she found one to squeeze into. She thought about what to say as she walked to the building.

"May I help you?" The receptionist greeted her when she entered.

She gave the woman a smile with a hint of sadness.

"I'm here to find out about the remains sent here this morning from Ingram Bay."

The receptionist checked her log and flipped through several pages.

How many deaths are there here?

"Here it is. Skeletal remains assigned to Dr. Anderson. Do you have information about the identity?"

"No. The remains were found near my parents' home, and I wondered if they'd been identified."

The receptionist hesitated.

"Let me check with Dr. Anderson. And your name?"

"Caitlyn Jamison."

It was her lucky day—a doctor on staff who might have time to talk with her. The receptionist was cautious, probably because she had to deal with gruesome curiosity seekers.

"Have a seat while I check to see if Dr. Anderson is available."

"That'd be great," Caitlyn responded.

While she waited, Caitlyn pulled out her tablet and jotted down ideas for SafeGrid's marketing plan. Her adrenalin flowed. She always enjoyed being part of a client's team, and the SafeGrid project was no different.

"Excuse me, are you Ms. Jamison?" a voice asked.

Caitlyn jumped, so engrossed in the world of transformers and electrical grids she momentarily forgot where she was. A white-coated woman with hands in her pockets stood in front of her. Was she expecting Dr. Anderson to be male? Composing herself, she responded, "Yes. Are you Dr. Anderson?"

The woman nodded, handed her a guest lanyard and motioned for Caitlyn to follow.

"We can talk in my office."

She followed Dr. Anderson through double doors and down a long hallway. Caitlyn had been in a morgue before and it wasn't a pleasant experience. She didn't want to come across any corpses today. To her relief, Dr. Anderson led her into a well-lit office. The curtain-framed windows overlooked the city streets. The opposite wall featured floor to ceiling bookshelves. An area rug in soft shades of blue and gray gave the room a homey feel to provide aggrieved families a comfortable space. Photos of Dr. Anderson and her family offset her professional certificates. She noted Dr. Anderson had a husband, three children, and an Irish Setter.

"What can I do for you?" Dr. Anderson asked. She sat behind her desk and motioned for Caitlyn to take one of the upholstered chairs in front.

"My parents live in the Forest Green community north of Ingram Bay. Conservation land borders the development where skeletal remains were discovered. Apparently, a developer had encroached onto that property."

"And?" Dr. Anderson asked, leaning forward.

"When my cousin was killed a couple of years ago, a passion for justice ignited inside me. I had to find out who killed him, and why. I had to bring him justice, and closure for our family. This passion for righting wrongs allowed me to meet and team up with the local sheriff. We solved my cousin's murder, and then went on to solve another crime, six months later. I'm a graphic artist. I see things different than most. When I learned about the skeletal remains, and that they were of a young girl, that passion for justice was rekindled. I want to make sure the girl is identified, and answer the questions of who and why."

Dr. Anderson nodded.

"I haven't had a chance to review the coroner's notes, so how were the remains found?"

Caitlyn cleared her throat. She'd only arrived in Ingram Bay yesterday. Her knowledge of the incident was limited.

"At daybreak a man operating a small bulldozer spotted a piece of cloth. He got off his machine and discovered he'd disturbed remains buried in a shallow grave. He called 911."

"I see," Dr. Anderson said. "What else?"

"The coroner arrived and confirmed the remains were human. So far I haven't heard that anyone in town knows her."

"Her?" Dr. Anderson asked.

"Sorry. The rumor is the remains are of a young girl."

"Go on," Dr. Anderson instructed.

"I'm not sure if the sheriff plans to investigate, or if the state police will."

Dr. Anderson sat back, her hands folded.

She's deciding how much to tell me.

Caitlyn, too, sat back, silent, waiting, hoping.

Dr. Anderson moved forward in her chair, her arms on the desktop.

"I was just arriving when the remains were brought in. I gave them a cursory examination. I believe they are of a fifteen or sixteen-year-old female, and I estimate death occurred about nine months ago, give or take a few weeks depending on soil and weather. Consequently, it is too early to determine the cause of death, and of course DNA hasn't been run."

"Isn't DNA done immediately?"

Dr. Anderson smiled at Caitlyn's naïveté.

"Unlike the popular television shows, those tests take time, especially the DNA. And since this type of case is not a top priority unless law enforcement deems it so, it could be months, maybe years, before we get to it."

Ignoring the facts, Caitlyn plunged ahead. "If you had to guess, would you say the young girl died of natural or unnatural causes?"

"I don't jump to conclusions, but I can tell you, and again, on *cursory* examination, I noticed a skull fracture."

"Could a blow to the head be cause of death?" Caitlyn asked.

"Possibly. I can't speculate," Dr. Anderson replied, not giving up any more information. "Now, you probably wonder why I offered to see you."

"It occurred to me."

"I, too, want the remains of this young woman identified. Thank you for filling in the story. A cold case is like putting a puzzle together. Every piece of information helps. I requested a search on missing persons for the time period that I estimate she died. Unfortunately, we are short staffed—a nation-wide problem, but it explains why I, or anyone else here, can't immediately focus on these remains."

"Can you at least keep me in the loop?" Caitlyn asked.

"I'll try, unless she is identified and her family requests privacy."

Dr. Anderson rose. The conversation was over.

"Thank you for your time. I'm glad the young woman is in caring hands."

"Wait."

"Yes?" Caitlyn asked, biting her lip. Could Dr. Anderson stop her from investigating?

"Why do you care?"

"Why do I care?"

"There's more going on with you than simple curiosity. You aren't in law enforcement, so why are you interested? You mentioned your passion for justice, but I sense there's more."

Dr. Anderson wanted her to dig deeper into her motives and it was a question Caitlyn hadn't thought about. She cared about the victim, but what was the answer?

"It's just who I am. I have a deep-rooted sense of justice. When I come across something like this I can't help myself," she replied. "I connected with this young person. When I was that age I had a love-hate relationship with my parents. I wanted to run away, join a cause, and make a difference. I have this uncanny feeling the girl was probably pursuing her dream of making the world a better place and she came across something or someone that got her killed."

"*You* have a vivid imagination," Dr. Anderson stated. "I asked because there are people fascinated with the morbid. They want to see corpses, want information on bodies. We've put procedures in place to deal with this, so I took a chance when I agreed to see you. I had a feeling you were genuinely concerned and I hope my intuition is right."

Dr. Anderson checked her watch.

"It's late. I'd better get back to work. Those waiting for their loved ones' autopsies don't care it's close to closing time. I'll try to keep you informed if I have more information, and I'd appreciate it if you would do the same."

~

Caitlyn sat in her car and watched Richmond's rush hour traffic pass by. She thought about the meeting with Dr. Anderson. She turned on her phone and heard the familiar ding of a text message. Before she entered her password, the phone dinged again with its second annoying alert.

All right already!

John Graves had sent a text an hour ago acknowledging receipt of the documents she'd sent earlier, but he needed clarification on several points she'd made. Immediately. Her meeting with Dr. Anderson had taken longer than planned.

She sent a text back promising she'd send him the information within the hour. With her phone in dictation mode, she dictated notes as she drove back to Ingram Bay.

Another text arrived as she pulled into her parents' driveway. She hoped it wasn't from John Graves. Over an hour had passed since she'd promised to get right back to him. She'd lose this contract if she weren't careful. As soon as she got to her room she'd type up the dictated notes and send them out.

With a sigh of relief, she saw the text was from Ethan.

Skeletal remains? Don't get involved! Busy on a case. Will be in touch.

A smile spread across her face and then she thought, *what case?* The last time they talked he hadn't mentioned a new case.

Her smile faded when she read the next text. John Graves had called an emergency meeting for seven thirty in the morning, the time she'd planned to head back to Arlington. She continued to worry about The Bay Foundation report. Her contact there hadn't responded to her latest email. Something was wrong.

Caitlyn went straight to her room, but instead of working on the SafeGrid materials, she went to her laptop and started a document labeled, "The Body in the Shallow Grave." When the victim was identified she'd erase the word "body" and replace it with the victim's name. She compiled a list of people to interview and knew it would grow as she talked with them. She'd start with the developer Vince Russell, Bud and Lilla Higley, Sheriff Goodall, Joan the waitress, and if she got enough courage, she'd try to find the Brown brothers. Those interviews would lead to more suspects.

She labeled the next page of her document, "Who had the most to gain?" She came up with a variety of scenarios and added names to match each.

The question was: what threat could a teenage girl pose—unless she came upon something illegal? Who or what did she see?

Ethan could advise her on how to proceed. She touched his number on her cell and waited for him to answer. Instead, the call went straight to his voice mail.

~ NINE ~

Ethan studied the map and checked the time. Four o'clock. Rush hour out of DC would be in full force, and that was confirmed when he tried to get onto I-95. Three lanes of traffic crawled. His car didn't have an HOV lane responder, which meant he'd have to travel with the workday traffic.

He got into the right-hand lane and took the first exit that advertised a restaurant. He'd eat and when the traffic let up, he'd head south. It was after seven before the traffic lessened enough for him to hop back onto the highway, but he hadn't wasted the time. He'd studied the information provided by Special Agent Jensen.

While in the restaurant he mentally composed another note to Caitlyn. He couldn't tell her what he was doing, but she'd worry about his lack of response. If she got involved in another murder investigation, she'd need his help.

Working a special assignment. Don't get involved in a case.

~

Seven miles north of Ingram Bay he slowed to look for the place the bureau had indicated he stay. He'd noted that this part of Virginia had few options for motels or gas stations.

The Moonshine Inn appeared five miles north of town. It might have been out of the Prohibition era. The motel was one story and had about fifteen rooms. In its day it probably was a thriving business, but now more likely served vagrants and other unscrupulous sorts. Perfect.

He had to find appropriate clothes to fit his new identity, and didn't know if the town of Ingram Bay would have a thrift store, but if it did, the store wouldn't be open at this hour. He needed to find a Goodwill or Salvation Army drop-off. He drove past the motel and noted one car in the parking lot. He continued on into town and after driving up and down several streets, he got lucky. Although the Goodwill store was closed, donations had continued to be dropped off. He parked at the back of the store and when assured no one would see him, he dug into the bags of donated clothing. It didn't take long to find two pairs of well-worn jeans, a faded flannel shirt, and several faded tee shirts, all his size.

With the pilfered wardrobe stuffed in his trunk, he drove back to the motel. To assume his new identity, he unbuttoned the top buttons of his shirt, pulled it out of his pants and rubbed dirt onto it. He did the same with his face.

The motel's small reception area was empty when he entered. Sounds of a televised baseball game filtered through from the back room. He stepped up to the dirt-encrusted counter and rang the bell. While he waited, he looked around the motel's office. Dated flyers decorated the dirty off-white walls. Grit covered the windows that faced the parking lot. After observing the scantily furnished room, he rang the bell again. The curtain parted and a man wearing a stained undershirt appeared. His extended beer belly indicated his favorite pastime.

"What can I do for ya?" the man asked, pressing his stomach against the counter.

"I'd like to rent a room," Ethan replied, slurring his words. He rocked on his feet, hinting that he might have had a little too much to drink.

The man cast an eye over Ethan to assess what kind of trouble he might be. After several seconds, he pulled a register from under the counter.

"Sign here. Name, address, license plate number and make of car."

Ethan took the pen and with a slight shake of his hand, he signed his name, Cody Braswell, Kentucky, no town listed. He turned towards the grit-covered window to check his license plate number.

Who remembers that?

"Didn't memorize it," he mumbled, "can't see out these windows." He looked the proprietor in the eye.

"Never mind," the guy stated, turning the register around to see what Ethan had written.

"How much?" Ethan asked.

"You related to the Appalachian Braswells?"

"Could be," Ethan slurred. "Don't know much about family."

His answer satisfied the guy or maybe he just wanted to get back to his baseball game.

"That'll be thirty a night. How long you 'spectin' to stay?"

"Depends if I find work. Anyone need a hand? Not fussy, can keep my mouth shut."

The man shook his head. "Not off-hand. I'll ask around. Here's your key. Number ten at the end."

"Thank you," Ethan replied. He steadied himself, turned, and walked out the door.

The motel room was small, sparsely decorated and dirty, but it'd have to do until he found something better. Ethan spread the briefing materials out on the bed, and cringed at the thought of what might be crawling through the fibers of the faded yellow bedspread.

He opened the file on Chloe Wright and read through the report. They'd taken statements from her parents, and a couple of school friends before the senator put a stop to the interviews. There was a list of items taken from her room, which included her laptop. He'd have to find out about her phone. The report on the laptop contained social media sites, popular singers websites, and several video games, but the last item caught his eye—the girl had been following an organization called *EnvironmentNow*!

No DNA reported.

Why not?

He made a note of the missing information. He put the folder aside and processed what he'd read. He checked her Facebook page. Nothing posted since August. Was she captured and her phone taken? He didn't have a good feeling about the outcome, and he needed to learn what the agents had found before they went missing.

He paced, thinking, aware of the ticking clock. Time was running out. He needed to recreate the path the agents had taken in trying to find Miss Wright.

He pulled out the map and studied the topography of the land and the history of the town. Ingram Bay had been incorporated in 1840 though the first settlers had arrived long before that. Large 19th century plantations, operated by slave labor, were now broken up into small farms growing mostly corn and soybeans. Only a couple of the large plantation houses still existed.

The Chesapeake Bay supported watermen, their families, and recreational boating. A peaceful locale, but he knew no place was immune to criminal activity.

Ethan picked up Special Agent Joseph Wheeler's dossier.

Joe Wheeler, twenty-eight, born and educated on Tangier Island, graduated from the University of Virginia, served in the military, and then joined the bureau. His father was a waterman. From what Ethan knew about watermen, the family would expect Joe to follow his ancestors' career path.

He'd be familiar with the area and a good candidate for the mission.

Ethan closed the dossier and opened the one on Tara Jones, age twenty-seven.

Both so young.

Tara was from Michigan, but when he saw her place of birth, Holland, it made sense. She'd grown up near Lake Michigan. He went back and forth between the two dossiers comparing and contrasting their experience.

Finished reading, he tried to get into their heads. Trained investigators in top physical condition, the agents wouldn't have been taken down easily.

A text alert on his personal phone interrupted his thoughts.

Where did I put it?

A second ding arrived just as he reached his phone.

Good job. Well hidden. Even I couldn't find it.

The text was from Caitlyn.

Waiting to hear from you.

He couldn't ignore her. His fingers remained poised over the phone as he thought about what to say. The answer—nothing. He'd put her off a while longer.

Busy here. Will be in touch when I can.

She'd assume he was still in New York. He hit "send." He hoped she'd be busy with her new client and wouldn't have time to think about his response, or lack thereof.

He flipped through the paperwork provided by Special Agent Jensen. What happened to the rest of the information on the assignment? He'd call in the morning. It was late. He'd better get some rest—there wouldn't be much time for that until the case was solved.

~ TEN ~

An enticing aroma from her father's grill wafted into the house. Caitlyn had closed her cold case file and had turned her attention to the SafeGrid account. Lost in the world of statistics on energy, she'd ignored her growling stomach.

"Dinner's ready," her father yelled as he entered the house from the patio.

She joined her parents in the dining room and enjoyed her father's grilled shrimp and vegetable ka-bobs. When her parents asked about her day, she responded, "My new client, John Graves, has called an early morning meeting. Could I stay another day or two?"

"Stay as long as you want. We love having you. Maybe you should move here," her mother replied.

"Thanks, Mom, but since most of my clients are in the DC area, I really need to stay closer."

"Just wishing," Ann said.

"If my client base changes, I'll give it some thought," Caitlyn said and placed a hand over her mother's.

She turned to her father, "Dad, have you met many locals?"

"A few. Why?"

"I'm interested in the history and culture of the town."

Herb rubbed his chin.

"Not sure what you're after, but I know that the area is experiencing growing pains. It's been undeveloped, and that's created a tug of war between the long-time residents who want to keep it that way and the newcomers who want to cut trees, clear land, and build houses. I heard there were protests aimed at this development. We're slowly being accepted into the community, in part because we add to the tax base without putting a strain on the infrastructure."

"Like having kids in school?"

"Correct. Although tension between the factions remains high, I don't think it would escalate to murder, if that's what you're thinking."

"If the girl *was* murdered, could she have seen something she shouldn't?"

"Like what?" her mother asked, putting her fork down.

"That's what I'd like to figure out. The historical society museum would have information on the town. Mom, could you do some checking the next time you volunteer there? Maybe ask the other volunteers?"

"Please don't get involved in another investigation," Ann said.

"I agree with your mother. You have responsibilities to your clients. You can't correct every injustice."

Caitlyn didn't want to start an argument or make a promise she couldn't keep. She got up to clear the table.

"Delicious dinner, Dad. Thank you."

"Don't bother with those," her mother said. "You have work to do. If your meeting is early tomorrow, and you get out in time, can you come with me to the new museum exhibit on Tangier Island?"

She didn't want to spend the day traveling back and forth to Tangier.

"I'm not sure how long the meeting will run, and I should get back to Arlington."

Her mother's expression tugged at her heartstrings. It wouldn't hurt to stay another day or two. She had her laptop. She could work from here.

"Okay. If the meeting ends in time, I'd love to go with you. I'll meet you at the Reedville ferry."

"Great," Ann replied with a smile. "The ferry leaves at ten."

Caitlyn reached over and gave her mother a long overdue hug.

"The meeting is at seven thirty. It should work."

While her parents were busy in the kitchen, Caitlyn headed to the couch in the great room. Summit curled up next to her. The view of the bay was distracting. She'd much rather sit and gaze out at the water, but instead she pulled up her case file.

How does one investigate a cold case?

Her fingers flew across the keyboard, putting in search terms to learn about the process. She listed the items to check: forensics, dental records, DNA, GedMatch. If Dr. Anderson put a rush on the DNA, a family tree could be started with the victim's DNA results. She went back to searching and found an intriguing website: The Doe Network.

What's that?

She clicked on the site. There was too much information for her to go through tonight, so she bookmarked it.

An email arrived from John Graves. Attached was a document that contained specific wording to use when contacting Virginia state legislators. She read it over twice. It didn't coincide with her marketing plan. She came up with ways to tweak it, but when she got to the bottom of the page it read: "Do not edit." She'd have to question that at tomorrow's meeting. In the meantime, she typed up ideas that rushed from her head to her fingers.

Then her creativity stalled.

Instead of thinking about electromagnetic pulses, scenarios of how a teenaged girl ended up buried in a shallow grave intruded into her thoughts. She needed to get out of the house and stretch her legs. Summit was fast asleep so she let him be. Without him she could walk and not wait while he researched every smell.

It was dark, but the streetlights lit the sidewalks. She passed several residents walking their dogs. She'd set out at a fast pace, but slowed when she noticed a woman, wrapped in a fleece blanket, sitting on her front porch. Tricia Reilly.

"Good evening," Caitlyn called out as she passed by.

"Hi there. Want to join me?" Tricia asked. "I've got another blanket. It's chilly, but too nice an evening to spend indoors."

"Sure," Caitlyn responded, her plan for a brisk walk pushed aside. She'd take this opportunity to learn more about Tricia and the town.

She wrapped a warm blanket around her and settled in.

"You look tired. Been working all day?" Tricia asked.

Caitlyn decided not to mention her trip to Richmond.

"Yes, and there's a lot to learn about my new client. I'd planned to head home tomorrow, but the CEO called a meeting for first thing in the morning."

"They must be serious," Tricia said. She reached into the insulated bag at her side and pulled out a plastic wine glass and a bottle of Pinot Noir.

"Do you always have a spare glass available?" Caitlyn asked, taking a sip.

"When you live in a community like this, you're prepared. I keep this bag by the door and bring it out whenever I sit on the porch. People are out walking, but what they really want is a chance to socialize. Now, tell me more about your new client."

"There isn't much to tell. They make replacement transformers that will better protect our power grid in the event of an electromagnetic pulse. I'm excited to be part of the team, but there's a lot of pressure because of the lack of funding to get these things built. Neither the government nor the utility companies want to bear the cost. The government says it is a civilian infrastructure responsibility and the utility companies should bear the cost. The utility companies say it is a matter of national security, so the government should pay. Neither will budge. And then when I try to focus on the job, I think about the girl buried in the shallow grave," she pointed towards the woods, "just over there."

"I'm sure the police will work the case at some point. You need to stay focused on your job," Tricia said.

"You mentioned you worked in Norfolk. Were you with the Navy?" Caitlyn asked.

"My entire career was with the military, and I ended up in Virginia. It's a good place to retire, and I have family in the area," Tricia responded. "Before you ask the next question, I was married, but it didn't work out."

"I'm sorry," Caitlyn responded. "I don't usually ask personal questions, but since you brought it up, you said your family is in the area?"

"Yes, but mostly I consider my neighbors to be my family."

It was evident Tricia didn't want to share more of her personal life, so Caitlyn changed the subject.

"Have you heard about The Doe Network? It's the International Center for Unidentified and Missing Persons."

"Not sure I have," Tricia answered, sipping her wine.

"I didn't have time to browse through the site, but I learned each missing or unidentified person is assigned their own unique number. The website has sketches of all their cases, and the victims are sorted by state and sex. It was unsettling to see the number of persons listed in each state. My first reaction was—this can't be true. Volunteers staff the network—amateur sleuths and genealogists. They try to identify people and connect them with family. I'd hoped to find the missing girl on that site."

"Leave the investigation to the authorities," Tricia warned. "Getting involved in a criminal investigation is dangerous, and you could be charged with obstruction."

Caitlyn frowned at the advice and didn't appreciate Tricia's tone.

"What if the authorities assign this as a cold case? And it isn't worked on for years," she countered.

"It's still none of your business," Tricia stated, and then to relieve the tension, she leaned over and poured more wine into Caitlyn's glass.

"Will you be heading back to DC soon?"

"No. Since I have an early morning client meeting tomorrow, Mom asked me to go to a museum exhibit on Tangier Island. I'll stay another couple of days."

"I suspect your other clients will be glad when you are back at your office."

Why did Tricia want her to leave town? She couldn't dwell on that now. It was getting late.

“I’d better call it a night. Thanks for the wine, conversation, and advice,” Caitlyn said.

“Any time,” Tricia replied, “And remember what I said about investigating.”

~ ELEVEN ~

Ethan woke with a start. Three a.m.—the time he woke most every night. During deep sleep his subconscious took over and revealed answers that eluded him during the day. Tonight was no different; he had the answer. When Special Agent King came into the room, he'd stuffed a folder of papers into the side panel of his laptop case. The missing information was probably there. He got up, pulled the laptop out from under the bed, unzipped the side pocket, and there were the papers. He flipped through the pages and put them back. There was the address of the place where the missing agents had stayed in Ingram Bay. First thing in the morning he'd search the agents' rental. That solved, he fell into a deep restful sleep.

The next time he woke it was after five. His nerves were firing. He was ready to get to work. He was also starving. On his drive through town last night he'd noticed a quaint eating establishment on the main street. He'd have breakfast and then find a room to rent. He didn't want to stay in this fleabag motel any longer than necessary.

He pawed through the clothes he'd taken from the Goodwill box and put aside the cleanest shirt and jeans. The short-sleeved light blue shirt had a slight stain at the hemline, but he could tuck it in. The faded jeans were a little loose, but the length was perfect.

~

Ethan walked into the Sunny Side restaurant and quickly surveyed the interior. Three men sat on stools that faced the kitchen and talked amongst themselves. To his right, booths lined the front windows. From his vantage point, only two booths were occupied. Two women sat in one booth, while the other held a family of two adults and two young children. The room to his left was dark. The restaurant lived up to its name. Yellow and white gingham curtains draped sparkling clean windows; clear vinyl protected pale yellow tablecloths on the dining room's tables. His observations complete, he turned his attention to the savory aroma of bacon and eggs.

"Good morning," a waitress greeted him.

"Good morning," he replied and followed her to a booth halfway down the right side of the restaurant.

"My name's Joan," she said as she handed him a menu. "Coffee?"

"Please," he responded.

When Joan returned with a mug and a small carafe of coffee, he ordered two eggs, sausage and a side of hash browns.

"No grits?" Joan asked with a smile.

She'd pegged him for a northerner. He liked her sense of humor.

"I'll pass on those this morning," he replied. "Maybe tomorrow."

"Sounds good," Joan replied, picking up the menu. "Be right back with your order."

On his way in he'd picked up the local *Pennysaver* to peruse the ads and looked for a room to rent. He circled possibilities and put the paper aside when his order arrived.

"Here you are," Joan said as she placed the hot platter in front of him.

"Thank you." While settling in last night he had forgotten to eat. The candy bar from the gas station vending machine had given him a sugar high, but no nutrients. He wanted to dig in, but work came first.

"Joan, I'm new to the area, need work, and a room to rent. Do you know of any rooms or jobs around here?"

Her hand rested on her hip and she heaved a sigh. Apparently this wasn't the first time she'd been asked that question.

"What kind of work are you looking for?"

"Anything. I'm strong, and can keep my mouth shut."

She scowled, nodded, and said, "I'll ask the guys in the kitchen."

He'd tapped into the right source. She'd know what was going on in town, hear all the gossip, and have connections.

The restaurant was getting busy, so he might not have a chance to talk with her again. He took a napkin and scribbled his contact information—the cell number with the Kentucky area code the bureau had provided, and handed it to Joan as he left the restaurant.

Back in his motel room, he made calls to the rental possibilities he'd found in the *Pennysaver*. The first three went to answering machines. He didn't leave a message. On the fourth call, a man answered. He had a one-room efficiency apartment for fifty bucks a week. Ethan jotted down the address and told the guy he'd be there in half an hour.

~

The efficiency apartment was one room equipped with a small refrigerator, microwave, toaster, and coffeemaker. The metal-framed single bed was pushed up against an inside wall. The faded chenille bedspread couldn't conceal the ultra-thin mattress. The loveseat-sized sofa was worn, and the frayed corners exhibited evidence that a previous renter had a cat. A small metal table and two straight-backed chairs took up the center of the room. No television; no Wi-Fi, which was fine. He wouldn't have used it. He had Internet access through the 4G Network on the bureau issued phone.

He put the address of the agents' rental in his GPS and drove through the town. The north and southbound lanes were separated by green space. The median was filled with yet-to-leaf out crape myrtles. He noticed that most storefronts were full. Ingram Bay had a healthy economy. He saw several construction sites on his way in, which made sense. This area was prime for development.

How will this lovely historic village adjust to the influx of new residents?

He passed a five-star hotel and marina complex at the south of town, and three miles further he turned west. Sparsely spaced large houses, probably belonging to the old plantations mentioned in the documents, had fallen into disrepair. He pulled off into one of the long driveways and jotted down notes about what he'd seen, routes taken, and observations. This dirt driveway showed recent use. Someone was using the outbuildings, probably for storing farm equipment.

His cell rang and showed a local area code. He pounded his fist on the steering wheel, frustrated he still had a couple of miles to the agents' rental, but the call could be about a job and a way to get information from the locals. He pulled over and answered.

"Cody here."

The caller didn't identify himself, just, "Hear you're lookin' for work."

"Yes sir. You got somethin'?" Ethan responded.

"Yeah."

The caller gave the directions. Ethan scribbled them down as fast as he could.

"Be there in an hour."

Ethan pulled out the roadmap to make sense of the directions. He wondered who the caller was and who'd spread the word.

Let the games begin.

~ TWELVE ~

The SafeGrid office was on a narrow tree-lined street in a mixed-use neighborhood. Residential homes sat alongside small office buildings. Caitlyn drove past a dental office, a hair salon, a veterinary practice, and three homes before she arrived at the one-story red brick building that housed SafeGrid's office. The parking lot was full, so she drove to the rear of the building and squeezed into the last spot.

The board members, their expressions grim, were seated when she walked into the room. They didn't have to wait long for the meeting to start. John Graves entered carrying a stack of papers.

"Thank you for coming on short notice. Last night I received a Department of Energy report about unusual solar ejection activity. The earth wasn't affected, but scientists and government officials are gearing up for a possible catastrophic geomagnetic event."

Caitlyn shifted in her seat. The pressure was on.

"There's concern that North Korea is increasingly unstable. If the Korean government explodes a hydrogen bomb over the western United States, it would take out the electrical grid of the states in the west, Midwest, and southern Canada. Those threats don't include hackers and terrorist attacks. We have to ramp up production."

He surveyed the board members.

"We need workers of all skill levels."

He turned to Caitlyn. "Additional funding. Follow up and convince the utility companies and federal government to pledge funding for the transformer production unit."

She had to think. Fast. How would she get those two entities to agree on anything? Didn't he know the phrase, "an act of Congress?" Before she could raise a question, he continued giving out assignments.

"Step up our legislative efforts to convince the state senators to lift the moratorium. Jack, Dan, contact our senators to put pressure on their colleagues and the governor. Bill Webber will broker the deals. The legislators won't act on this unless there's something in it for them. We'll do whatever is reasonable."

What moratorium?

While he talked, her internal alarm went off. Again. Now they were talking about state legislation not federal. What was that about?

She resented being put in this position.

"Caitlyn, you're on the team now. You need to get up to speed."

He didn't give her an opportunity to respond. He continued to rant.

"You have your assignments. Keep me in the loop about progress."

He picked up his papers and left the room. It was only eight o'clock, and the meeting was adjourned. The men picked up their folders and chatted amongst themselves as they left. Caitlyn gathered her folder, but got as far as the door when she decided to ask John Graves to explain the moratorium and exactly what he expected of her. As she turned back, she noticed William Webber enter John Graves's office where an animated conversation began. The door was left ajar. She took a couple of steps towards the office and stopped. She didn't catch everything, but what she did hear had nothing to do with the manufacture of transformers.

~

Caitlyn had an hour before she had to meet her mother at the ferry—enough time to pay Vince Russell a visit.

On her way to the meeting she'd noted his office was on Main Street. She pulled up to the curb and observed the surroundings. A light was on inside. She approached the door and peeked in the window. No one sat at the reception desk. She turned the knob, but the door was locked. She knocked. When no one answered, she cupped her hands against the window and peered inside again. She took a step back and knocked, this time louder.

A tall handsome man, in his forties, with an athletic build, appeared from a room off the reception area. Could he be Mr. Russell? She'd pictured him as short and flabby.

The door opened a crack.

"Is Mr. Russell in?"

"I'm Vince Russell. How can I help you?"

She recovered from her surprise and responded, "Do you have a minute?"

"I'm not discussing yesterday's event, if that's why you're here," he stated and started to shut the door.

"I'm not here to talk about that. I'm writing an article on housing developments, and would love to do a profile of you and your company. Do you have time to answer a few questions?"

Seconds passed, and then the door opened.

"I suppose. Come in," he said.

Caitlyn straightened her shoulders and walked into the reception area.

"Mr. Russell, my name is Caitlyn. It's nice to meet you."

He showed her into his office.

"What magazine do you work for?"

"Actually, I'm freelance."

He seemed to buy her story; she breathed a sigh of relief.

"I was about to pour myself a cup of coffee. Would you like one?" he asked, warming up to her.

"That would be great, thank you," she replied. She didn't need another cup of coffee, but she did want an opportunity to check out his office.

The room smelled of fresh paint, the color similar to the sea foam blue she'd chosen for her efficiency apartment. A framed display of large houses and condominium complexes with pools, spas, and gorgeous sunsets decorated one wall. The dark walnut frames were a nice contrast to the lighter color of the walls. Framed articles about his projects were interspersed among the photographs. Vince Russell appeared to be a successful businessman.

Her tour around the office brought her to the back of his cluttered desk. She didn't mean to snoop, but one paper stood out. She recognized the letterhead. She glanced at the doorway and listened for his return. When she heard nothing, she glanced down at the letter. She lifted the first page and noticed William Webber's signature. Ingram Bay was a small town. It would be natural for businessmen to know each other, but . . .

"Here's your coffee," Vince Russell said as he entered the room holding two china mugs.

His entrance startled her, and she hoped he hadn't seen her looking at the papers on his desk.

She recovered quickly and took a seat on the small couch. She took a tentative sip of the hot brew.

"Your photos are impressive."

"Thank you. I'm proud of what I've accomplished, and hope to do the same in the Northern Neck," he said as he glanced with pride at the photos displayed on the wall.

He sat in a side chair that faced the sofa. He leaned over and placed his mug on the coffee table and then leaned back with his hands folded on his lap.

"Where do you want to start?"

"Tell me about yourself, your background, and what brought you to this area," Caitlyn said, pulling out her steno pad.

"I grew up in Boston, Massachusetts, attended college there, but I've lived and worked in Chicago, San Francisco, and New Orleans. From those experiences I learned about various lifestyles and architecture. Virginia is attracting more businesses and drawing retirees from all over the United States. I'm incorporating designs that I hope most will find comfortable and intriguing."

"Why did you choose Ingram Bay?"

"I'd visited the area many years ago, and then a former associate from Boston suggested I check out the area. This part of Virginia is ripe for development. As I mentioned, it's becoming a popular residential and retirement destination. I rented this storefront, hired local contractors to renovate it, and then worked with a local real estate agent to find the most suitable land for development."

She jotted down notes as he talked.

"Since you mentioned the recent event on your property, will you be altering your plans for that site?"

Vince shifted in his seat.

"I'm disturbed by the event, obviously. It's unfortunate the discovery was near property I'm developing. The fact that one of my contractors misread the plans and went over onto the conservation land is upsetting. I'll have to supervise my contractors more closely."

Her questions were making him uneasy. A silence came between them.

"What did you say your name was?" he asked.

She tensed. She'd intentionally not given her last name in case he made the connection with her father. But she'd misled him enough.

"Caitlyn Jamison," she replied.

Before she could ask another question, he rose, smiled, and said, "I'm sorry, Ms. Jamison, but I don't have any more time today. I have client calls to return."

He'd made the connection and now she was dismissed. She'd try another time, assuming he'd see her again. Once he did a little research on her, he'd find out she wasn't a freelance writer. She packed up her pad and pen, and turned to leave, but she was not about to give up.

"One more question. Were you aware your condo plans were too close to conservation land?"

Vince stopped short, his fists clenched, his expression grim.

"Of course not."

~

Vince Russell didn't have phone calls to return. It was just a ruse to get rid of her. Instead, he sat at his computer and clicked through various condominium plans. The plans he'd filed with the town showed no violation of the easement. Then he'd altered the plans, just a bit, pushing the driveway out away from the units, which made for better aesthetics. He thought no one would notice that the driveway crossed over the easement by a few yards.

Just my rotten luck. He sighed and thought about his next step.

He'd arrived in Ingram Bay with grandiose plans. The Northern Neck had miles of undeveloped land with shorelines that bordered two rivers and the Chesapeake Bay—a location to lure boaters, fishermen, and nature lovers. It had easy access to Richmond for those who enjoyed shopping and excellent restaurants. On his drawing board was a new yacht club with an upscale housing development.

He wished Bud had called him first. They could have talked. Maybe he could've convinced Bud not to report what he'd found, but Bud was an honest man. He wouldn't have agreed.

When he arrived at the site, Sheriff Goodall had greeted him with, "My God, Vince, I thought you had more sense than to plan a condo complex on state land."

He'd asked himself the same question. He didn't normally violate property lines, but this lot was narrow, and after he altered the plans, buyers liked the design and had put their deposits down.

Then there was NIMBY—not in my backyard—an outcry every developer dreaded. The last people in wanted to shut the door. The Forest Green residents were no different. Retirees were the worst. Most had too much time on their hands and wanted to share their expertise. Their comments at the town board meetings had been tedious. He'd tried to integrate into the community and be a good neighbor by using local contractors, but as much as he tried to win over the locals they resented his intrusion into their peaceful locale. Could it be because they couldn't or wouldn't trust a Yankee?

Bill Webber was the one who suggested he come to Ingram Bay. They'd worked on projects in Boston, but he hadn't seen Bill in at least five years. Bill had called and told him about the development opportunities here, and then he'd met John Graves. He'd done his research and agreed this area was ripe for development. He now worried that Bill and John were getting too aggressive with their plans.

He looked at the papers strewn across his desk. A note from Bill Webber on SafeGrid letterhead requested funding for one of their projects. It wasn't a project he could condone. It would ruin his business model. Besides, he didn't have the money they were asking for.

Had the Jamison woman seen the letter? He shoved it into the top drawer and he'd deal with it later. He had no desire to organize the rest of the mess or pay bills. Instead, he turned back to his computer and clicked through more plans.

The designs enticed him to get moving on another project, but he had to rescue his current project first. He had to work out the driveway problem, and figure out a way to stop Webber and Graves. If they were successful in getting the moratorium overturned, the area's housing market would crash. They were working at cross-purposes.

The incessant ringing of his cell phone interrupted his thoughts. He paused, debating whether to answer it. He didn't want to talk to any government officials or the press. Not until he talked with his attorney. He pulled the phone across the desk and checked the caller ID. John Graves. Just before the call went to voice mail, he picked up the phone.

"John, what's up?"

"Vince, heard about the remains uncovered by one of your contractors. Did you know he was over into the conservation easement?"

Vince took a deep breath. How many times would that question be asked? This was a chink in his armor that John would latch onto.

So what's the real reason for his call?

~

John Graves hung up the phone, and turned to William Webber.

"Our friend has gotten himself into trouble. We've got to convince him to help with our legislative efforts."

"We have to give him incentives. He's a good guy, and if our plan goes through, it'll ruin his business. We have to come up with a compromise."

"You're right. We'll scout out property south of the town and pressure the locals to sell. Vince can build there, but we can't waste too much time and effort on him. He can always find another section of the country to develop," John said.

~

Caitlyn sat in the parking lot of the Reedville Ferry and waited for her mother to arrive. The assignment John Graves gave her this morning weighed on her mind. She couldn't afford to spend the day traveling to Tangier Island, but she'd promised her mother. They hadn't spent much time together in recent years, so this was something she had to do.

Caitlyn opened her briefcase and found the numbers for the major utility companies and for congressmen that served on the Committee for Energy and Commerce. Herbert Wright was the chairman. She started with the utilities, where she introduced herself and explained the reason for her call. As suspected, she had to leave a message. She'd follow-up these calls with letters. Next were calls to congressional offices, and she followed the same procedure.

A knock on the car window startled her.

Her mother had arrived.

~ THIRTEEN ~

Ethan didn't have much time to search the place where the agents had stayed. He had to meet the guy in an hour. According to the GPS, the Airbnb where the agents' rented a room was fifteen minutes away, and it would take at least that long to get back.

Their rental was a small cottage set back from the main house and was several miles west of town. The lock was easy to work, and within seconds he was in. The space was similar to what he'd rented, except it had two small rooms off the main living area.

Ethan pulled on gloves and moved quickly around the room, searching every conceivable space for any clue the agents had left behind. Their training would have precluded them leaving a trace, but everyone makes a mistake, especially if caught by surprise. He needed something, anything, to put him on the right trail.

Finished with the living room, he entered the small alcove that served as Joe's bedroom. Shaving kit and duffle stuffed with clothes remained on the bed. Ethan rifled through the bag, and checked the side zippered pockets. Nothing.

Tara's room was much the same. She was a minimalist. No makeup or shampoo. In the bathroom, only a bar of soap was left in the shower, towels hung haphazardly on the hooks. Her duffle much the same.

Ethan went back into the living room.

Where else?

He walked over to the kitchen counter and stood at the small sink. The open shelf above it held a small bottle of dish soap, and to the right, an assortment of single-serve boxes of cereals. The refrigerator had a half full bottle of milk. He turned back to scan the living area for what he might have missed on his first pass through when something pulled him back. Cereal boxes. Two were missing, pulled from their packaging. The empty boxes were in the wastebasket. The next box was slightly askew. He pulled it from the cellophane wrapper and checked the seal. It appeared untouched, but on closer examination, he detected a small wrinkle. He wedged his fingernail under the flap and with minimal pressure the box opened. He unfolded the inside wrapper and moved the corn flakes aside. He felt around the box, careful not to spill any of the flakes. When he swept his finger across the bottom, he felt something solid. With two fingers, he lifted out a flash drive. He pulled it from the box and slipped it into his jacket pocket. He gently shook the box to resettle the cereal, refolded the interior wrapper, and sealed the box up as best he could before putting it back into place.

His burner phone chirped, reminding him of his appointment.

Damn.

He needed to get to his computer to read the flash drive, but if he didn't show up at the job, he'd lose his chance of gathering information.

He arrived at the pre-arranged meeting place—a closed gas station where two state roads crossed—a few minutes early. He parked where he could see vehicles coming from either direction. He wore jeans that had a small tear at the knee, a faded tee shirt, and a warm flannel shirt.

He didn't have to wait long. A mid-sized black sedan pulled in. A man who appeared to be in his mid-fifties, tall, and with thick black hair tinged with gray, got out. The guy was dressed casually, but the quality of his clothes gave him away. Ethan stepped out of his car, but remained behind the door. The man approached.

"Cody?"

"Yeah," Ethan replied.

"Thanks for coming. Heard you're looking for work."

Ethan moved away from the car's door and let it close.

"Yeah. Traveling and looking for some lucrative employment," Ethan said, hoping the man would read between the lines.

"I may have something."

"You know my name. Can I have yours?" Ethan asked.

The man considered the request, judging him.

"JR."

JR, right. Like JR Ewing in the show Dallas. Maybe we're related.

A chill ran down Ethan's spine. Did this guy know who he was? Had his cover been blown? Was he mocking Ethan with the reference to JR? He'd have to stay on high alert.

"Okay, JR," Ethan said, stretching out the pronunciation of his name. "What've you got?"

"Follow me. I've got a storage shed down the road with boxes to load."

JR was right. The small metal building was just "down the road." Two men worked in one section. They appeared to be in their mid-twenties. They wore thin flannel shirts, faded blue jeans and steel-toed boots. Each wore a filthy baseball cap backwards with greasy neck-length hair sticking out the back and sides.

Introductions weren't given. JR told him what to do. He suspected the other two would keep an eye on him. At the first opportunity he'd introduce himself, assuming JR didn't stay.

The boxes, stacked three high and three deep, were to be loaded into a small white box truck that was backed-up to the building. The license plates were crusted over with dirt so the numbers weren't visible, but they looked like Virginia plates. He'd have to get the numbers *and* find out what was in the boxes. He bet the other two men knew. When the time was right, he'd ask.

"The boxes are heavy, so place them carefully in the truck," JR said. He turned and pointed to the opposite corner of the room. "See those longer ones?"

Ethan nodded.

"Those take two men to move. Don't do it by yourself."

"Yes sir," Ethan responded.

"If you have questions, just ask them," JR said, pointing to the next room. "If you do a good job, I may have more work."

"How do I get paid?"

"You'll get paid when I'm satisfied with the job."

After JR left, Ethan carried boxes while straining to overhear the conversation of the other two. When he'd loaded a fair number, he approached them. He timed his arrival at the back of the truck at the same time they were loading.

"I'm Cody," Ethan said as he stood back to allow them to load.

The men didn't respond, but continued to work.

"I'm new 'round here. Wonderin' where I can get a cold beer? After work, of course," he laughed.

One started to respond until the other struck him hard on the chest with the back of his hand.

"We're not supposed to talk to you, unless it's about work," the slapper stated with authority.

"Okay. I get it, but we're working together, right? That makes us part of a team; a team sticks together. They share information, like, well, where to get the best beer." Ethan leaned against one of the stacks to put the men at ease and to see if he could find a label.

He had to move this conversation along and find out who these two were and what was in the boxes. His nerves were firing. He had to find out what was on the flash drive.

"Sandy's is the best place."

"Billy Bob Brown, that's not the best," the other jumped in, stamping his foot.

"Shut up Henry," Billy Bob replied, his face turning red.

"We gotta get back to work," Billy Bob said, and pushed the other man back into the building.

Ethan studied the two and saw the similarities.

"Are you two brothers?"

"What of it?" Henry retorted.

"Nothing. Just noticed how you look alike. What else do you do for the boss? This is pretty mindless, and we," he motioned to the three of them, "are more on the ball than just moving boxes."

The men straightened their posture.

Ethan had hit a nerve. These guys had probably suffered put-downs for years. This was their chance to be in control.

"We do important stuff," Henry replied, puffing up his chest. "We're do'in retrievin' and . . ."

Billy Bob whacked his brother again and said, "Shut up."

Before Ethan could question them further, a pickup truck with a trailer that carried an older model bulldozer pulled in. The sign on the truck said Higley Excavating. An older man climbed out, and with an arthritic gait, he approached the men, but stopped short when he saw Ethan.

Billy Bob spoke first.

"What do ya want . . . Higley?" Billy Bob drew out the syllables of the last name. Then laughed. "We're taking a break. We got only a couple boxes left to load."

"I've only got a few," Ethan added.

How does he fit in?

Higley addressed the men. "You're expected at the other site."

To Ethan he said, "Not you."

At that he turned and limped back to his truck.

"What was that all about?" Ethan asked.

"Another project."

The men had said enough to give Ethan more to go on, especially the "retrieving" comment that got Billy Bob upset with his brother. What were they retrieving, and did it have any connection to Joe, Tara, or Miss Wright?

"What now?" Ethan asked as they finished loading the truck.

"*We* go to the next job. You wait for another call," Billy Bob replied.

Not the response he wanted, but he had things he could do while he waited.

"Does JR come back with our pay?"

The boys laughed.

"When he inspects the truck and sees the building empty and tidied up, he'll find you," Billy Bob said.

Relieved he wouldn't have to stick around for the inspection, Ethan got into his car and drove into town to find a quiet spot where he could access the flash drive. He could care less about the paycheck, but what worried him was the fact JR might be checking him out.

~ FOURTEEN ~

Caitlyn stood next to her mother as the ferry pulled out of the Reedville harbor.

"We'll have to come back and visit the fishermen's museum," Caitlyn stated.

"Definitely. The town is named for Elijah Reed. He came from Maine and started his menhaden fishing operation here. The museum has an excellent historical display, and I learned that two of the fishing vessels are in the National Register of Historic Places," Ann said, and then pulled a brochure out of her purse.

"You sure are learning a lot about the area," Caitlyn said.

"This brochure explains the Tangier Island museum's special exhibit," her mother explained, handing it to Caitlyn.

Caitlyn looked over the brochure and handed it back.

"Looks interesting. I'm glad you talked me into coming, but if you don't mind, I've got some work to do."

"I'll come inside with you. I figured you'd need to work, so I brought a book."

Caitlyn pulled out her tablet and worked on SafeGrid's website for the next hour and a half. When they were close to Tangier, Caitlyn turned to her mother and asked, "Mom, did you notice the dead fish about a half mile from the mainland shoreline?"

"I did, and a sulfur smell. Is it red tide?"

"Not sure. It could be a contaminant in the water."

On their walk to the museum Caitlyn told her mother what she'd read about Tangier Island.

"The island is only four to five feet above sea level. Tangier has lost about two-thirds of its landmass since 1850. It's being threatened by what they call thermal expansion and there's discussion about global warming. There are watermen and their families living here, with family lines going back for generations. It'd be a shame to see the island and its culture disappear."

"There's been discussion about that at our museum. It's been suggested that Virginia tax dollars be used to secure Tangier's shoreline," her mother replied.

"It *is* part of Virginia," Caitlyn stated. It was a difficult situation, but right now her mother was eager to get to the museum and not talk politics. They only had two-and-a-half hours before the ferry would make its return trip to Reedville.

With their museum experience over, they walked back to the docks and stopped at the ice cream shop.

"That was worth the trip. I loved every minute," Ann said between licks of her chocolate ice cream cone.

"I love their Elizabethan accents," commented Caitlyn. "And their dress, and the creative exhibits."

"This ice cream is a perfect ending," her mother added.

Caitlyn watched the ferry passengers make their way towards the boat. Since she'd worked on the way over, she hadn't paid attention to any of the other passengers. Scanning the area, she noted a short stocky man with a familiar gait walking towards them. She couldn't place him, and she didn't want to stare, so she turned her attention back to the harbor.

"Excuse me, aren't you Caitlyn Jamison?"

Caitlyn turned to her left. The man she'd noticed stood next to her.

"Yes, and you are?"

"Chad Owens. We met last fall in the Finger Lakes."

It took a couple of seconds for Caitlyn to connect the name.

"Dr. Owens. I'm sorry I didn't recognize you," Caitlyn responded.

"And I didn't expect to see you on Tangier Island. What brings you to this lovely place?"

Caitlyn nodded towards her mother.

"My parents moved to Virginia and bought a house overlooking the Chesapeake."

"Ingram Bay," Ann said.

"I'm familiar with the area," Chad said with a smile.

"Dr. Owens, this is my mother, Ann Jamison. Mom, this is Dr. Chad Owens. He's a marine biologist from the State University of New York at Stony Brook on Long Island. He was monitoring the Finger Lakes last fall when I was working there on a winery brochure."

"It's nice to meet you, Mrs. Jamison," Chad said, stepping forward to shake Ann's hand.

"And you," Ann replied. "Did you come over for the museum exhibit?"

"No. My wife Emma did. I came to talk to a few of the watermen. Did you notice the amount of dead fish floating in the bay?"

"Yes, and a weird smell. Is it red tide?" Ann asked.

"No. It's the latest crisis I'm dealing with. I've sent samples to the lab at Stony Brook. I hope to get results soon. At the rate the dead zone is growing, we don't have much time."

"Sounds serious," Ann stated.

"It is. If we can't find a solution within the next few days, shorelines along the Chesapeake Bay, the Potomac and Rappahannock Rivers will be quarantined. Fishing will be restricted."

"I had no idea. Tell us more," Caitlyn said, patting the bench next to her.

Chad appeared relieved to have a seat. He glanced at their ice cream cones and then glanced down at his expanding waistline.

"My wife Emma and I are staying at the hotel south of town while I'm on a consulting job for The Bay Foundation this week."

"Really? I'm . . ." Caitlyn started, but decided not to mention her connection with the foundation.

"It's a lovely hotel," Ann jumped in. "Why didn't we run into you on the ferry?"

"Emma gets a little seasick, so we sat in the back of the boat."

"Ah, sorry to hear that," Ann said.

"We're under a time crunch. The foundation needs the latest data sent to its graphic arts department to finish its annual report.

The meeting is in less than two weeks, and with this new dead zone, I don't know what they'll do."

Caitlyn smiled. If only he knew she was the foundation's "graphic arts" department.

"My consulting contract ended, and Emma and I were about to head home when the new dead zone appeared, so I've extended my stay."

"Is this something we should be worried about?" Ann inquired.

"Not sure, and since the foundation is short staffed now, I'll stay on for a few more days. Emma will return home soon. She can't stay away from her high school librarian job much longer."

When Chad finished telling about the crisis in the bay, Caitlyn told him about the skeletal remains found near her parents' home.

"I heard something about that. Is there any more information? Have they identified the remains?" Chad asked.

"Not yet, but I'm curious and want to follow up. I've been in touch with the medical examiner in Richmond. Their caseload is overwhelming, so it isn't a top priority."

"I bet Sheriff Ewing is helping you with this mystery," Chad stated with a wink and a smile.

Caitlyn hesitated, getting her emotions in check.

"No," she stated.

"Wasn't his office digitizing cold cases?"

"Yes, but I don't want to bother him and besides, he has no jurisdiction here." A little white lie never hurt. She didn't want to admit that Ethan had been evasive in answering her texts and that she didn't know where he was or what he was doing. "I'll see what I can find out and then I suppose the state police will take the case. I want to be sure the person is identified and the culprit is caught."

Chad gave her a knowing look. "Does that mean you're headed into another investigation?"

Ann exclaimed, "Oh, please. We're trying to convince her to stay out of it."

"Good luck. I've heard she's tenacious," he replied and then looked up as a woman approached.

"Emma. Come and meet some new friends. This is Caitlyn Jamison and her mother Ann," Chad said as he introduced his wife.

"It's nice to meet you, Emma," Caitlyn said. The woman wore tan linen slacks with a cream knit top and coordinating sweater. Her dark hair cut short to accentuate her oval face.

Ann nodded her greeting and offered Emma a seat.

"What have you been doing this week while your husband works?" Caitlyn asked.

"I'm writing a history of the bay's ecosystem. The Chesapeake Bay and Tangier Island are wonderful resources."

"I told them about the latest issue," Chad said.

"Your book project sounds interesting," Ann said.

"Thank you. We thought we'd have a relaxing time at the end of his consulting contract, but that's not to be."

"I was just telling your husband about the skeletal remains found near where my folks live," Caitlyn said.

Before Emma could comment, Ann rose and said, "It's time to board the ferry."

Caitlyn turned to Emma as they hurried towards the dock.

"Let's continue this conversation. I'd love to hear more about your book."

"And I'd like to hear more about how the skeletal remains were discovered," Emma replied.

Emma and Caitlyn walked ahead while Chad and Ann trailed behind.

"Ann, why don't you, your husband, and Caitlyn join us for cocktails this evening?" Chad asked.

"I'm sorry, but Herb and I are committed to an event in our community, but I'm sure Caitlyn would love to join you."

~

The ride back to the mainland was not as calm as on the way over for two reasons. A strong wind was blowing from the southeast, meaning a storm was brewing. Another storm was brewing in Caitlyn's mind. She didn't want to have cocktails with the Owens that evening. Already behind in her work, she'd planned to hunker down and get caught up. The wave action made typing on her tablet difficult. To calm herself, she closed her eyes and mentally drafted the letters to the utility companies and Congress. Then her thoughts wandered to scenarios of how and why a teenage girl ended up buried in a shallow grave.

As the boat docked, a text arrived from The Bay Foundation's marketing director. Dr. Owens mentioned the foundation wouldn't have the data she'd need to finish the brochure in time. Her mind raced. How could she rearrange the annual report's documents and get it done in time for its meeting?

They'll want the brochure copy to proof before I send it to the printer.

She read the text as they debarked the ferry and then read it again when on solid ground. The Bay Foundation had postponed its annual meeting until further notice. More information would follow. She tried to catch up with Chad Owens.

"Wait," she yelled and waved her arms, but he drove off.

Although concerned about the growing dead zone and the dire consequences if Chad and his team couldn't solve the issue in the bay, relief washed over her. Pressure from The Bay Foundation was off. She could concentrate on SafeGrid and solve the mystery of how and why the girl had died.

When they got home, Ann reminded her about the cocktail invitation and offered to provide a hostess gift. Caitlyn hid her frustration.

"Thanks, but I can't stay long," Caitlyn stated, as client deadlines and a murder investigation swirled through her head.

~

Ethan parked on a side street a few yards from the library. He pulled the laptop from the trunk and put in the flash drive. One file folder appeared. Using the pass code the bureau provided, he gained access and found case notes on the kidnapping, and scanned through them, again noticing the lack of information.

Once notified about the ransom note, Joe and Tara were sent directly to the Northern Neck while another agent talked with Chloe's parents and only a couple of her friends until the senator put a stop to those interviews. The notes were sketchy. The girl's father stated the investigation was to be confidential. How could the agents work from the lack of background information? The senator must be one powerful dude. Then a note at the end caught his eye.

Following lead to activity near the bay. Girl seen heading there.

It wasn't much and left him with more questions than answers.

He closed the laptop, put it back in the trunk, and then walked around the corner and down the street to the sheriff's office.

He stopped short as he opened the door. Although there wasn't a vehicle parked in the lot, there was an intense conversation between the sheriff and an older African American man. A quick glance told him it was Mr. Higley, the same guy who came to tell the boys about their next job. Now he had a connection between the sheriff, JR, the metal storage facility, the Brown brothers, and Mr. Higley. It had been a productive morning.

Ethan backed out and quietly shut the door. He walked down the street to a drugstore where he purchased a candy bar. When he saw Higley's truck drive by, he walked back.

The office was sparse. The counter to separate the public from the sheriff's desk was covered with cheap brown laminate. There wasn't a switchboard, only a phone on the sheriff's metal desk. This was definitely a one-man operation. Maybe not much happened in this sleepy town. Or were things happening that were being overlooked or out of the control of the lone law enforcement officer?

Sheriff Goodall sat at his desk, leaning over his phone and squinting as he touched the numbers. He hung up as Ethan entered.

The sheriff appeared to be of retirement age. He was overweight, and the large open potato chip bag and bottle of soda on his desk indicated he wasn't interested in doing anything about that. He rose from his chair with some difficulty. Arthritis or maybe gout was a problem.

"What can I do for ya, young fella?" he asked.

"I was wondering . . .," Ethan began, but before he could finish the sentence, the sheriff pulled out a map from under the counter.

"If you want directions, this map will help," he said and shoved a Virginia state map across the counter. He turned back to his desk where he picked up the phone again.

Ethan accepted the map and said, "Actually, I'm new in the area, and want information."

Sheriff Goodall sighed and put the phone down.

"What kind of information?"

"Name's Cody," Ethan stated. "Lookin' for work. I figure your office would know everything that's going on in the area." He turned and looked out the front window. "Nice town you have here. I see you got some new developments starting up. Besides housing, anything else going on in the area? Short-term jobs?"

Sheriff Goodall shook his head and shrugged.

"Nothin' that I'm aware of."

The man's patience was being tried. In a sharp tone he stated, "This is the sheriff's office, not an employment agency. If you don't mind, I've got paperwork to do."

"I had a chat with a couple young guys this morning that seemed to have work. In fact, they told me they were brothers. And they had another job to go to."

Sheriff Goodall stiffened.

Ethan jotted down his name and phone number.

"If you hear of anything, let me know. I'll be around for a few more days."

As Ethan walked out the door in *sotto voce* he said, "Paperwork? You have no idea."

Deep in thought and his head down, Ethan hurried back to the library where his car was parked.

"Excuse me?"

Ethan stopped and looked up in surprise.

"Ethan?" the man asked.

The guy was familiar, but he couldn't place him.

Where have I seen him before?

The man put out his hand and introduced himself. "Chad Owens. We met last fall. I'm the marine biologist who was monitoring the Finger Lakes."

Just my luck.

What were the odds he'd run into someone he knew in this small Virginia town? It was hard enough to make sure he didn't run into Caitlyn.

"Oh, yes. Nice to see you," Ethan replied, giving Chad's hand a quick shake.

Chad hadn't picked up on his hesitation, so he continued to explain his presence in town.

"I'm here on a consulting job for The Bay Foundation, and was ready to leave when a mysterious dead zone appeared in the bay. Now I'll have to stay a few more days until we get the results back from the lab. The foundation's scientists are at a convention in L.A., so it's up to me."

Ethan smiled and tried to continue walking towards his car, but Chad walked alongside until his phone rang.

After checking the caller ID, Chad said, "Just a minute." He touched the accept icon and turned to Ethan, "Sorry, gotta take this call. Nice to see you, Ethan."

"No problem, and good luck with the dead zone," Ethan said, relieved their conversation ended. Before Ethan could escape, Chad put his caller on hold and said, "Ethan, why don't you join us for cocktails this evening. We're staying at the Chesapeake Inn just south of town."

Ethan looked down at his grubby clothes, and the time, which was close to five o'clock.

"I'm here only a short time and didn't pack for cocktails, but thanks, anyway."

Chad shook his head. "Don't worry about dress. We'll have drinks and appetizers sent to our room. It's 204. Emma will be excited to meet you. See you about six-thirty," Chad said as he hurried away, talking on his cell phone before Ethan could come up with another excuse.

I don't have time for socialization, though it could be an informative evening. Chad would know what's happening in and around the bay.

~ FIFTEEN ~

Billy Bob and Henry James Brown were deep into a competitive game on their new Xbox. The game's semi-automatic weapons were plowing down each other's players at rapid speed. The brothers yelled and hit each other while taking great pleasure in their make believe massacres.

"We need to get ourselves one of those," Henry James stated. "Wouldn't it be fun to walk into a shopping mall in Richmond . . ."

"Don't be stupid," his brother interrupted. Billy Bob was the more pragmatic of the two. "Do ya know the planning that'd take so we didn't get caught? Besides, we have our hands full with the dives and the mine."

"I'm tired of doin' that," Henry James whined. "I want to hear the rat-a-tat-tat and feel the power."

"Are you willin' to tell the boss that you quit?" his brother asked.

"Well, no. Though you could," Henry James replied, salivating at the thought of murdering a group of innocent shoppers.

"Henry, what do you see in this room? I'll tell ya. The newest Xbox, largest flat screen TV, gas allowance. The boss even bought mom a new stove. Are ya willin' to see all that go away?"

"I guess if you put that way," Henry said. "But I'd still like to take down a whole crowd of people. Then come home and watch it all on TV."

"You're dreamin'," Billy Bob said, slapping his brother on the back of the head. "Go tell ma to get off her fat behind and bring us somethin' to eat."

As Henry got up to find their mother, he noticed the sheriff's car pulling into the driveway.

"Ah oh, trouble," he warned.

The boys met him on their front steps.

Sheriff Charles Goodall faced his nephews, the offspring of his only sister. He'd promised her years ago that he'd keep an eye on them, but that was when they were two. Now they were twenty-five, and it took everything he had to keep them in line. They were complete screw-ups.

"What brings you out here today Uncle Chuck? Don't you have criminals to chase, speeders to catch? Oh, it's a weekday. You do that on the weekends," Billy Bob said, his lip turned up in mockery, his hip jutted out with both thumbs wedged in his belt.

"I heard a rumor a waterman saw you coming down the path near the mine. Tell me it's not true," Sheriff Goodall stated, his voice raising a notch.

The boys had no response. They shuffled their feet in the dirt.

"How many times do I have to tell you—be careful. *No one* can see you down there."

The sheriff clenched his fists, trying to retain control. He didn't expect an answer. His nephews hung their heads, their way of asking forgiveness. Today he wasn't in the mood, and tempted to slap them both. He took a deep breath and turned towards the house. His sister peered out the window. He turned back to his nephews and lowered his voice.

"You know how careful you have to be, right?" He let that statement hang in the air.

"Geez, Uncle, it was only one of those old watermen from the island. We figured he wouldn't remember seeing us," Billy Bob responded.

"I thought we should get him off the boat and smash his head," Henry James added, hoping that would appease his uncle. "I didn't want to let him go, Uncle Chuck."

"Shut up," Billy Bob said, turning to his brother, fist raised.

Henry James stepped back. Once again his attempt to stand up to his brother had failed.

"That's not what I meant," Sheriff Goodall said. "No one should get hurt. Just do the job and keep a low profile. Do you understand?"

"I do," Billy Bob responded, his hips swaying with renewed confidence. "We appreciate your advice and for looking after us," he said, always the diplomat.

"We're sorry," the brothers said in unison.

Sheriff Goodall shook his head in dismay. These two would be his downfall, and if he wanted the payments to continue, he'd have to come up with a better way to supervise them.

~ SIXTEEN ~

Ethan cleaned up and drove into town. He found a grocery store, and hoped it sold fresh flowers. It did. The selection was small, but he found a bouquet that would do.

With the flowers secured on the front seat, he headed south until he saw the sign for the Chesapeake Bay Hotel and Marina. He drove down the meticulously landscaped parkway and continued past the hotel to the marina where he found a parking spot at the rear of the property. As he got out of the car he noticed that several boats were docked and ready for boating season to begin.

He located a side door into the hotel and climbed the flight of stairs to room 204. The door opened immediately.

"Glad you could make it," Chad Owens greeted him.

Chad took Ethan's coat and then led him into the sitting area.

"And you know Caitlyn," Chad stated.

He froze. *Big mistake.*

Hearing her name, Caitlyn rose to greet the new guest, but then she, too, froze.

"This is awkward," Chad said as he looked from Ethan to Caitlyn and noticed their shocked expressions. "Neither of you knew the other was in Ingram Bay?"

Although he knew Caitlyn was in Ingram Bay, he'd hoped he wouldn't run into her while he was here on assignment. To maintain his cover, Ethan responded with a curt, "No."

Caitlyn remained silent, too stunned to speak, but a million questions went through her mind.

"If this is embarrassing, I'm sorry. I didn't mean to . . ." Chad continued and turned as Emma entered the room.

Ethan recovered and handed the flowers to Emma.

"You must be Ethan. I'm glad you could join us. Please sit while I put out drinks and appetizers. I'm glad we have a refrigerator and microwave with this room, and the hotel's catering is convenient," Emma stated.

"Emma, we have a problem," Chad said, holding up his hands.

"No problem," Caitlyn said, finally able to speak. "It's just that neither of us knew the other was in town."

Ethan felt her eyes bore into him as she spoke.

The room was silent as they waited for his response.

"It's complicated, and I'm not sure I can explain."

"Emma, we could all use a drink," Chad directed.

While they sipped their drinks, Emma tried to recover from the awkwardness that had clouded the evening.

"We're enjoying this hotel very much. While Chad is at work, I've taken full advantage of what the hotel has to offer. There's a lovely sitting area on the first floor that has a view of the water. I work on my book there." For Ethan's benefit she explained. "I'm writing a history of the bay."

"That sounds like an interesting project," he replied. He swirled the drink in his glass and knew he had to address the elephant in the room.

"I'm in the area on special assignment. I hope you understand that I can't tell you more."

That would satisfy Chad and Emma, but not Caitlyn.

"That's intriguing," Emma responded to break the silence. She understood his predicament and wouldn't push for more information.

"Maybe when it's finished you'll share the details with us?" Chad asked.

"If I can," Ethan responded, eyeing Caitlyn. He turned to Chad and asked, "What's going on around the bay?"

Chad slid forward on his seat, eager to share his research.

"I serve as a consultant to The Bay Foundation. I review data on the health of the Chesapeake. The foundation board needs an outside evaluation to make sure the calculations are correct. The reports were fine and I signed off on the numbers. The data is then turned into graphs and charts."

"Is it The Bay Foundation with headquarters in DC?" Caitlyn asked.

"Yes, why?" Chad replied.

"They're my biggest client," Caitlyn stated. "I'm the graphic design person who turns the data into the graphs and charts. I add the photos and arrange the text. Now I know why they haven't sent the final figures. I've been under a lot of pressure to turn that project around. I didn't know why they postponed the meeting."

Chad nodded.

"The day we were to head home information arrived about a new dead zone. I rechecked the numbers, and they were correct, but we couldn't release the data until we checked out the new report. We hired a boat to Tangier Island to meet with Joseph Wheeler, the waterman who found the dead zone. We collected our own samples and shipped them off to SUNY Stony Brook for analyzing; we're awaiting the results. During our interview with Mr. Wheeler, he briefly mentioned his son. Apparently he's working for a law enforcement agency here on the mainland."

Ethan's head jerked up at hearing the waterman's name.

"Did Mr. Wheeler tell you any more about his son?" Ethan asked.

"Very little. Joseph mentioned the bureau, so I assumed he meant the FBI, but I could be wrong," Chad replied. "I'd planned to go back to the island to talk further with Joseph, but he's ill. A doctor flew over from the mainland and took blood samples. We're waiting the results to see if it has anything to do with the new dead zone."

"Isn't there a medical facility on the island?" Caitlyn asked.

"There's a fully equipped medical facility, but no doctor on staff. Medical personnel fly over by helicopter once a week for regular checkups, and to attend to any other medical issues that have arisen," Chad explained.

"Interesting," Caitlyn said.

"I've been doing research on the information he supplied. It's quite a mystery, and all I know at this point. Caitlyn, how are you coming on your investigation?"

She gave Ethan a sideways glance.

"Not well, actually. Ethan, it's why I *needed* to talk with you."

"I'm sorry I couldn't be more forthcoming in my replies. Tell us about the skeletal remains."

"A contractor uncovered them when he was clearing a driveway for a condo complex. The guy was over onto a conservation easement, and there's disagreement over who's at fault—the contractor or the developer. When the contractor, a man named Bud Higley, discovered the remains he called 911. The coroner arrived and confirmed the remains were human and sent them to the morgue in Richmond. I talked with the medical examiner, and she confirmed they are of a teenaged girl, and," she looked at Ethan and then Chad, "the medical examiner encouraged me to find out what I can about the girl."

Ethan shook his head, his lips tense. "And?" he asked.

"I talked with the developer, Vince Russell. It's his project that called for the driveway to go over onto conservation land. When I asked about the remains, he abruptly ended the conversation."

"There might be another reason," Ethan said.

"I'm sure he wants to get legal counsel before he says too much," Chad added.

"It's possible, but something doesn't feel right. I don't think the sheriff is working the case, and so far no one has come forward to identify the girl. And to complicate matters, I'm having concerns about my new client," Caitlyn said.

"What do you mean?" Ethan asked.

She shifted forward in her seat.

"They hired me to develop their marketing materials, but then the CEO, John Graves, decided I should also be responsible for getting the government and utility companies to pay for the manufacture of replacement electrical transformers. Then there are snippets of conversation about overturning a moratorium in Virginia."

"Could the company be operating with a new name or be from another country?" Emma said.

"That would explain why there isn't much about them," Chad added. "It could be their mission has changed and they want to shed the old image."

"I agree," Ethan said. "You might be interpreting the snippets out of context, plus, there're a lot of environmental regulations and permits to go through."

"It bothers me that I have these questions that I am not getting answers to," Caitlyn stated.

"Caitlyn, tell us about your background," Emma said. "And then we'll each share a little about ourselves as a way of getting to know each other better.

~

After an hour of sharing stories about their jobs and families, Ethan stood.

"I'd better call it a night. Thank you both for your hospitality."

"Where are you staying?" Chad asked.

Ethan laughed as he glanced around the Owens' spacious and elegant hotel room.

"It's quite a contrast with this suite. I'm renting a room a few miles north of town."

"Do you want to stay at my parents?" Caitlyn asked.

"No, thank you. I can't," he responded.

His tone meant that conversation was over.

Caitlyn, too, stood and thanked their hosts.

They took the stairs down to the parking lot and stepped out into the brisk night air.

"I'm parked over by the staff entrance where no one's likely to see us. We need to talk," Ethan stated.

"I agree."

He took her hand, and when they reached his car he turned, gently touched her face, and drew her into an embrace.

"I've missed you," he whispered in her ear, "and sorry I haven't been forthcoming with what I'm doing."

She melted at his touch.

"I've missed you, too," she replied.

Ethan scanned the area to make sure no one was watching.

"Let's get in the car."

She sat in the passenger seat, hands on her lap waiting.

"I know you can keep a confidence," he began.

"Of course," she responded. He was scaring her. Various scenarios ran through her mind.

"I've taken a position with the FBI."

Caitlyn's eyes went wide with disbelief.

"The FBI? When did that happen? I don't know whether to be excited or angry that you didn't tell me."

"It *just* happened. A friend convinced me to apply. The bureau needs experienced investigators. I didn't want to say anything until I had the job, and when I found out, they immediately sent me here on a kidnapping case."

"Kidnapping? That's horrible," she replied. "Does it mean you're no longer sheriff of Riverview?"

"Correct. Tom Snow is acting sheriff and should be appointed to the position soon."

"Since you can't give details, is there anything you can say, and can I help?" Her curiosity piqued.

"I'm working for a federal agency, so no, you can't be involved. But do you remember what Dr. Owens said about the Tangier Island waterman?"

"Of course. What does it have to do with your case?"

"The waterman's name is Joseph Wheeler."

"So?"

"Two agents arrived here a few days ago on this same case, but haven't checked in recently. I'm to find them, too. One agent is Joe Wheeler, who grew up on Tangier. He's familiar with the bay and the geographic area of the Northern Neck. It's too much of a coincidence. Chad's Joseph and the agent must be father and son, and whatever the father witnessed floating on the bay's surface might be connected to what the agents came up against."

"What do you think that is?"

"I don't know and I'll have to talk with Dr. Owens again."

"Do you think this ties in with the skeletal remains?" she asked.

"Anything's possible. Whatever's going on has been in progress for a while. The FBI and Homeland Security have been monitoring this area, but haven't pinned down anything. Another reason the agents were sent," Ethan said.

"Do you have any idea what happened to the agents?" she asked.

"No, but what I learned this evening from Dr. Owens gave me ideas to pursue."

They sat in silence, neither wanting the evening to end.

"We need to talk," Caitlyn began. "About our relationship."

"I agree and I think it's time to take the next step. Long distance isn't working for me. We need to live closer together and have opportunities to get to know each other better," Ethan said.

"Like dinners that aren't interrupted with calls from the police station?" Caitlyn said, laughing.

"Yes, and concerts, hiking, kayaking, visiting all the wonderful Washington museums," Ethan added.

"Now that you work for the FBI, does it mean you'll be moving to Virginia?"

Ethan put his finger on her lips and whispered, "I hope so."

He withdrew his finger and moved towards her, but Caitlyn pulled back.

"First, is your divorce final?"

He settled back against his seat and closed his eyes.

"I'm not proud of that situation, and it's the reason I never talked about it. Jennie walked out six years ago. I felt I'd failed her, and for a time I thought we could work things out. Then I got the job in Riverview and my life in New York City faded. She'd made a new life for herself in Wisconsin. For some crazy reason we never became legally separated. Last year she showed up at the office and suggested we get back together. Jennie is controlling; our reconciliation had to be on her terms. She wanted me to move to Wisconsin. I no longer loved her, so the day you left Riverview, I started divorce proceedings."

"And?" Caitlyn asked and wondered why he never mentioned this in their phone conversations. He still hadn't answered her question.

"Jennie signed the papers. The divorce became final at the end of December. I'd planned to fly to Virginia and tell you, but then my colleague called about the FBI job. The last three months I've been consumed with paperwork, interviewing, and attending training sessions, plus keeping up with my job as sheriff. I didn't want to say anything to you until I knew for sure. If I didn't get the job, then I'd have to come up with another solution. When I interviewed, they inferred I'd be stationed at Quantico, but now I'm not sure. They need field agents. I could be sent anywhere, but right now my job is to find the missing girl and the two agents. Whatever happens, we *have* to make our relationship work."

~

Caitlyn pulled into her parent's driveway and decided to say nothing about running into Ethan.

Her parents were in the great room. Her mother was reading with Summit curled up next to her. He opened one eye to acknowledge her presence.

Her father was asleep in his Lazy Boy.

"How was the visit with the Owens? I bet the hotel is lovely," Ann asked.

"The visit was nice. The hotel is beautiful and their room spacious," Caitlyn replied.

"You had cocktails in their room and not in the hotel lounge?" Ann inquired.

"Yes. It was pleasant and we didn't have to compete with bar noise. How was your event?" Caitlyn asked, changing the subject.

"Fine. Just a bunch of neighbors getting together at Tricia's, but we'd offered to help set up and clean up after."

Caitlyn looked over at her father, asleep in his chair.

"Is Dad all right? He doesn't have the spark I remember."

Her mother sighed.

"Since his heart attack last year he's been declining. I try to keep him from overdoing, rest more, eat better, but you know your father."

Caitlyn nodded. Her parents were aging, a fact she didn't want to acknowledge. The move to Virginia a few months ago had also taken its toll.

"Will you leave him there all night?" she asked.

"No. I'll wake him soon," her mother replied.

"Okay then. I'm glad you had a good time tonight. I'm off to bed."

Summit hadn't moved. Her dog, snuggled in close to her mother's thigh, had found another soul mate.

"Did someone drive in?" Ann asked.

"You have great hearing, Mom. I didn't hear anything, but I'll check."

As Caitlyn entered the front hall, the doorbell echoed through the house. She ran to the door and hoped the intrusive sound hadn't disturbed her father.

She opened the door and a police officer, whose nametag stated he was Sheriff Charles Goodall, stood on the front porch.

"Good evening. It's Ms. Jamison isn't it?" Sheriff Goodall said as he tipped his hat.

"Yes, is there a problem?" Caitlyn asked.

"Are your parents at home?"

Herb and Ann joined her in the front foyer, her father shaky after being roused from a sound sleep.

"What's the matter?" Herb asked, stepping around Caitlyn to take control of the situation.

"I have questions for you and your daughter," Sheriff Goodall responded, looking from one to the other. "Is there someplace we can chat?"

"Yes," Herb said. He led the sheriff into the room they had just vacated. "Please, take a seat."

Caitlyn was nervous about the sheriff's presence. Had he found out about her investigation into the remains? If so, he'd soon find out she was tired and in no mood to be chastised.

Being the polite hostess, her mother asked, "Would you something? Coffee, tea, water?"

"No ma'am," the sheriff responded, sitting at the edge of a chair, fingering the rim of his hat. He turned to address Herb.

"Someone attacked Vince Russell earlier today."

"What?" Herb exclaimed.

"Oh my," Ann said as she sat down.

Caitlyn leaned against the doorframe, stunned at the news. She had just talked with Mr. Russell.

"When?" she asked.

"Late morning. One of his clients arrived at his office around noon. When they entered, he was sprawled over his desk, unconscious and bleeding from a cut on his head."

"Will he be okay?" Ann asked.

"We hope so. The ambulance took him to a hospital in Richmond. I'll know tomorrow if he's well enough to talk."

"So, why are you here?" Caitlyn asked.

The sheriff cleared his throat.

"I consider you both persons of interest in Mr. Russell's attack. Neither of you is to leave town."

Caitlyn glanced at her father then back at the sheriff.

"Mr. Jamison, you threatened Mr. Russell at the last town board meeting," Sheriff Goodall stated.

"I may have said things in the heat of the moment," Herb replied. "But darn it, sheriff, you know Vince Russell is clear-cutting the land, putting houses and condos in everywhere, destroying the beautiful landscape. There's no stopping him. I knew his condo project was too close to the conservation easement, but no one at the town board meeting would listen. Are they getting paid off?"

"Herb, what an awful thing to say," Ann said, trying to pull her husband back before he said something he'd be sorry for.

Sheriff Goodall stiffened, but instead of replying to Herb's accusations, he turned to Caitlyn.

"Ms. Jamison, I learned you were the last known person to see him before the attack. You visited him earlier today, correct?"

Her father's eyes bored into her.

"Is that true?" Her father blurted out.

She turned to address her father and to calm him down. "Yes, Dad, it's true. I wanted to learn more about him and his business."

"You're not investigating those remains are you?" he said.

"Herb, calm down," her mother stated, placing a hand on her husband's arm.

"Sheriff, how did you know I was in Mr. Russell's office?"

"It's a small town, Ms. Jamison," Sheriff Goodall responded, not answering her question. "What exactly did you and Mr. Russell talk about?"

She thought back to their brief conversation.

"Actually, not much. He offered me something to drink and when he left the room, I wandered around the office. He had pictures of houses and condominiums that I assumed were his projects, but now I'm not so sure."

"What do you mean?"

"Anyone can hang photos of houses on the wall, but it doesn't mean the photos represent *their* construction," Caitlyn explained. "To answer your question, our conversation was brief. As soon as I asked him about the remains found near his construction site, he got tense. He stood and said he had client calls to make."

"What makes you think he's something other than what he says?"

"He says he's worked on high-end construction projects all over the country, but he comes here and violates conservation land. That doesn't make sense."

"I'll check into his background, but in the meantime, I want to remind you that solving crimes is for law enforcement professionals."

"Yes, sir, I understand," Caitlyn responded with her fingers crossed.

"Back to your visit with Vince Russell, what did you do next?" Sheriff Goodall asked.

"I met my mother at the Reedville ferry."

~ SEVENTEEN ~

Caitlyn woke early and immediately started work on the SafeGrid account, though still shaken by the sheriff's visit and learning about the attack on Vince Russell. The sheriff had a lot of nerve considering them persons of interest in the attack. She needed Ethan to help sort this out, but he was busy with his own investigation. She shouldn't bother him.

She thought about the letter from William Webber she'd seen on Vince Russell's desk. How were they connected? To send a letter on company letterhead indicated the subject was business and not personal. Was Mr. Webber the colleague that had enticed Vince Russell to the Northern Neck?

It was time for a break. A drive through the countryside would clear her head and that is when she came across Bud Higley.

Within three blocks of town, the landscape became vast newly planted fields. She slowed and opened her window to savor the fragrant earthy spring air. Lost in thought she almost missed a sharp curve. She cranked the wheel to the right, and when she gained control, she noticed a bulldozer at the far end of a field. The cleared parcel was in stark contrast to the planted fields and the woods beyond. An old pickup truck with a faded "Higley Excavating" written on the side was parked close to the road. A small sign, stuck into the newly cleared land, stated it was the future home of Colonial Estates. The builder was Russell Construction Company.

She turned into the temporary drive and navigated around the muddy potholes. She heard the dozer's engine strain as it pushed through the heavy clay soil. The machine turned and headed her way. When it drew near, she felt the intense heat that radiated off the engine. Bud Higley climbed down, being careful not to fall. When he approached, she noticed his limp.

The man wasn't tall, under six feet, and probably weighed around a hundred sixty pounds. His weathered face and hands represented years of hard work. His brown coveralls were threadbare in places; the bottoms coated in red Virginia clay.

"Whatda ya want?" Bud asked as he headed to his truck, though not waiting for an answer.

He pulled a can of engine oil from the truck's bed and walked back to his dozer. He poured the oil into its rightful place, and when the can was empty, he returned to his truck. He then reached into a cooler and pulled out a sandwich.

"You still here?" he asked, as he took a bite.

She approached him.

"Mr. Higley. I'm Caitlyn Jamison. I met your wife Lilla the other day at the restaurant in town. She mentioned it was you who discovered the skeletal remains. That must have been quite a shock. I don't mean to bother you during your lunch break, but could you spare a minute to talk about that?"

Bud's expression hardened. Would he walk away? He stood his ground and looked her over. He placed his sandwich on the hood of his truck, and wiped his hands on his coveralls.

"Lilla mentioned she'd met someone who was askin' about the discovery. Did she tell ya she'd warned me not to go?"

"Lilla told you not to clear that parcel?" Caitlyn asked, urging him to explain more about Lilla's warning.

"Yeah, she has these premonitions and most of the time she's right," Bud stated. "I just needed to get that small job done so I could start on the bigger projects that are lined up. I don't always agree with what Mr. Russell and them other developers are doing to our land here in the Northern Neck, but I, as well as the other small contractors in town, need the work. Lilla keeps telling me it's progress, but I don't like it."

"Can you tell me about Mr. Russell?"

"I heard he was attacked, but I know nuthin' 'bout it. So what do ya want to know and why? You a reporter?"

"No, sir. My parents live at Forest Green and their property abuts the conservation land. I'd like to find out who the girl was, why she was killed, and buried there. You folks have lived here a long time. I thought you might have an idea about the identity of the victim. Could she have been one of the protesters in the area last summer?"

Bud shoved his hands into his pockets and shifted his weight off his lame leg.

"A bunch of kids were around last summer protesting. It was probably one of them. They're long gone now. You don't think I had anything to do with it, do ya?"

"Of course not."

"Or it wouldn't surprise me if the Brown boys were involved. They're nephews of the local sheriff. He and I have had our differences over the years and mostly because of those boys. In fact, I was just in his office complaining about them."

"Mr. Higley, what can you tell me about the protesters that were here last summer?"

Bud shook his head.

"Ma'am, I don't have time to talk about that now, but I will give you a piece of advice."

"And that is?"

"Don't poke your nose where it doesn't belong. It could be dangerous."

Bud turned and walked back to his dozer.

~

Caitlyn sat in her car and thought about the conversation and Bud's warning. Everyone warned her to stop the investigation. She could have done a better job with her questions. She could have engaged him in conversational foreplay, but she didn't have the experience to interview suspects. When she had worked with Ethan, he interviewed while she took notes on what was said and observed the body language. That was her strong suit—observation, details, and thinking outside the box. She was good at putting pieces of the investigation's puzzle together quicker than anyone else. How was she going to solve the mystery of the murdered young girl if she didn't have the other half of her team?

She decided her next stop would be the library to research the local newspaper and find out what was going on in town last year.

The Ingram Bay Library, built in 1895, was located on Oakwood Street, two blocks from the main thoroughfare. The large brick structure featured a shared space with the historical society. Her mother had mentioned the tension between the two entities. The library needed more space, and its board hinted it might expand into the back of the building now used by the museum. More small town politics.

As she made her way through the library to the reference department, she admired the interior woodwork. Talented craftsmen had put their heart and soul into the details of this old building.

"Can I help you?" a white-haired librarian asked.

"I'd like to read past issues of the local paper. Are they digitized?"

The librarian shook her head.

"That's on our wish list, but we don't have the funding. We do have the paper on microfilm."

Caitlyn followed the woman to a small alcove in the back of the library. Five tan metal cabinets stood against the wall, their drawers neatly labeled. A table nearby held two microfilm readers.

"Is there anything in particular you are looking for?" the librarian asked.

"I'd like to read the local paper for the past year."

"That would be," the librarian scanned down the drawers, "here." She pulled out the drawer and stepped back to let Caitlyn find the box of film she needed.

Caitlyn checked the labels on the boxes and chose the two she wanted. She followed the librarian to one of the microfilm readers and the librarian showed her how to use it.

"Thank you. These machines are different, and it's frustrating trying to get the reel in."

The librarian smiled and nodded. She'd heard that before.

"Good luck," she said and left Caitlyn to peruse the film.

She started with January and by the time she got to July she needed a break. Microfilm readers were hard on the eyes and neck. She walked around the library, shaking out her hands, and massaging her aching neck. When she'd had a good stretch, she came back to the machine and looked for anything that might give a clue as to the girl's identity.

The August 22 edition featured articles on protests in the area. A group of young environmentalists had arrived in town to protest the new housing developments. They demanded a stop to the practice of clear-cutting land that caused unchecked runoff into the bay. She read through the article and then went to the next week's edition. The protesters were still in town and causing much angst among the locals. She leaned in to study a photo of the group. She was sure the photo was taken in front of Vince Russell's office. She scanned the faces, read the placards, but no names were listed. She continued scanning the paper. She found nothing on a missing girl. She sat back letting out a sigh.

She scrolled through to September and stopped at an article in the September 12 edition about the town's Labor Day parade. A town-wide picnic followed.

What a nice tradition.

She'd tell her parents about it and mark her calendar to return for this year's Labor Day celebration.

She looked through the photos to see if she recognized anyone. She was going to the next page when a picture caught her eye. She stopped, scrolled back, leaned in and squinted. The grainy photo was of a group of women watching the parade. A teenaged girl, about five feet tall with wispy blond hair that hung just below her shoulders, stood at the end of a line of parade watchers. Her eyes were wide; her expression intense. Was she one of the protesters? Caitlyn read the names of the group and the girl at the end was identified as Cassie White. None of the women had the last name of White. The girl stood a bit apart from the others, her body language saying, *I don't belong here.*

Could this be the victim?

She hit "print," and then checked her watch. She'd spent too much time reading through microfilm. She had to get back to the house and catch up on her work. John Graves expected a report each afternoon, but she had one more thing to do.

She asked the librarian where the local high school was located. She put the address into her GPS and arrived at the location within an easy ten-minute drive.

The high school office staff did not recognize the girl, and when they checked their enrollment lists they found no one by the name of Cassie White. Disappointed, hungry, and behind in her work, Caitlyn returned to the house.

~

When she entered, the sweet tangy aroma of orange cranberry muffins welcomed her. Her mother was bent over the oven, pulling out the last batch. Two muffin tins sat cooling on the counter. Caitlyn's mouth watered. She'd have to be careful or she'd gain ten pounds.

"Are these for us?" she asked as she approached the counter where the muffins were cooling. It was a question she'd asked since age ten after she and several of her friends had helped themselves to a batch of double chocolate brownies her mother had made for a special garden club meeting.

"Yes," Ann replied with a laugh, humored by the comment that had been asked ever since the brownie-snatching event.

"They smell delicious." Caitlyn approached the counter and gingerly picked up one.

"Wow, warm," she stated as steam poured out of the muffin from her first tentative bite.

"There's an extra tang because I added a zest of lemon to the recipe this time," her mother said, placing the last tin on a large wooden cutting board that served as her hot pad. "Do you like it? I'm always trying something different."

"Yes, delicious, but first, how's Dad feeling?"

"About the same. He insists on going out and doing errands and he keeps tinkering around the house. It's good he keeps busy. He's still upset about the sheriff's visit last night. How could the sheriff think you or your father had anything to do with Mr. Russell's attack?"

"It's a shame about Mr. Russell and I hope the police can catch the culprit soon. When I was out for a drive I ran into Bud Higley. I talked with him about finding the remains and he told me that his wife, Lilla, had warned him not to go that day," Caitlyn said.

"Really?" her mother responded.

"Apparently she has these premonitions. He didn't want to talk about the protesters here last summer, so I went to the library and researched the newspaper archive. I found several articles about environmental protests in the area a few weeks before the town had its Labor Day parade. I was looking at the photos and noticed one of a young girl, about the same age as our victim." Caitlyn pulled the copy of the clipping from her purse and placed it on the table.

"Do you think this is the victim?" Ann asked.

"I don't know. No one at the school knows her, and if she's not a local, and no one has come forward to identify her, then the girl must have been visiting the area or she was part of the environmental protesters group," Caitlyn replied.

"Why wasn't the girl reported missing?" Ann asked.

"That's the all important question and the crux of the mystery."

"For a cold case, such as this one, what would be the next step?" her mother asked.

"When you're at the museum, look for documents, newspaper clippings, anything that might have information on what else was going on in town last summer and early fall. Ask the other volunteers and any locals you come across. Someone has to have noticed the girl," Caitlyn responded.

Ann nodded, sat back and crossed her arms.

"You know how your father and I feel about you investigating this incident. Why don't you call your friend Ethan? He's in law enforcement. If you don't think the local police are doing anything, maybe he can talk to some people. He's probably had experience with this type of thing. Maybe he could come down for a few days and consult with Sheriff Goodall, or at least give you advice."

Caitlyn nodded, remembering his embrace. She still hadn't told her parents Ethan was in the area.

His advice would be to stay out of it!

"That's a great idea, but he's very busy," Caitlyn responded, and then put down her half-eaten muffin.

"How about we start now."

"Start? How? On what? Don't you have work to do?" Ann countered, confused and then afraid of what Caitlyn was suggesting.

"I'm a visual person. Instead of talking about what we *think* happened nine months ago, let's sketch it out so we can *see* what happened."

"I don't want to see anyone murdered," her mother replied, shivering.

"Not that. Mysteries are puzzles. We'll make notes on everything we know about the remains, age, sex, time of death, suspected cause of death, suspects, and what they'd each gain from committing this crime. It's about motive and opportunity," Caitlyn explained.

Ann paused before responding.

"Who would gain anything from murdering a teenaged girl?"

"That's the question that'll make this murder difficult to solve. Remember, I solved my cousin's murder when there seemed to be no reasonable explanation."

"His death was an accident," Ann stated.

"This might have been an accident, too, but we have to figure out why it happened, who did it, and why a missing girl wasn't reported. Do you have something we can use to post our ideas?"

"I've got an old corkboard. It's still packed away, but I'll find it," Ann replied and headed to the garage.

"I'll get paper and a couple of pens," Caitlyn said.

Her mother returned with a large corkboard and a plastic box of colored pins. They cleared a workspace on the counter, propped up the corkboard, and set their supplies on the kitchen table.

"What do we know?" Ann asked, as she reached for a piece of paper.

"Our victim is female, approximate age, sixteen," Caitlyn wrote "Jane Doe" and stated the age and sex. She pinned it at the top of the board.

"This will be fun," Ann said. "How about you state the facts, I'll write them down, and then you put them on the board?"

"Good idea. The next fact is death date approximately eight or nine months ago, August or September."

She stuck the note next to the first on the board.

"Label one as 'Suspects,'" Caitlyn said.

"Bud Higley discovered the remains. Did he know they were there and reported them so he wouldn't be under suspicion? Did Lilla know and was that the reason she'd pleaded with him not to do the job?"

"Wait. He's the one who found the remains. He wouldn't have done that if he was the one who murdered her," Ann stated.

"It's a good way to ward off suspicion. Maybe his conscience bothered him and he wanted her found and properly buried. Since he found her, and acted surprised, he wouldn't be suspected."

"I'm afraid to ask how you know all this," her mother stated. "Go on. Who's the next suspect?"

"Vince Russell had a lot to lose if the girl saw him developing in protected land. But murder? How would the girl, apparently not a local, know about the conservation land? Unless she was one of the protesters."

"I've only seen Vince Russell at a few town board meetings, but I can't imagine him doing anything like that," Ann said.

Caitlyn continued to dictate the notes.

"Sheriff Goodall plays the persona of a good ole boy, but I think he knows more, especially where his nephews are concerned. Is he part of whatever this young person saw? Is he protecting someone? Is he being coerced?"

"That's a reach," Ann said as she dutifully wrote down the sheriff's name. "Do you really want to talk with him after he accused you and your father of being persons of interest in Mr. Russell's attack. Should I write your names down as well?"

Caitlyn gave her mother a sideways glance and continued, "Then the Brown brothers."

"Who?" Ann asked.

"Two brothers that live in the area. I saw them when I was in the restaurant one day. They thought it funny when they almost knocked Lilla Higley down."

"How does that make them suspects?" Ann asked.

"They're disrespectful," Caitlyn replied. "It's a shallow reason, but let's list them."

"Is Lilla Higley a suspect?"

Caitlyn rubbed her forehead in thought. "Add her to the list. If she were involved, maybe it was an accident, so Bud got rid of the body."

"This isn't a very long list, and several names are a stretch," Ann stated.

"I agree, and the other option is none of the above. Does this town have secrets, with many people keeping them? Or was this a random act of violence committed by a passerby now long gone?"

Caitlyn plunked herself down next to her mother and studied the board.

"It's a start, and as we learn more about the town and what's going on, it will lead to more names."

Ann checked the time.

"I've got to get to the historical society. I promised to continue the indexing project this afternoon as well as be backup if the museum gets busy."

"Thanks, Mom. Would Dad be willing to talk with his friends and come up with more ideas?"

"I'm not sure, and he's not going to be happy about this," Ann stated, pointing to the corkboard.

"You're right. I'll store it in my bedroom closet."

~ EIGHTEEN ~

The president of the Ingram Bay Historical Society wheeled two large cardboard boxes into the society's workroom.

"Muriel, what do you have?" Ann asked.

Muriel Lowman lowered the cart's wheels and came to an abrupt halt. She slipped the boxes off the dolly onto the floor to Ann's right, straightened and caught her breath.

"You shouldn't be lifting that much," Ann gently chastised her colleague. "Why didn't you ask me to help?"

Muriel ignored Ann's comment and replied, "It's another box delivered by the guy who's cleaning out his mother's house. I don't think he ever came around when she was alive, so now he comes to clear out. I suspect he wants to sell the house and be done. A sad situation, but I'm thankful he donated her papers to us and not to the dumpster."

Ann checked to see how the boxes were taped together, then walked over to her work area, pulled out a drawer and extracted a pair of scissors. She slit open the boxes to check the contents. They contained family photographs, papers and news clippings, all items the museum could use.

"It's a shame the family doesn't honor this woman's history, but I'm glad he's giving it to us. I'll add this material to the indexing project. It's a fast way to learn about the area," Ann said.

As a newcomer she knew not to be critical or judgmental about the way things were done. When she approached Muriel for a volunteer position at the museum, she'd kept that in mind. With that attitude, she'd been accepted as a regular, and it felt good to be part of a team.

"What did you say?" Ann asked, embarrassed she was lost in her thoughts.

"I said I've been feeding that cat that's been coming around," Muriel repeated. "A small black cat has been hanging around the back of the building. It's a cute little thing. Seems content with life, though I'm sure it would be more content to have a home."

Ann ignored the hint, and instead said, "I'm sure it would. Now, what do you want to do with these boxes?"

"Leave them. I'll find someone to go through them. Oh, I hear the bell. Visitors. Better welcome them. It's been a busy afternoon for early April," Muriel stated as she headed into the museum proper, her dolly forgotten.

Ann sat down and stared at the computer. She couldn't get her mind into the indexing project. She was curious about the contents of the boxes.

Most of the clippings in the box had no citation. She wouldn't be able to identify the paper, the month, day, or even the year. Indexing this material would be a challenge. When she had time, she'd use the library's subscription to Ancestry.com to search the articles. Next, she'd have to figure out the best way to preserve the clippings. She'd discuss it with Muriel and then it'd come down to funding. Archival material cost money, and the museum operated on a shoestring budget.

Ann pushed the clippings aside and pulled out ribbon bound letters. She put those aside and dug down to the bottom of the box until she touched something solid. She pulled out a black leather journal that looked in perfect condition.

She debated whether to open it. Muriel was giving a tour of the museum, and the bell had just rung announcing more visitors had arrived. It'd be awhile before she'd be available. Ann flipped the book back and forth, observing everything about it. It was soft leather with a thin gold trim around the perimeter. She inhaled the leather's fragrance. There were probably more journals within the boxes, but to get a flavor for what the woman was recording, Ann flipped through and read the last entry written a few days before the woman died.

As she read the woman's personal and intimate thoughts she felt as if she was violating the woman's privacy. But this person was dead, and apparently her son didn't care about his mother's memorabilia. Ann cared and the museum would treasure this piece of local history.

When Muriel returned thirty minutes later, Ann held up the book and said, "Curiosity got the better of me, so I checked out the boxes and found letters bound in pink ribbon, and one of the woman's journals."

"Wonderful. I'll let you take charge of this project."

~ NINETEEN ~

While Ethan waited for JR to call, he reread the notes on the agents' laptop and jotted down key words that might be a clue as to where they'd gone. He'd also follow-up with Chad Owens about the dead zone in the bay. As he reached for the phone, it rang, and when he recognized the number, he closed his eyes, took a breath, and became Cody Braswell.

"Cody," he answered.

"I have another job. Be at the building at two o'clock."

"Yes, sir," Ethan said before the call disconnected.

While he waited, he'd check out the local paper to learn what was going on in the area.

When he entered the library, the reference librarian showed him where the microfilm and readers were located at the back of the non-fiction section.

"This area's been busy lately. We rarely have researchers here, but you are the second one. Follow me. The cabinets are in the back. I'll let you find the film you need."

"Thank you," he said.

The librarian couldn't tell him who the other person was, but he had a good idea.

She's working the case.

He scanned the file labels and found the drawer that held the time period he needed. He pulled out the two microfilm boxes that contained the local paper from the last year. He threaded the film into the reader and started the slow task of reading.

After thirty minutes, he sat back, rubbed his neck, and got up to check out the small rural library. For its size, the library had a great collection, both in fiction and non-fiction. A small children's room was off to the side. Red beanbags decorated the room where children could relax and enjoy a good book while their parents browsed in the adult sections.

Back at the microfilm, he found a few articles on the town meetings to discuss the pros and cons of hydraulic fracturing, but nothing else helpful. He saved several articles on his flash drive just in case. Articles on environmental protesters that had arrived in town appeared in the August and September issues. He'd noticed several articles about SafeGrid and its owner, John Graves. Since this was Caitlyn's new client, he read the articles. The company was relatively new in town and energy oriented. The story had information about the critical need for replacement electric transformers and the country's future energy needs.

What else are they into? The article didn't mention background information on this company or its officers.

Did Caitlyn do a thorough background check?

~

Ethan arrived at the shed five minutes past two. Henry James was the only one there.

"Howdy," Ethan said as he swaggered in.

Henry James glared at him.

"What's in the boxes? And where's Billy Bob?"

"You're late," Henry James replied.

"Well I'm here now. What's the job?"

"Boss wants us to load these boxes. Takes both of us, so wait a minute." Henry James ordered.

"Okay, then let's get to it." There weren't many boxes; the job would be quick. He'd have time to check in with Chad Owens.

He walked to the nearest box. It was long and narrow. When he tried to pick it up he realized it was heavier than he expected. The heat and humidity of the day and the enclosed space had caused him to sweat. When he put the box down, it slipped out of his hands and clanked to the floor with a loud thud. He then remembered JR's strict warning.

Henry James rushed over, his face horror-stricken.

"What the hell do you think you're doing? Didn't I tell you to wait?"

"I, well, I didn't mean to drop it. My hands are sweaty," Ethan said as he wiped his brow. "Sorry. I hope there isn't expensive china in there."

"These are way more valuable," Henry James replied.

There were only three long heavy boxes to load and several smaller ones, also marked fragile. The whole process took less than half an hour. He wondered what Billy Bob was doing.

"Who'll move the truck?"

"I'll drive it to the meeting point," Henry James responded. "Then another guy takes it to the buyer."

He hesitated, looking Ethan up and down.

"You lookin' for more work?" Henry James asked as he opened the driver's side door.

"You got somethin'?" Ethan pulled the piece of grass he'd been chewing out of his mouth.

"Me and Billy Bob could use help, but you can't say nothin' to nobody. You wouldn't know it, but we are like, what's the word . . . independent business men."

"Entrepreneurs?"

"Yeah. That's the word. You must be educated or somethin'."

"Not really. Just been around folks like you and your brother and heard the term used before. What's the job? I can keep my mouth shut. Hell, who am I gonna tell? I'm new in this hick town."

A satisfied smile crossed Henry James's face.

Ethan stared at the woods to hide his excitement.

Henry James pulled a wadded up napkin from his pocket, smoothed it out and drew a map.

"Here're the directions. Show up noon tomorrow," Henry James instructed as he jumped into the cab of the truck and started the engine.

~ TWENTY ~

Summit trotted up the carpeted staircase to the loft and into Caitlyn's bedroom. He sat at her feet, looked up, and stared. His walk was overdue.

Caitlyn agreed, because she also wanted to talk with Tricia. If she had a military background, did she have resources that could help with solving this case? Tricia would have to be convinced the case was worth looking into, and that was going to be a hard sell.

Summit stood still while she put on his collar and leash.

Caitlyn picked up her tablet and followed him down the sidewalk. She waited while he relieved himself several times after sniffing out just the right spot.

When they arrived at Tricia's, Caitlyn rang the bell. No response. She rang again. Nothing.

"She's not home, fellow, let's continue our walk. Maybe she'll be here on our way back."

Summit trotted ahead in agreement and they continued to check out the community.

The first time she'd visited her parents was in late January. It had been a quick trip, and she'd helped her mother unpack boxes. The weather was cold and snowy, so they'd stayed in the house and in the evenings enjoyed visiting, warmed by the natural gas fireplace.

Her parents had purchased a resale in a completed section of the development that saved them from the noise and dirt of construction. The community's lodge was large and beautifully landscaped. Caitlyn wasn't a resident, so she couldn't enter the building without a fob, and especially not with Summit.

They meandered back and checked Tricia's house again. Still not home.

When they reached her parents' house, Summit pulled at his leash. He was ready for a nap. She was not.

"Let's not go in yet. I want to check out the crime scene."

She steered Summit past the house and into the woods. Would there be any clues left to help her identify the remains? It was a long shot, but she had to try.

When they got to the edge of the conservation land, she let Summit off leash and tried to keep up with him as they pushed their way through the vegetation and into the wooded area. When she came to the yellow police tape, she watched Summit sniff around. She, too, "sniffed" around. She shuffled her feet in a circular motion and pushed aside dead leaves and twigs, careful not to trip on the vines that weaved their way along the forest floor. She walked around the perimeter of the tape looking for anything that might be helpful. She ducked under the tape and studied the area where the remains had been found. The coroner's staff had done a good job of scouring the area. She squatted down and sketched the scene on her tablet. She took a few photos of the area to use on her crime board.

"Well, boy, I guess there's nothing here."

Summit stopped at the sound of her voice and then trotted off. He wasn't ready to go. He seemed intrigued by something close to where the remains had been unearthed. He started to dig.

"Summit!" Caitlyn exclaimed. "That's enough. You're getting dirty."

She went over to where the little dog frantically dug. Dirt, leaves, and debris flew out of the hole he was making. She took hold of his collar and pulled him back. She was about to give him a lecture when she spotted something shiny in the freshly dug hole. She pulled a tissue from her pocket and picked up the object. It was a thin metal bracelet with CW engraved on the inside.

Does this belong to the victim? CW could be Cassie White, the girl in the photo.

Caitlyn was excited about Summit's find. She pocketed the bracelet and urged the dog out of the forest. When they got to the edge of the woods, she stopped to brush leaves and burrs from her clothes. She did the same on Summit.

"What are you doing?" A stern male voice greeted her as she made her way out of the woods.

She stopped and looked up. Sheriff Goodall, arms folded across his chest, stood near his patrol car that was parked at the curb. A deep scowl darkened his face.

Caitlyn took a last brush across her jeans and then faced him.

"I was out for a walk," she replied.

"That area's a crime scene. Didn't you see the tape?"

"Yes. I did." Caitlyn responded as she fingered the bracelet in her pocket. Her answer implied she'd stayed clear, but she suspected the sheriff knew the lure of crime scene tape would beckon to her. Should she hand over the bracelet? No. She'd keep the bracelet and figure out what to do with it. She didn't want to impede an investigation, but she was sure the sheriff wasn't investigating, and not sure that he wasn't complicit in the crime.

"Don't go into that area again, and keep that dog on a leash," the sheriff warned.

She nodded, not promising anything.

Caitlyn watched him return to his patrol car and drive off. She walked towards her parents' driveway and noticed Tricia Reilly standing on the sidewalk in front of her house, hands on her hips. Caitlyn waved to get her attention.

Tricia frowned, shook her head, and went into her house.

What's that all about?

It didn't appear to be a good time to talk with Tricia, so Caitlyn went to her parents' house and worked on the SafeGrid account for several hours. To work out the kinks in her shoulders and neck, she went downstairs and stood before the windows that looked out at the bay. She was determined to continue her investigation despite the sheriff's warnings. Tricia's attitude confused her. Did Tricia think she was poking around the crime scene? She put on a sweater and walked up the street.

Caitlyn rang the doorbell. The door opened and Tricia waved her into the foyer.

"Is something wrong?" Caitlyn asked. "If looks could kill . . ."

"Come in," Tricia said, cutting her off.

"Why such a grim expression earlier?" Caitlyn asked as she entered Tricia's living room.

"Let me answer your question with two of my own. First, what were you doing in the conservation land, and, what did the sheriff say?"

"I took Summit for a walk, and when we returned, the sheriff warned me to stay away from the crime scene."

"Isn't that what I advised?" Tricia said, hands on her hips.

"Yes, but . . ."

"No buts. You're putting yourself in danger. You have no business getting involved."

Tricia's tone was confusing. The woman was angry, and until she knew where that anger was coming from, she'd have to be careful about what she shared. Now was not the time to tell Tricia that the sheriff considered her a person of interest in the attack on Vince Russell.

"The medical examiner said it could take months or even years before a determination on the cause of death is made and a DNA report comes through. I don't want to wait that long, so I researched newspapers at the library and found interesting articles from last summer. Were you here when the environmental protests were happening?"

"I hadn't moved in yet, but I heard about them. Friends told me about the protests. Forest Green was targeted," Tricia responded.

"The town's Labor Day parade was about the time of this girl's death, and an article about the parade included photos. One showed women watching the parade and a girl who was identified as Cassie White."

Tricia shifted in her seat.

"Do you have it with you?"

"Yes," Caitlyn replied, pulling the article from her pocket along with a magnifying glass she'd borrowed from her father's study.

She handed the photo and magnifier to Tricia to let her study the faces.

"If you compare her with the women, you'll notice the difference in stance and dress."

"I disagree with that conclusion," Tricia stated, handing the newspaper article back to Caitlyn. "Besides, there are a lot of young girls around town with a similar look. And any kid that age is trying to disengage from the older generation."

"True, but it's a possible lead."

Tricia shook her head.

The conversation was going nowhere. Caitlyn left Tricia's house discouraged, but by the time she got to her room, the continued pressure to drop the investigation made her even more determined to follow through. She fired up her laptop and with the newspaper photo in hand checked to see if the girl resembled anyone on The Doe Network website. She clicked on Missing Persons, United States, and then Female. Each state listed how many females were missing in that state. She'd learned from her earlier search that each person had a specific Doe Network numerical identifier with name, race, age and date they went missing. Many women had been missing or unidentified for years.

She'd start with Virginia; only fifty-two females were listed in their missing persons database. As she scrolled through, she noted the entries were old. She went back to the introductory page and read that the site was in the process of being transferred to NamUs, a website of the Department of Justice. The new site was set up differently than The Doe Network. A person had to register, and she didn't want to do that just yet. Stymied, she sat back and developed a new plan.

~ TWENTY-ONE ~

Caitlyn searched for her phone, and then remembered it was in her purse that she'd thrown on the couch. She wanted to tell Dr. Anderson that she'd made a possible ID of the victim. But before she could make the call, her phone dinged with an incoming text from John Graves.

She read the text—*a meeting at my house at* . . . Caitlyn checked the time.

Oh my God, about now!

She checked her purse for her keys and made sure the SafeGrid file was in her briefcase. She got as far as the front door and stopped.

Will this meeting be just the two of us?

She thought about what to do. There was no time to find out.

What's the address?

He'd given her his card with his home address written on the back. She rummaged through her purse until her fingers lit on a business card. Twelve Bayside Court. She put the address into her GPS and drove as fast as she safely dared—the sheriff might be watching for her—to the home of John Graves.

The house was three miles east of town. She was a few minutes late, but not the last to arrive. She was about to ring the bell when she heard a car approaching. As it drove past the front entrance on the circular driveway, she recognized William Webber driving a Maserati. She'd heard about these cars, but had never seen one. She tried not to stare.

She hoped to learn more about Mr. Webber's relationship with Vince Russell. They were both driven businessmen. How close were they and were they capable of murder? Was there an unholy triangle between William Webber, Vince Russell and John Graves, and did the girl witness something she shouldn't have?

She was getting carried away and had no basis for her suspicions. Her intuition had served her well in the past, but she couldn't let her imagination take over. She had to focus on the task at hand—get the word out about SafeGrid, identify funding sources, and secure grants to allow the company to ramp up production.

Damn politics!

The job would be easier if the federal government and the utility companies would stop pointing fingers at each other and join forces to ensure the safety of the country's electrical grid.

An attractive young female dressed in black with a crisp white apron answered the door and offered to take her coat.

Caitlyn tucked her phone and keys into the coat's pocket and handed it to the housekeeper. She followed the woman into the large gathering room. The room had a vaulted ceiling with a fieldstone fireplace that took up an entire wall. Beautiful teak bookshelves lined the opposite wall. Floor-to-ceiling windows provided a spectacular view of Chesapeake Bay. A man, professionally dressed, stood there admiring the view. She walked over to join him. As she approached, he turned and acknowledged her presence, but didn't speak. Caitlyn recognized him as one of the board members, though she couldn't remember his name.

"Hi, I'm Caitlyn. We met at the board meeting," she said, hoping he would repeat his name for her. He didn't. He shook her hand showing little interest. Before she could say anything more, William Webber entered the room, followed by John Graves.

"Jack, Caitlyn, let's get started," John stated.

Jack, the bank president.

"Thank you for coming, especially on such short notice. Bill has informed me of a cash flow problem. We spent more in the transformer production unit last quarter than we took in. We have to increase sales and funding this next quarter. Caitlyn, what progress have you made getting the federal government and the utility companies to come up with a plan to fund replacement transformers?"

"I have calls into the Department of Energy and our state congressmen. I've contacted the three largest utility companies in the country and have followed up the calls with letters and info packets. I've also researched foundations that focus on energy and made initial contacts. We can't wait for a funding cycle, so I put in special funding requests," she explained.

"Good," John replied. "Keep the pressure on. I need you working 24/7 on this. We've hired three lobbyists to get the moratorium lifted. Everyone agrees it's critical, but they're afraid of the environmentalists. The protesters here last summer are an example of how powerful the environmental lobby is, especially when they are youngsters. We need to brainstorm how to overcome our deficit, prove ourselves in the market, get our legislators to remove the ban on mining, and become attractive to investors."

John Graves passed around the budget sheets.

This was news to Caitlyn.

Legislators, lobbyists, mining? What are they talking about?

She'd had enough.

"I have a question about the mining."

"We'll explain that later. Right now I want to get through these budget sheets," John stated.

William Webber looked at her over the top of his glasses.

She studied the budget sheets and noted potential customers and their geographic areas. Most were on the west coast, probably because of North Korea's recent threats to explode a hydrogen bomb in the atmosphere. The east coast needed protection as well, but that would be a topic for another day. She had to focus on the report in front of her and get answers to her questions.

Then she noticed the discrepancy. An account number that was different from the others. Before she could ask, the housekeeper approached and whispered something in John's ear.

He rose abruptly and stated, "That's all we have time to discuss today. Send your comments to me via email with a copy to Bill. Please excuse me, but I've got to take an important call."

To his retreating back, Caitlyn said, "I've got a question on a budget line, an account number is different from the rest, and . . ."

She turned to look at William Webber and Jack.

"Can you answer my questions?"

William Webber moved over and sat next to her. He looked at the budget sheets in her hand and commented, "Budgets are complicated and not everyone can understand them. I'll put it into a more readable format, and that might help you understand it better," he said as he took the papers from her.

She was reluctant to give up the folder containing the budget materials, but he was right. The financial documents should not be out where they might inadvertently be left for others to see, though she noticed that Jack had tucked his into his briefcase.

William Webber packed up his paperwork and disappeared into another room. Jack had already retrieved his coat and was out the door. Meeting over. When she got to her car, she pulled out her phone. Did she dare text Ethan? Would he have his personal phone with him? She went ahead with a cryptic note.

Something fishy with S-G accounts.

Caitlyn pretended to be busy organizing her tote as she kept watch on the front door, but William Webber didn't come out. If she stayed longer, it'd be obvious she was spying on them. She started her car and headed back to her parents' house. She'd have to decide what to do about her new client.

~

Back at the house, Caitlyn wasn't especially hungry, but stress made her eat. She pulled out a yogurt and walked around the kitchen deciding her next move. As she pulled open the refrigerator door, her phone rang. The caller ID display was Richmond City Morgue. When she answered, Dr. Anderson was on the line.

"Dr. Anderson. Do you have more information?"

"Unfortunately, no. The chief medical examiner had reassigned the intern that was to do the database search to a higher priority project. When I asked for the search report, he informed me it hadn't been done. I put in another request. In the meantime, I requested the FBI Laboratory Trace Evidence Unit in Quantico to develop a facial model. There are many cold cases ahead of this one, but I've cashed in some favors and have my fingers crossed we don't get bumped out of the queue."

"How does that work? You only have skeletal remains and some fabric."

"We have enough to allow the forensic anthropologist to determine sex, age range, ancestry and physical stature. I hope there will be enough DNA to run comparisons with the details the forensic anthropologist finds. Several cases have been solved using this method, but, again, it comes down to priority."

"Sounds like science fiction to me," Caitlyn stated.

"Very close," Dr. Anderson replied with a laugh. "Do you have any news on your end?"

"I did a newspaper search and found a photo that features a young girl about the age of our victim, and about the time of death. The paper identified the girl as Cassie White. I visited the high school to see if anyone recognized her. No one did. Last summer a number of protesters were in town and she might have been one of them. They created quite a stir and tempers flared."

"Email me the newspaper clipping."

"I'll do that now," Caitlyn replied, "and let me know if your staff finds anything. In the meantime I'll continue to ask around to see if anyone recognizes her."

"Caitlyn, I know I encouraged you to find information on this girl, but I didn't intend for you to investigate. That job is for law enforcement."

"I don't think the sheriff or the state police are doing anything. I understand there are many open cases ahead of this one, so that's why I'm gathering information that might help. I'll take your advice and proceed with caution."

Caitlyn took a photo of the newspaper clipping and emailed it to Dr. Anderson. With that done, she walked back to the kitchen, and as she entered the room, her phone alerted her to a text. She picked it up. A text from Dr. Anderson.

Database search done. No matches.

~ TWENTY-TWO ~

Despite the negative database search results, Caitlyn's talk with Dr. Anderson had given her an adrenalin rush. The fact a facial construct could be done, and that Dr. Anderson would shepherd that process was exciting news.

She washed out the yogurt container and placed it in the recycle bin.

Bud and Lilla Higley knew what was happening in the town. Now that she had a *possible* name for the victim, she'd talk with the Higleys. She headed to the door, but a soft whimper stopped her. Summit sat with his head tilted.

"Okay, boy, you can ride along, though you'll have to stay in the car."

Summit heard the word "ride" and danced around.

Not trusting the accuracy of her GPS on the rural roads, Caitlyn memorized the directions to the Higley's home that she had found through maps on her laptop. Using both resources, she located the doublewide mobile home several miles west of town. She hoped to catch them both, but suspected that Bud would still be at work.

The Higley's driveway was long and disappeared deep into the woods. She stopped near the mailbox to rehearse how she'd approach the subject with Lilla, assuming the woman would talk to her.

There was a pull-off halfway down the drive where Bud parked his truck and trailer, and further down the driveway ended to the left of the mobile home. The home had faded beige siding and equally faded dark brown trim. A ramp to one side of the front porch would allow Lilla easy access. Sheer curtains hung across the windows.

A cool breeze came up as she stepped out of the car. She reached for her sweater.

"Stay, Summit," Caitlyn instructed. She rolled down the windows to give him adequate airflow. He understood and lay on the passenger seat, head resting on his paws.

Caitlyn approached the house, looking around as she did. The mobile home sat in a small clearing surrounded by dense woodlands. Tall pine trees towered over the home, encroaching onto the once cleared land. The forest was reclaiming its rightful space, and allowed little sunlight to filter through. The place gave her an eerie feeling, but she'd come this far. She couldn't just drive away. She walked up the ramp and knocked. The door opened almost immediately, which surprised her since Lilla had trouble walking.

"Good afternoon, Lilla," Caitlyn said. "Do you remember me? We met at the restaurant the other day."

"I remember," Lilla responded. "What do you want?"

"Do you have a few minutes? I have something I'd like to show you."

Lilla nodded and then repositioned her cane.

"Why don't you bring your dog in? An animal shouldn't be left in a car."

"How did you know Summit was with me?"

"I heard something, got up, and saw you drive in."

Caitlyn nodded. That's why she was at the door.

She did as Lilla requested and brought Summit into the house.

Lilla was unsteady, so Caitlyn took one arm and helped her into the living room.

"Where would you like to sit?"

"My special chair, there," Lilla stated.

She got Lilla settled in her recliner, and when Lilla had her feet elevated, Caitlyn picked up the soft multicolored blanket that had fallen to the floor and laid it gently across the woman's legs.

"That's a nice little dog," Lilla said, reaching her hand towards Summit.

Caitlyn loosened the leash so Summit could approach Lilla and sniff her hand. While Lilla and Summit became acquainted, Caitlyn asked, "Is Bud around? I had hoped to talk to you both."

"No. He's doing some work for Vince Russell. A yacht club," Lilla replied with sarcasm.

"Will the projects slow down now that Mr. Russell is in the hospital?"

"Mr. Russell will be out of the hospital soon and the projects will continue. The contractors have enough work to keep them busy for a while. Then there will be more development, more people and more traffic. Since it upsets me, Bud doesn't tell me much these days, but I hear what's going on in town."

"And that's what I wanted to talk with you about."

"What do ya want to show me?"

"It's a newspaper clipping from last year's Labor Day parade. I found it in the local paper. I hoped you could tell me about the women," Caitlyn said as she pulled the newspaper clipping from her purse.

Lilla's eye's widened and her posture straightened as she studied the photo. A smile spread across her face and her finger paused as she touched each person in the line of parade watchers.

"There's Bertha Thomas. She died in December after a long battle with cancer. I miss her. Fanny Carver is next. She's lived here a long time. Husband passed, but Fanny's still going strong. She has a friend, Tricia somebody, who visited often. Guess Tricia wasn't around for the parade.

Caitlyn froze.

Tricia?

'Next are sisters, Gladys Cole and Delia Brown. Gladys rarely has much to do with the family, and the reason is Delia's two boys are always in trouble. We got no use for them. Their uncle, Gladys and Delia's brother, is the sheriff, and he tries to keep 'em out of trouble, but he just covers for them. Poor Delia."

Lilla handed the clipping back to Caitlyn.

"Lilla, who's the girl at the very end of the line?"

She'd be a great poker player. What's she thinking?

"Who?" Lilla asked.

"The girl. Do you recognize her?"

Lilla shifted back in her recliner.

"It was an interesting time in town," Lilla began.

Caitlyn waited for Lilla to continue.

"Tell me."

"That's Cassie. She came to town with the protesters sometime mid-August. Those kids raised an uproar. Bud had a run-in with them several times as he did his work, clearing land for Mr. Russell."

"Did you get to know her or any of the other protesters?"

"We tried to stay away from town when those kids were around, but one day Bud saw a couple of young girls sitting under a shade tree. He stopped and asked them what they were doing. They were kinda cocky, like we were lower class or something. They told us they were eighteen, but we knew better, and we knew they were part of that protester group and would need a place to stay." Lilla stopped to catch her breath. "We heard most of them were sleeping in the woods. Bud offered the girls a place to stay."

"Did both girls stay with you?" Caitlyn asked.

"The girls were like peas in a pod, but only Cassie stayed. The other girl, and I don't remember her name, went back to town. Bud took her, though we were reluctant to let her go. It was a dangerous situation, and those kids didn't have any idea how dangerous."

"Go on."

"I didn't want the girl staying here. There are tricksters out there, so while she was here I hid our money and valuables. We let her stay in the extra room that has an old sleeper sofa. I told Bud two nights and then she'd have to go. We didn't know how long the group would be in town. We didn't want trouble, or have the rest of 'em showing up here expecting room and board. There were rumors of looting."

"How long did Cassie stay?"

"Only a few days. The group stayed in town a few days after Labor Day weekend. With all the summer folk still here and parade watchers, the protesters had a large audience."

"If you felt the girl was younger than she said, did you report her to the authorities?"

"Bud talked with the sheriff, but he had his hands full with keeping the peace in town and couldn't be bothered."

"This group, do you know if there were leaders? Someone in charge?"

"I heard it was an environmental organization that targets specific areas and then transports youngsters to demonstrate. I don't know if there were any adults. Kids will be kids and if they did have supervision, I don't think it was enough to keep them under control," Lilla explained. "I don't think the organization was as reputable as they wanted people to believe."

"What were they protesting?" Caitlyn asked.

"They were against development that was clear-cutting forests and creating instability in the banks bordering the rivers. There have been mudslides with debris running off into the bay because of that retirement community. More and more houses are being built without an adequate conservation plan, at least not good enough for us. Bud cringes every time he's instructed to clear land near the water."

"Has he discussed his concerns with Mr. Russell?"

"Yes. Mr. Russell listens and then tells Bud waterfront property is what people want. It's all about the business. We heard rumors the moratorium on uranium mining might be lifted. It would be disastrous, but money usually wins out," Lilla stated with a sigh.

Mining moratorium. SafeGrid. Caitlyn's stomach tightened as the pieces of information came together.

Caitlyn turned the conversation back to the victim. She'd deal with SafeGrid later.

"Describe Cassie. What else do you know?"

A smile crossed Lilla's face as she tilted her head and thought.

"Cassie was full of life. I'd say she was about five feet two inches and a slight one. She had blond hair and blue eyes.

Reminded me of Scandinavian descent. Her eyes sparkled and she came to life when she talked about the group and environmental issues. She was passionate. She wanted to save the world as many young folks do."

"Did she talk about her family?"

"We tried to get her to tell us, but she'd clam up. We figured she'd eventually tire of traveling and go home. Most of them were school age. We figured once the school year started, they'd return to their homes."

Lilla pointed to the clipping. "Can we get a copy of that?"

"I'll make a copy and drop it off," Caitlyn replied. She leaned forward, resting her elbows on her knees, as she waited for Lilla to gather her thoughts as well as her energy. She didn't want to create any more anxiety than she knew Lilla was already feeling.

"You said the group left after Labor Day?"

"Yes. We assumed Cassie left with the group. Never said goodbye. Bud went out looking for them, but heard they had moved on. Someone said they went to North Carolina. Like I said, it was time for school to start."

"That must have hurt."

"It did. It sounds silly now, but I liked her. We talked to the sheriff, but he couldn't do anything. She was traveling with a group of protesters."

Lilla sat back and took a deep breath.

"I wonder what I could have said to make a difference and convince her and her friend to go back to their families. Both had blond hair and beautiful blue eyes. Almost like twins. So why are you interested in Cassie?"

"I saw the photo and wondered if . . ." she stopped, not sure how to share the information.

". . . if the remains that Bud uncovered are her?"

"Yes. I have no proof, and you said there were other young girls in the group that were similar looking."

"Yes."

"Then I will continue my search. You mentioned Delia Brown. What can you tell me about her boys?"

"They're a handful, those two."

"I saw how they treated you at the restaurant."

"Oh, pay no mind. That's just how they are. A couple weeks ago Bud was out fishing, near the shore. His boat is small, and since the motor isn't reliable, he doesn't venture too far out. As he sat there and waited for a fish to bite, he noticed those boys dragging a heavy metal object out of the water. They had diving gear on, and a pulley contraption set up. Bud wanted to help, so he pulled in his line, started the motor, and headed to where the boys were. When he got close, they looked surprised, and then angry. Told him to go away. Bud was suspicious about what they were up to and about the heavy metal object. He decided to tell their uncle, the sheriff."

"Did he?" Caitlyn asked, needing confirmation of the players.

Lilla closed her eyes. Caitlyn was getting impatient, but knew if she rushed Lilla, the woman would shut down completely.

"No," she sighed. "Their uncle would cover for them, so Bud had to decide when it's important enough to report their behavior to the sheriff."

"Picking his battles," Caitlyn stated. "Did Bud know what the object was?" Caitlyn asked.

"He figured they'd probably found one of the World War II munitions. Some were dropped in the Atlantic and occasionally currents bring them into the mouth of the bay. And then there are some coming down river from the Naval Surface Warfare Center in Dahlgren."

"Could the munitions still be 'live' after all these years?"

"Some are. Some have mustard gas and other biological weapons of that time."

"What do you think the boys are doing with them?"

"I suppose they could be sold to . . . anybody," Lilla replied.

Caitlyn thought about the possibilities—terrorists, or kids seeking a thrill, both dangerous. She thought of Ethan and the case he was following. Maybe it was time to combine their efforts.

"And Bud didn't think that wasn't important enough to report?"

Her outburst didn't bother Lilla.

"You said it; pick your battles."

"Did the protesters know about these munitions?"

"Can't say. Those kids were all over the town, and even rented boats to survey the rivers and shores of the bay."

"Thank you, Lilla. You've given me a lot of information. I have to get going. I'll be in touch if I learn the whereabouts of Cassie."

Caitlyn had more questions, especially about the moratorium, but they'd have to wait. Lilla showed signs of fatigue. She motioned for Summit to follow her as she gave Lilla's hand a pat and headed to the door.

"Wish I was doing better and could help," Lilla stated wistfully. "But I think the cancer has finally won."

"I'm sorry," Caitlyn responded, taking a seat next to Lilla. Before she could respond further, a noise from the back of the home startled her. She tensed. The dense forest that surrounded the property had spooked her, and it would be easy for someone to break in and no one would see. Summit's fur raised, a soft growl emanated from his throat. Caitlyn's fight or flight instinct kicked in. She looked around for a weapon, but before she could react, Bud Higley entered the room. He wasn't pleased to see her.

"What are you doing here?" he demanded.

Lilla put her hand on Caitlyn's and responded, "She's here to talk about Cassie. She's got a newspaper article of last year's Labor Day Parade when Cassie stayed with us."

Tears formed in Lilla's eyes as Bud approached her. He sat down next to her.

"There's nothing more we can tell you. Please leave. My wife is not well and additional excitement and stress is not good for her."

Caitlyn didn't argue. She rose and picked up her dog.

"Thank you, Lilla, for allowing me to visit. I hope you feel better soon."

She turned to Bud.

"Mr. Higley, I'm sorry if I've upset you or Lilla. I didn't mean to."

In the car she sent off a short text to Ethan.

Call me.

Back in her room, she typed up notes on her conversation with Lilla, her impressions of Bud—his angry request that she leave. If she was going to identify the victim, and for Lilla's peace of mind about what happened to Cassie, she needed more information. Lilla's mention of mining came to mind. Was someone starting to mine a dangerous ore illegally and without proper procedures in place? Did Lilla go near this mine and it triggered her disease? Was SafeGrid involved? Is that what got the girl murdered? She still believed the victim to be Cassie White. She put the finishing touches on her case journal now labeled "The Death of Cassie White."

A text message arrived from John Graves.

Come to the house. We have something to discuss.

~ TWENTY-THREE ~

Caitlyn hesitated as she gathered her SafeGrid material, the questions about the financial discrepancy, and what other business interests SafeGrid was involved with. She wouldn't be involved in anything illegal.

Why aren't we meeting in the office?

John's earlier suggestion that they meet in "a more comfortable setting" ran through her mind. Would other members of the board be there? She didn't like being ambushed, and her instincts warned her about being alone with him.

Stop being paranoid. I have a job to do.

Summit watched her getting ready to leave. He sat at the door with tail wagging.

"Sorry Summit, stay. After this meeting we might be headed home."

His sad eyes told her he understood. Apparently the dog enjoyed living in a retirement community.

John Graves met her at the door.

"Thanks for coming over to the house. I prefer working from my home office rather than the building in town. I'm sorry the earlier meeting ended abruptly. One of our state senators called to update me on the status of the moratorium, and I wasn't sure how long it would take. I remembered you had a question on the budget, and I wanted to clear that up."

The housekeeper appeared with two crystal glasses and a bottle of Perrier. Caitlyn breathed a sigh of relief. They weren't alone.

John poured their water and sat back into the plush leather chair that faced hers.

"I realized that in our haste to get things up and running, we haven't been completely forthright with you," he stated.

She sat, sipping her water, giving him time to explain.

"And you're probably wondering about the moratorium legislation."

"I am, but first I also found an anomaly in the budget lines. One of the account numbers isn't the same as the others and contains a sizable sum. Does the company have an offshore account?"

When he didn't answer right away, she continued. "Is the manufacture of electrical transformers all that SafeGrid does? I can't do my job if I don't have the full story."

John Graves cleared his throat and shifted in his seat.

"SafeGrid was originally a Canadian company in the business of mining uranium, and Virginia has a large uranium deposit. We approached the state years ago to get the permits, but when news got out, residents were vocal against mining. Legislators felt pressured to declare a moratorium on uranium ore mining, but we didn't give up. We kept after the legislators, explaining what a financial boon this would be for the state, and the jobs it would create. Last summer we almost had them convinced to lift the moratorium when a group of protesters arrived. The legislators backed down. It was an election year. They didn't want this issue brought up."

"Isn't mining uranium dangerous?" Caitlyn asked, wondering if her parents should move to another state.

"The ore isn't dangerous when it's underground. The hazard is when the ore is separated from the hard rock, a process called milling. Done correctly, which SafeGrid would do, Virginia's uranium deposits could provide power to every nuclear power plant in the United States for over two years. The entire mining process would provide jobs and an increased tax base for the state."

"There's no guarantee on safety, and I believe the reason for the moratorium is that the risk is too great for residents and the water supply. And another problem is the waste has to be stored for up to one thousand years. If anything goes wrong in the mining or milling process, water source pollution could occur," she added.

"SafeGrid has a team working on this aspect. The bottom line here is that people want *and need* power, affordable power."

"Is SafeGrid still a Canadian company?"

"No. I brought it to the states several years ago, renamed it, and added the replacement transformer unit. That is another critical need. It will be a disaster if the country's old and outdated transformers are not replaced. Our business plan is solid. The company's mission is to *supply* energy through nuclear power, and to *protect* the country's power grid by updating the transformers that transmit that energy to the end users. Since this has political overtones, some of our investors did not want to be named. To accomplish that we needed an off shore account."

"But . . ." she began, but he continued.

"I assure you that we're working to develop a safe method for extracting, milling, and storing. We've identified a parcel of land to bury the tailings. We have to get enough state legislators on board to reverse the moratorium. The country's power needs will only increase, and we need to lessen dependence on foreign oil. Nuclear power is the best way to accomplish those goals. That is why we need someone with your skill set to help us market our products."

"Your intent was to get me onboard with marketing the replacement transformers and then use my skills to get the moratorium lifted?"

"Yes."

She couldn't believe this was his plan. She'd never been in favor of nuclear power. Too much was at stake if something went wrong. But he had a point. Energy was a growing issue. Solar farms and windmills had their own problems, and could never provide the amount of power of a nuclear plant.

"I'm not convinced that nuclear power is the answer, and we can't put people in jeopardy if something goes wrong. I will honor my contract and continue to work on getting start-up funding for the transformer replacements. I cannot, however, get involved in the political process. If you'd like to find someone else . . ." she let the sentence drop.

He didn't look happy, but she had to do what she felt was right.

"Please stay. I'll talk to the board and see what other arrangements we can make."

He stood. The meeting was over. As he walked her out he said, "Let's not let our fundamental differences on nuclear power keep us from having dinner while you're still in town."

She hesitated. John Graves was handsome, charming, and with their business connection, they'd have a lot to discuss, even argue about.

"I'd like that," she replied. "I'm pretty busy now, but maybe on my next trip?"

"I'll make sure that happens," he replied.

~ TWENTY-FOUR ~

The morning sun was on the horizon when Caitlyn walked out onto the patio. She loved this time of day. She wiped the early morning dew from the plush cushions and curled her feet up under her to keep them warm. She took in a refreshing breath of the cool air and set her cup of steaming black coffee on the side table while Summit researched all the nighttime smells.

"Hello," a voice called out.

Caitlyn turned to see Tricia Reilly walking through the backyard. The peaceful morning was now interrupted, but since she felt Tricia hadn't been honest with her, it would be an opportunity to find out why.

"Hi," Caitlyn responded. "Coffee?"

"Love to," Tricia said, looking over the seating area.

"The cushions are damp," Caitlyn stated. She threw Tricia the cloth she'd used to wipe down her seat. "I'll be right back with your coffee."

"I take mine black," Tricia called after her.

They sat in silence for the first few minutes, sipping their coffee, absorbed in their thoughts.

"Sheriff Goodall paid us a visit Tuesday night," Caitlyn said.

"Did he discourage you from playing amateur sleuth?"

Caitlyn ignored Tricia's sarcastic comment.

"He told us someone attacked the developer, Vince Russell."

"Oh, my gosh. I hadn't heard," Tricia exclaimed. "Why did he come here?"

"He considers Dad and I persons of interest in Mr. Russell's attack."

"You've got to be kidding. What's up with that guy?"

"He's just doing his job. I was the last known person to see Mr. Russell before his attack, and Dad had threatened him at the town meeting. But, do we look like the kind who attack people?"

"It seems a bit ridiculous," Tricia replied.

"I think the visit was because the sheriff wants to scare me away from investigating the skeletal remains."

"Does he know you're continuing to investigate and you might have identified her?"

"No. There's no database match. It is only my gut that tells me the remains are the girl in the photo."

Caitlyn put down her mug and faced Tricia.

"Which brings me to my next question. Why didn't you recognize anyone in the newspaper clipping? Your friend Fanny was in that photo."

Tricia put her mug down and faced Caitlyn.

"Are you accusing me of something?"

"Of course not. I'm just asking."

"The answer is I didn't look close enough and I was focused on the girl."

Caitlyn watched the steam rise from her mug as if it would provide the answers. Did she believe Tricia's story?

"I've been thinking about the situation with the skeletal remains," Tricia continued, interrupting Caitlyn's thoughts. "It could have been an accident. If she were out traipsing around in the woods, tripped, fell, hit her head . . ."

"According to the medical examiner, on 'cursory examination,' her words, there was evidence of a blow to the head. Then someone buried her. It was no accident. It took motive *or* opportunity, or both. Something is going on here and we need to find out what."

Caitlyn rose and said, "Come inside. I've set up a crime board."

"A what?"

"A corkboard, actually. Mom and I have added information about the crime."

Tricia shook her head. "*You* are unbelievable," but she got up and followed Caitlyn into the house.

Caitlyn brought the corkboard out of her room and propped it up against the fireplace.

"We keep it out of sight so Dad doesn't get upset," she explained.

Tricia nodded that she understood, and then stepped forward to study the information on the board.

Caitlyn watched to see if any of the notes provoked a reaction. Tricia's jaw clenched a couple of times, but Caitlyn couldn't tell if it was habit, or if it was from something she'd seen on the board.

"I've recently learned that the government is investigating suspicious activity around the bay," Caitlyn explained.

"How do you know that?"

"I can't say, but one of my contacts is a scientist working on a new dead zone that's spreading in the bay. We're beginning to think the cases might be connected."

"What do skeletal remains have to do with a new dead zone in the bay?" Tricia asked as she read the notes on the corkboard.

"The protesters were here because of clear-cutting and pollution of the waters. If the issue in the bay that is appearing now can be linked to any issues last fall, then the cases might be connected. At this point we can't rule anything out. I talked with Lilla Higley, and she identified one of the protesters as Cassie, the girl in the newspaper photo. There was another girl traveling with her, similar looking. The Higleys offered lodging. Cassie stayed a couple of nights, and was out during the day. She might have done exploring on her own and came upon something that got her killed."

"You're assuming way too much."

"What are you two talking about?" Ann asked as she entered the room.

"I was filling Tricia in on the case. I have to add what I learned from Lilla Higley," Caitlyn said as she found a piece of paper and started writing.

"And the attack on Vince Russell."

"Right," Caitlyn responded.

Caitlyn tacked the additional notes on the corkboard. She let out a sigh.

"Do you have something else on your mind?" Tricia asked.

Am I that easy to read?

"My new client, SafeGrid. They're involved with more than I was originally told. The president, John Graves, explained the company has another business plan that I'm not comfortable with."

"And what is it?"

"I can't say, but one thing I can say is I don't trust his chief financial officer William Webber."

Tricia turned her attention back to the board. "May I?" she asked.

"Sure," Caitlyn responded, not sure what Tricia meant.

Tricia read the notes following the thread Caitlyn had developed.

"Those remains might be of someone passing through. Transients."

"I've considered that scenario, but it's more likely she was one of the protesters," Caitlyn said, standing her ground.

Tricia turned away from the board. "I'm sure the police will investigate when they can. In the meantime, when the sheriff talks with Vince Russell he'll know it wasn't you or your father who attacked him, and I also doubt your client is involved. Thanks for the coffee, but I've got to go."

"Thanks for the help," Caitlyn responded, staring at the corkboard.

When Tricia had left, Ann said, "My, that was an abrupt departure."

"I agree. Wonder what's going on with her."

Further conversation was interrupted by Summit's whimper—his alert to her first priority.

~ TWENTY-FIVE ~

When Caitlyn had first checked out the location of the remains, she'd noticed a clearing to the south of the construction site. She assumed it went down to the bay. Now was the time to find out if that assumption was true.

The path into the conservation land showed signs of wear that was not there when she first explored. How many people from the community, besides her, were curious about where the remains were found?

"Come on Summit. We're going for a walk."

They entered the conservation land and walked through the woods giving the crime scene tape a wide berth. The yellow tape that had been strung from tree to tree now sagged.

The sheriff has probably forgotten about it and it will end up in the bay.

When she neared the backside of what was to be the new condo units, someone had posted a No Trespassing sign. She ignored that and let Summit off leash so he could run ahead and follow his nose. She tagged along, noting that the path to the bay hadn't been mowed recently.

The path had several switchbacks. She didn't see any obstacles that would have prevented a straight shot, unless used by a vehicle and they didn't want a steep incline.

Summit reached the shore first, running back and forth, keeping an eye on the water as it lapped against the rocky shore. She watched him play tag with the waves, and then she found a stick for him to chase. After a few minutes, he stopped, turned, and his ears went up. He let out a soft growl.

Caitlyn, too, heard a sound. She was trespassing. She didn't need more trouble, so she looked for a place to hide.

~

Ethan wanted to check out the area a little more before he joined the Brown brothers and learned what else they were up to. He'd driven west for several miles and then circled back. He noticed a sign announcing the future site of Chesapeake Condominiums. He pulled in. Woodland surrounded the property. The building's footers had been poured, but nothing else had been done. He walked around the construction site and then followed the newly bulldozed path and came upon crime scene tape.

This must be where the skeletal remains were found, and the reason construction had stopped. He'd noticed a sign up the road indicating the Forest Green development and assumed that was where Caitlyn's parents lived. He ducked under the sagging tape and inspected the area. He didn't think he'd find anything of value, but it never hurt to have another pair of eyes. He circled around outside the taped area shuffling his feet as he went. As he reached what he felt was the farthest perimeter, he hit something hard.

He pulled a glove from his pocket and brushed the leaves and debris away from whatever his foot hit. He pulled a handkerchief from his pocket, gently brushed the dirt away from a metal shovel blade. The tip was a rust color. Could it be blood? He walked back to his car and put the blade in the trunk.

He continued his walk, and as he passed by the conservation easement, he came to a clearing and a narrow path to the south. He walked over to see where it went, assuming it went straight to the bay, but within a few yards the path made a hairpin turn.

He walked to the first curve, and then a few more yards to another hairpin curve. When he reached the next section he could see water. At the shoreline, the view was breathtaking.

He tore his eyes from the expanse of water and focused on the details of his surroundings. Something heavy had been dragged onto the shore. He knelt down and examined the sand. Metal shavings and rust. Tire marks meant a four-wheeler had been parked nearby. There wasn't a dock, but he had an idea of what the object was and who was involved.

~

"What are you doing here?"

Ethan turned, startled, and then relieved when he saw Caitlyn.

"I could ask you the same question," he replied. This was so like her.

"I was out for a walk. This property borders my parents' home."

Summit raced out of the bushes, where Caitlyn had had a tight grip on him, and ran over to greet his friend.

Ethan bent down to acknowledge the dog and then walked over to where Caitlyn stood. He took her hand to help her over the rocky shore.

"And I believe that why?"

She smiled. "Okay, you got me. I wanted to explore the path down to the bay, same as you. Did you see the crime scene tape?"

"I did."

"Did you have a look around?"

"I did."

"And?"

Ethan smiled. "I found something."

"You did? What?" Caitlyn asked, unable to contain her excitement.

"I'm not at liberty to say," Ethan said, eyebrows raised.

"Stop it."

"Okay, you win. I found a rusted shovel, or at least part of one. That might have traces of blood. I've put the blade in the trunk of my car and will ship it to the FBI lab as soon as I can."

"Could be the murder weapon," Caitlyn said.

"That we don't know. At least there might be fingerprints on it or identifying marks that would tell us who owned the shovel."

"If there is blood on it, what about jurisdiction on this case? It's not related to what you are working on, and the locals might be annoyed if the FBI gets involved."

"That's a good point, but the more I learn, the more I think there's got to be a connection between the cases. Dr. Owens told me that Joseph Wheeler said his son told them he was being sent to the Northern Neck, and that he might visit them."

"So confirmation that one of your missing agents is the son of the waterman."

"Yes. And the agents were searching in the woodlands near the water. Like, right over there," Ethan said and pointed to where he'd seen the metal fragments.

"When I first searched the crime scene area, I found, or I should say Summit dug up, a bracelet. It had the initials CW on it. I think it belonged to our victim, and that the victim is Cassie White, who was in town over Labor Day weekend."

"Did you mention this to the sheriff?"

"Of course not. He's not interested, and besides, I don't trust him."

Ethan shook his head. "Then give me the bracelet and I'll have it tested."

She didn't want to relinquish the bracelet, but it was the right thing to do. "It's at the house. The next time we get together, I'll bring it along."

Ethan checked his watch.

"I've got to go soon."

"Then let's walk back. You can get the bracelet and send it along with the shovel."

~

Caitlyn joined Ethan on her parents' couch and handed over the plastic bag that contained the bracelet.

"This is what I found in my newspaper research," she said handing him the clipping. "The photo was taken last September at the Labor Day parade. See the girl at the end? I think she's the victim and her name is Cassie White."

"Who identified her and what do you know about her?" he asked.

"Lilla Higley confirmed the identity. The girl stayed with them a few nights while the protesters were in the area. Cassie was part of that group. She found housing with the Higleys but came and went as she pleased. I think she went off on her own and witnessed activity that got her killed. Probably the same activity that your agents came upon."

"You're assuming a lot. This Cassie White could have just moved on with the group." Ethan placed the clipping on the coffee table.

"You're right. But I have a feeling the remains are Cassie. I just have to prove it. And then figure out the why and by whom. When you get results from the shovel and bracelet, we'll know more. When can you get the items to the lab?"

"I'll make the call and arrange a pick-up," he responded. "You need to slow down. This is a dangerous situation and you can't interfere with an investigation."

"I don't get the impression anyone is following up on this case. Dr. Anderson would have mentioned it if they were," Caitlyn countered.

"Law enforcement agencies are overloaded, so this case will get assigned a number, and worked when they can."

"So I've been told," she responded but decided not to mention the facial reconstruction. "But it's not good enough. This victim needs justice."

Ethan checked his watch. "I don't have time to argue. We'll talk about this later. Talk with the sheriff. Don't approach him as an outsider. Each community is different and before you barge in you have to learn and respect the culture."

"I don't just barge in," she said in defense.

Ethan knew better, but decided to be politic.

"I'm not saying you do; I am just saying . . ." Ethan countered.

"Yeah, yeah, tread carefully and that is not something I do, right?"

"I'll refrain from answering that," he responded with a smile. They both knew Caitlyn could be impulsive when she got onto something, like chasing down criminals. Her sense of justice overtook her common sense.

"Ingram Bay has one sheriff. Small towns have to share law enforcement services as a cost cutting measure. I stopped in to see Sheriff Goodall, using my alternate identity, posing as a guy down on his luck looking for work."

"How did that go?" Caitlyn asked.

"Not well. When I inquired about whether there was any mining or drilling in the area, he cut the conversation short. Or it could mean he didn't want to say, or he doesn't have time to answer questions from the public."

Caitlyn nodded in agreement. Ethan made sense. She'd have to adjust her modus operandi and learn to assess situations better before she jumped in.

"There's another situation," she began.

"And I have to leave," he stated.

"It's about my latest client."

Ethan looked stunned when she finished telling him about SafeGrid. She showed him the website that explained the business and the situation with the country's electrical grids.

"I don't know what to do," she said. "The transformer part is important, and I want to be part of it, but I'm uncomfortable with their mission of ending the moratorium on uranium mining. It would ruin this beautiful area."

Ethan was silent. She waited for his advice.

"That might be the answer," he said as he grabbed his coat and prepared to leave.

"What's the answer?"

He turned and came back to her. He held out his hand, helping her from the couch. He pulled her close and gave her a hug.

Her timing wasn't always the best, so as they embraced she said, "Did you hear someone attacked the developer Vince Russell and Dad and I are persons of interest?"

~ TWENTY-SIX ~

Ethan took a step back.

"You've got to be kidding."

He looked into her eyes to make sure she wasn't joking.

"Is there a reason you kept this information until I was ready to leave? Actually, I'm late."

"I didn't mean to. It was just . . ." she stopped, seeing the look on his face. "At one of the town board meetings my father was a little hotheaded and he threatened Mr. Russell. It was about the condo units planned on the other side of the conservation easement. And then I went to Mr. Russell's office to get information about him and his company. As you said, it is about knowing the players in town and then putting those pieces together."

"That adds another dimension to the investigation. For now, why don't you stick with your clients' work and let me work this tangled mess of cases."

Caitlyn knew he was right, but she wouldn't let it go. The girl's death was *her* case. Besides, he had his own case, or cases, to solve.

"Maybe you're right," she stated with fingers crossed behind her back.

"I've got to go."

"Where?" she asked.

Ethan hesitated. She was good at inserting herself into his investigations.

"I'm working with two local boys."

"Is their name Brown?"

His expression confirmed she had it right.

Caitlyn held his arm.

"They're trouble."

"How do you know?"

"I saw them at the restaurant. They came out of the bathroom, smelling of pot, and nudged Mrs. Higley as she was leaving. She almost fell. They made a disparaging remark and then drove off in their filthy truck. The waitress said they were trouble. And then Bud Higley said he wouldn't put it past them to be involved in a murder. Maybe they attacked Vince Russell."

"Stay away from them. Is that clear?"

"Clear," she responded.

~

He'd driven several miles north of the Forest Green development before he noticed a small break in the woods. He turned in and drove down a narrow pathway. Deep ragged holes pockmarked the dirt road down to the bay. Any vehicle traversing this lane would be a perfect candidate for transmission and alignment work. Branches whacked the windshield and scrapped the sides of his car as he followed the map Henry had drawn. The steep grade told Ethan their job was near the water.

His tires skidded on the wet clay soil as he came to an abrupt stop after navigating a hairpin turn at the bottom. There was little room to maneuver. How would he get out of there? It wouldn't be easy to back up the narrow twisting drive. He'd worry about that later. Billy Bob, standing near his boat, motioned to him.

He walked along the shore, which took him, at times, out into the water. Ethan's mind raced. What were these guys into that they had to keep so well hidden? He didn't have to wonder long. He walked towards Billy Bob, pushing branches aside as he went, and came to a clearing. A small shed sat against the woods. An old boat bobbed against a rickety dock.

"You're late," Billy Bob stated.

"Sorry. Got held up."

"Follow me."

Billy Bob pulled a key from his pocket to unlock the shed. Ethan stood back, not wanting to appear overly inquisitive.

"This here's where we store the stuff until it's shipped out," Billy Bob explained.

"What kind of stuff?"

“The stuff we recover from the bay, stupid,” Henry James responded. He stood close behind and Ethan almost gagged from the body odor.

“Right. Tell me what to do.”

“We have to load the boat with our diving gear. You dive, don’t you?”

He hadn’t dived since he was a teenager.

“Sure. Let me help with the gear.”

Billy Bob laughed and slapped his brother on the back until he, too, laughed at a joke that Ethan didn’t get.

“You’re not diving us with,” Billy Bob stated when he got himself under control. “We need you inside.”

When Ethan stepped inside the shed, he understood some of what the boys were involved in. Two rusted cylinders were propped against one wall. If his memory served him correctly, these ordnances could still be live, contain mustard gas and possibility other biological weapons. Could that be what’s creating the dead zone in the Chesapeake? Is this what Joe and Tara discovered?

“Where do you get these?” he asked.

“In the water. Some come in from the Atlantic, and some from upstream,” Billy Bob explained.

“We didn’t know what they were at first. A guy in town heard us talking about what we found and he offered us money if we could find more,” Henry James added.

“Shut up,” Billy Bob said. “You talk too much.”

Henry looked down in shame.

“Don’t worry,” Ethan said. “I won’t be tellin’ anyone.”

Ethan walked around the shed and noted the quality of the diving gear they had ready to put in the boat.

“I’m impressed with your gear. Must have cost you a bundle.”

“It’s provided,” Billy Bob responded, his chest swelling with pride. “We need good equipment for what we’re doing.”

“That’s what our ‘entrepreneurial’ is about,” Henry James stated, proud to remember the big word he’d learned from Ethan.

"Yeah. We got us a gold mine," Billy Bob said, nudging his brother. They both started to laugh.

"What do you want me to do?" Ethan asked, showing his impatience.

The boys stopped laughing, turned sober, and Billy Bob gave his brother a warning.

"If we let you in on this, you get a small cut. And if you tell anyone, we'll kill you. Got it?"

Ethan looked at the boys, their expressions grave. They weren't kidding.

"Hey, I'm new here, and yeah, I'm game for getting a small amount of anything. When do I start?"

They showed Ethan a cabinet at the back of the shed. Billy Bob pulled out a map of the bay and its tributaries.

"We're diving for the munitions at the mouth of the bay. When we find 'em, we drag 'em to shore, then up to the warehouse where they're boxed and ready for shipment. The boss has customers, and he said he'd give us 10% of the income from the munitions and he paid for our dive equipment. One day when we were out searching for more, and going along the shoreline, we noticed bones and other junk."

"Go on," Ethan urged.

"We found an Indian burial ground," Henry James blurted out as he danced around.

"Like I said, we didn't know what the bones and junk was worth, but it's a gold mine. We ain't told the boss. It's all ours," Billy Bob said.

"Good thing my brother's smart," Henry James stated, smiling at Billy Bob.

"Why's that?"

"Because he found a buyer. We met some guy in a bar. He's from New York. We started talking about diving for stuff. He was interested and gave us his card. He said if we ever came across any early Indian artifacts to contact him," Henry James stated.

"I gave the guy a call, and it worked out," Billy Bob said with pride.

"I guess it did," Ethan replied. "When's your next dive?"

"Later this afternoon if we can get the boat running," Billy Bob said.

"If I'm not diving with you, what do you need me for?"

"We need someone who can research the stuff we bring up . . . and how do they say . . . catalog it. We want to make sure the guy is giving us fair value. We ain't about to be taken advantage of. You know about computers don't ya? Can you make a list?"

"You're right. They shouldn't take advantage of you. You're doing the work and I know about computers. Where are the items and how should I list them? Word or Excel?"

The boys didn't seem to know what he was talking about. Instead, Henry James ran over to a rusted file cabinet, opened the bottom drawer and took out a new HP laptop. He turned to Ethan with a satisfied smile.

"We stole this." His smile faded, as he added, "but we don't know how to use it. We hoped you would."

Nothing about these two would surprise him.

"I can make that work, but we'll have to figure out a way to get a printout."

Henry James gave him a slap on the back and lifted the laptop's lid. "Don't worry. We'll figure that out another time. Just need the information in that thing so we can look at it."

Billy Bob stood at the doorway with a satisfied smile on his face. "You're gonna do fine. The top three drawers have items you can get started on."

"Okay," Ethan said and walked over to the table. He pushed the power button, and the laptop came to life.

"We gotta work on the boat," Billy Bob stated.

When the boys were at the dock, Ethan continued his examination of the storage shed. Rusty shelving units lined the walls with a variety of tools, motor oils, gasoline containers, and detritus. When he came to the shovels, he checked to be sure the boys were occupied. He picked up each one for a close examination, but didn't see one with a missing or new blade. If he had a can of Luminol he could test each tool for blood, but since that wasn't an option, he'd have to use his eye.

He replaced the last shovel when he spied a large crowbar and another tool of some sort wedged up against a metal shelving unit. He couldn't get it free without spilling everything onto the floor. The boys would certainly hear that.

He carefully removed the heavier items and placed them behind another cabinet. The space was still tight, so he pressed his back up against the wall and maneuvered his left hand to reach the tool. He felt something plastic wedged behind it. He worked the tool and the piece of plastic towards him, but before he could see what it was, a voice behind him said, "What the hell are ya doin'?"

"I found a tool," Ethan explained, startled.

He moved his hand away from the crowbar, held his breath, and reached for the tool that had a claw at the end. He moved his hand over to that and pulled it away from the wall, palming the small square piece of plastic as he did.

"This."

Billy Bob took the tool from Ethan, examined it, and then yelled to his brother.

"Henry, look what the newbie found."

Henry came running into the shed.

"Wow. And we thought we lost it."

Billy Bob gave Ethan a stern look.

"What we need is that inventory, not you digging around for tools."

Ethan nodded and walked over to the file cabinet where the items were stored. He opened the top drawer, astonished at what he saw. Artifacts, sharpened wooded stakes, and pieces of bone were intermixed. He took out three pieces, sat down at the computer and started the list. The boys didn't understand that the computer had no Internet to research the worth of the items, if there actually was a website with that kind of information. He'd have to guess at the worth of each item.

When the boys were back outside, Ethan pulled the piece of plastic from his pocket. It was an ID card imprinted with the name Tara Jones.

He had to find out what the brothers knew about the agents. He glanced out the door. The brothers were at the shore, working on their boat and arguing. Ethan looked around to see what else they stored. A second rusted three-drawer metal filing cabinet sat against the back corner. Making sure the brothers didn't notice, he walked over to the cabinet and pulled out the top drawer. Rusted tools, hammers, pliers, and screwdrivers that hadn't been used in a long time were piled haphazardly on top of one another. That drawer closed, he tried the next one where he found more of the same, along with nails and nautical equipment. Nothing hidden. This cabinet was a bust. No wonder it was pushed into a back corner. He tried the bottom drawer. Protective headgear, facemasks, and lead vests. Besides desecrating an Indian burial ground, these boys were dealing with something dangerous.

Maybe Joe Wheeler and Tara Jones had found out.

~ TWENTY-SEVEN ~

The black cat sat at the museum's entrance waiting for Ann to arrive.

"Good morning, little one," Ann said as she bent down to pet the cat, a positive step in their relationship. At first she'd put down a treat and walk away. Then she'd stay and talk to the animal. The cat was warming up; a bond had been created.

At the museum, she'd work as a docent, and when there were no visitors, she'd continue the indexing project. Since she started volunteering, she'd rush in, go to the back room, and work on an assigned project. Today, she'd take time to look around. The museum was comprised of four rooms. The largest held most of the exhibits, arranged in a timeline fashion, from the earliest history of the Northern Neck, its Native American inhabitants, to the establishment of Ingram Bay, and up to present day. To the left of the door was a counter with displays of tee shirts, local history books, and a few children's books.

Ann was nervous about using the credit card machine, and if anyone visited the museum and wanted to purchase something, she prayed they'd use cash, which reminded her to put out the donation jars.

Two smaller rooms were off to the right. One served for the revolving displays, like the one on the Native American cultures, the history of Christ Church, and the early settlers. The second small room was for research. A wooden rectangular table with four chairs occupied the middle of the room. Along the walls were file cabinets and bookshelves. The room at the back was where Ann usually worked, but today she didn't want to index or sort through old papers.

What do I feel like?

She checked the exhibits to see if any needed cleaning. When everything looked shipshape, she walked into the workroom. It was then she remembered the woman's journal.

"It's just what I need, a fun diversion while I wait for visitors," Ann said to the empty space.

She skimmed through the journal and then started with the last year. She was curious. Did the woman have a premonition about her death? Ann settled back in the chair and started to read. She came to September and read about the town's Labor Day festivities. She sat up, eyes wide.

I wonder if Caitlyn knows about this?

Ann went over to her purse and searched for her phone.

It has to be here somewhere.

Her anxiety rose and then subsided as she touched the phone's case. Her fingers found the device and scrolled down her contacts to find Caitlyn's number. She touched the number, but the call went directly to voice mail.

Where could she be? Why isn't she answering?

Caitlyn asked her to help with the case, and now she had important information to share. The museum had been quiet. Maybe she could close early. In her creative groove, she'd have her phone off, or wouldn't pay attention to it.

As Ann walked to the front door with the intention of closing the museum, the first visitors of the day walked in.

Frustrated, but doing her best not to show it, she said, "Welcome to the museum. Have you been here before?"

~

It was a perfect spring afternoon. Trees and bushes had started to leaf out, and the colorful spring bulbs took turns cycling through their individual blooming seasons. Goldfinches were yellow again, having shed their drab winter feathers. Hummingbirds would arrive soon, and they were a favorite. Caitlyn noticed the sun was getting low in the west. It should be dinnertime, but she wasn't hungry.

"Honey, I'm home," her father shouted, trying to be funny, as he came through the garage door into the kitchen.

He came out onto the patio where Caitlyn sat and noted her somber expression.

"What's the matter?" he asked.

"I've been thinking about Lilla Higley."

"Are you still fussing about those skeletal remains?"

"Yes. The Higleys housed one of the protesters, Cassie White."

"Who?" Herb asked, wiping his brow. He sat down, his breathing shallow, his face pale.

"Dad, you don't look good. Let's go inside where you can lie down."

"I'm fine," Herb responded. "And as far as the Higleys, there's nothing you can do. Let the police take over the case. They'll find out who killed that girl. Get on with your life."

She didn't expect any other response from her father and regretted bringing it up.

"Okay, then let's talk about your health. Have you forgotten how you ended up in the hospital last year? Mom and I want you to stay healthy, and getting yourself worked up at these town board meetings isn't a way to do that. I'm sorry I posed as a freelance writer in order to talk with Vince Russell, but it was the only way I could think of to question him. He's new in town, a big time developer, and some developers will do anything to get around building codes. I thought maybe the girl caught on to what he was doing."

"I, too, am ashamed at my behavior at the town board meeting. I guess we're even."

"We'll be even when you agree to slow down a bit, and start eating right," Caitlyn countered, and then turned when she heard the garage door open.

"Mom's home. She's going to notice your shortness of breath."

Ann rushed into the house, eager to share what she'd learned from the woman's journal, but stopped when she stepped out on the patio.

"Am I interrupting something?" she asked, and then noticed her husband's color. "Herb, are you all right?"

"I'm fine. Just overdid it a little. Now, tell us your news."

"I read something in that woman's journal that might be important."

"Really? Tell us," Caitlyn said

"The woman wrote about a group of environmentalists and the disruption they caused. Apparently, food and other items were stolen and the woman was afraid of a break-in. She mentioned that the Brown brothers liked to follow some of the protesters around, especially the girls. She also caught rumors of mining and drilling, which upset her. I can show you the entry if you come to the museum."

"Thanks, Mom. I would love to read what this woman wrote. Did she mention any names?"

"I didn't notice any, but visitors to the museum interrupted me and couldn't finish reading the entry."

"I'm glad she kept a journal. Keep reading and let me know what else you find of interest, especially any names."

Caitlyn glanced at her father.

"Dad, do you have something to say?"

Ann sat next to her husband, a worried look on her face.

"Herb, it's time you took your condition seriously. I've been after you to see a doctor here."

"I know," Herb replied. "I'll make an appointment soon, but right now, I have to get on a conference call that the oil company asked me to participate in. There's a crisis brewing in the Middle East and there's a good chance our oil supplies will be cut. We're ramping up production here, but we're also exploring investing in alternate energy sources."

"Like nuclear power?" Caitlyn asked.

"Yes," Herb responded, getting up. "The country has a good supply of uranium. It just has to be mined. Now, I'd better get to my office."

~ TWENTY-EIGHT ~

Caitlyn arrived at the Lazy Days Diner near the bridge that spanned the Potomac River over to Maryland on the opposite shore. Ethan had sent a text and asked her to meet him there. She checked the time—eight p.m. At eight ten he drove in and parked around the back. When he approached the front entrance, she joined him.

"What if someone sees us?" she asked.

Ethan shrugged. "Don't worry. I've got a plan if that happens."

They headed to a booth farthest from the door. When they were seated a waiter brought them menus.

"What did you want to see me about?" she asked.

"I discovered something today. The Brown brothers took me to a shed where they're bringing items they've retrieved from the bay."

Caitlyn moved forward on her seat. "What are they finding?"

"They're retrieving . . ."

"Are you ready to order?" their waiter asked.

They glanced at the menus, made a quick choice of peach pie à la mode.

"And a cup of herbal tea," Caitlyn added.

"Make mine coffee, black," Ethan said, handing the menus back.

When the waiter disappeared into the kitchen, Ethan continued.

"The boys have found and are retrieving items from an Indian burial ground."

"Isn't that illegal?"

"It certainly is. Removing artifacts is a misdemeanor, but they've brought up bones, and that's a felony."

"Are you going to report them?"

"Not yet, because what I also found is Tara Jones' ID."

"One of your missing agents."

"Now I can tie these two into the disappearance, but I need more time to figure out what happened, and if they murdered the agents and dumped their bodies in the bay, or if the agents are being held somewhere."

"What would be the purpose of that?"

"A trade. Whoever is running the show is planning something big, and they might need a bargaining chip. The Brown brothers don't have the mental capacity to plan the dives, or the funds to purchase the equipment, and find buyers. Someone else is orchestrating and bankrolling their activities."

"Will the ultimatum come soon?"

"If I'm right and Joe and Tara are alive, I don't know for how much longer. I have to find them before they're no longer useful."

"What about your kidnap victim?"

"I've been working on that. I received permission to talk with the father. I also learned that the Brown brothers are retrieving munitions from the bay."

"Munitions? Like military? Lilla Higley mentioned that, but I thought she was mistaken. If they get into the wrong hands . . ."

"The munitions are mostly harmless, but a few could still be live and some contain biological weapons."

"Do you have an idea who the mastermind is?"

Their waiter approached. Caitlyn sat back and smiled at Ethan to appear as if they were there to enjoy each other's company. Not far from the truth.

The waiter set their pies down, followed by their beverages.

"Is there anything else I can get you this evening?" he asked.

"No. Thanks," Ethan stated, his tone sharp.

Caitlyn glared.

When the waiter left, Ethan said, "Sorry. I didn't mean to be rude. I'm just under a lot of pressure."

"How can I help?"

Ethan's phone buzzed. He checked the caller I.D.

"I have to take this."

When Ethan concluded his call, he said, "That was Dr. Owens. He's received reports from the lab and wants to meet with me. He thinks, and I agree, that the cases are connected—the cold case, the kidnapping, the dead zone issue in the bay, and the missing agents."

While they ate, Caitlyn shared information she had gathered on Cassie White.

"Lilla Higley told me what she knew about Cassie. Cassie and a friend were traveling with a group of environmental activists. I wonder if Cassie stumbled upon what the Brown brothers were doing and got caught. I need to get to the library and do more newspaper research. My first time there I had blinders on, only scanning articles about a runaway girl. I missed a lot of other news that would be pertinent to our cases. And coincidentally, today Mom found information in a journal donated to the historical society. The woman mentioned articles from the paper about the protesters, the disruption, and where they went after Ingram Bay."

"Will you contact the medical examiner again?"

"Yes. I want to tell her what I've found."

"Any word on Vince Russell?"

"No, but I have him on my list to talk to. He arrived in Ingram Bay just months before the girl was murdered. When I talked with him, my goal was to find out about his background, his temperament, and if he has anger issues. When I brought up the remains he ended our conversation, and said he had clients waiting for a call back."

"Why am I waiting for a but?"

"I noticed something on his desk."

"You were snooping on his desk?"

"No! I was walking around the room looking at the framed pictures of his projects and bumped into his chair. I went to straighten it and noticed SafeGrid letterhead and the signature was of William Webber. He's the finance person at SafeGrid, my new client. Before I could read the details, which I tried to do, I heard him coming back with our coffee."

"It's also possible the sheriff is part of whatever is going on. This town is too small for him not to know. His warning to you and your father was to stay out of the town's business," Ethan said.

Their conversation came to an abrupt halt when the waiter arrived with the check.

Caitlyn leaned in. "Do you think Bud and Lilla Higley are involved?"

"I think it's interesting she told you so much," he responded. "And it might be her way of diverting attention away from them."

"Or, they're trying to figure out how to tell someone what they know. They depend on the businessmen for their livelihood, and I can't believe they would harm a young girl," Caitlyn said.

"You don't know the circumstances. Focus on that. If the remains are those of a protester named Cassie White, then her movements in town will tell us why she was murdered."

They got up to leave and on the way out, Caitlyn said, "I'm worried about Dad. He was out of breath and very pale when he arrived home this afternoon."

"Then you better get back."

~

Caitlyn arrived at the Bay Hospital and found her mother in the waiting room.

"Mom, I got here as fast as I could," she stated and put an arm around her mother. "Why didn't you call me sooner? How is he doing?"

"Slow down," Ann said. "There was nothing you could do, so I waited until I knew more. They're running tests and if he needs surgery, he'll go by ambulance to Richmond."

Caitlyn held her mother's hand. Her mother appeared strong, but Caitlyn sensed she was on the verge of breaking down.

"He'll be fine. He has a strong system and a will to live."

Her mother's expression did little to relieve her own anxiety. She didn't want to think about her parents getting old, getting sick and dying. In her mind they always stayed the same. Her father's first heart attack should have been a warning, but it was a warning he refused to heed.

A doctor finally appeared and told them Herb was being transferred to a hospital in Richmond. He advised them to go home, get some rest, and check in with the hospital in the morning.

"Mr. Jamison needs to rest," was the doctor's advice.

Caitlyn walked her mother to her car.

"I can't let him go there alone," her mother said.

"The doctor says he needs rest, and so do you. Do as he says and we'll drive over first thing in the morning."

Her mother nodded. "You're right, but I won't sleep a wink."

~ TWENTY-NINE ~

As promised, Caitlyn had the car warmed up at eight and waited for her mother to gather her things.

"What about Summit?" Ann said as she slipped into the passenger seat.

"Tricia will stop by and let him out in a couple of hours. I left the back door open and I'll stay in touch with her about when we'll be home," Caitlyn replied.

They arrived at the Richmond hospital at nine and went immediately to Herb's room.

Caitlyn stood back to let her mother have a moment with her husband. While she waited, she noted the hospital wasn't far from the morgue where she'd met with Dr. Anderson. If the opportunity came she'd slip away and see if Dr. Anderson was available.

Herb was taken into surgery at noon. Caitlyn and Ann waited in the hospital lounge area.

Caitlyn's phone vibrated. She checked the caller ID—Dr. Anderson.

"Mom, I'd like to take this. Will you be okay?"

"Of course," Ann replied, resting her head against the wall and closing her eyes.

Caitlyn walked down the hall and found a secluded spot.

"Dr. Anderson. Good to hear from you. Do you have any news?"

"We retrieved a DNA sample from the bones and my staff is running it against databases."

"Any news on the facial reconstruction?"

"Not yet, but I have a good feeling that we'll find this girl's family soon and can release the remains."

"That's great news. Thanks for the call," Caitlyn said.

She walked back to join her mother. "Mom, I have to run back to the house. In my rush to get Summit fed, walked, and get out of the house this morning I forgot to bring my laptop. I've got a couple of deadlines coming up."

"No need to explain. Your father will be in surgery for a while, and then in recovery. We won't be able to see him for hours, and if he is in ICU, which I suspect he will be, they may only let me in."

"I'll hurry," Caitlyn said as she picked up her purse and headed to the door.

She drove east and tried to remember the shortcut she'd taken on her last trip to Richmond. The route numbers were confusing. She was lost. She looked for familiar markers and slowed at one intersection deciding which one to take.

Keep driving east.

She spotted a familiar landmark, an old plantation house.

She turned and drove down the road and slowed as she approached the driveway. She stopped to have a quick look. The drive was long with weeds covering this once magnificent entrance. In her mind she saw fields of crops on either side, and out buildings to house the slaves—a horrible time in our country's history. She'd love to see the inside of the house. Would it still have elements of grandeur or had the years and war taken their revenge? She couldn't explore now, but maybe take a quick peek on the way back.

~

It was almost two o'clock when she got to the house. Summit needed attention and there was an email from John Graves asking for a clarification on several points she'd made in her last communication. Several neighbors dropped by asking about her father—apparently word spreads quickly in a retirement community. At five o'clock she called her mother.

"Mom, I'm still at the house. How's Dad?"

"He made it through the surgery with a couple of minor issues to be resolved. He's in recovery now, and then in ICU. When he gets there, I can see him for a few minutes. Why don't you stay home? One of our neighbors sent a text saying she was in town for dinner with friends and could bring me back."

"When will they have the prognosis?"

"Soon, I hope."

"I'd rather come get you. I'll have a bite to eat and drive back to the hospital," Caitlyn responded.

She cleaned up the kitchen from her snack and got back on the road. She found the shortcut that passed by the old plantation house. She was still curious about the structure, and although it was getting dark, she'd have just enough time to peek inside. She drove down the long overgrown driveway.

~ THIRTY ~

While he worked at creating an inventory of the Indian artifacts the brothers had retrieved, Ethan came up with a plan. The boys continued to work on their boat, so he walked out to see what they were doing. It was getting late. They wouldn't have time for a dive today.

"Some interesting items you've found," Ethan said.

Billy Bob nodded. "Yeah, and the stuff is bringing in some serious money. Stay with us and you'll earn enough to replace that junker of a car."

Ethan laughed, and said, "Will you be looking for more buyers?"

Billy Bob stood up and faced Ethan. "Why are you so nosy?"

"Not nosy. Just curious," Ethan responded, shrugging his shoulders, and walked back into the shed.

Billy Bob turned back to the boat. The only sound was Henry's cough that seemed to get worse by the hour.

Ethan fingered Tara Jones's card in his pocket. She'd either been here, or the boys had taken it as a souvenir. They were either involved in the disappearance of the agents, or at least they knew about it.

He'd moved his worktable closer to the door. When questioned, he told the brothers the heat inside the metal building would ruin the computer. It needed air. They believed him. Now he could eavesdrop on their conversation. If the two agents were alive, and these guys were involved, they might lead him to them. He listened for some hint and didn't have to wait long. Between coughing spells, Henry said, "It's getting' late. We gotta git to the deli."

"You don't have ta remind me," Billy Bob responded. "We have to finish this coat of varnish if it's going to dry before tomorrow."

"It ain't going to be good if they die," Henry stated.

"They ain't going to die because a meal is late or forgotten," Billy Bob replied, his tone sharp. Then he laughed.

"Like a couple days ago," Henry added, laughing.

They finished the last coat of varnish and came into the shed.

"That's good enough for today," Billy Bob stated.

Ethan stepped to the back of the shed and pretended to be searching for another item from the file cabinet. When he turned back, Billy Bob was within inches.

"We're done for the day. You can go. Keep your mouth shut or you'll regret it," Henry James instructed.

"Should I come back tomorrow?"

Billy Bob walked over to the computer and looked at the screen. He nodded.

"Yeah, you did all right," he said, giving Ethan a critical look.

He's looking for bulges to make sure I haven't taken any valuables. If they searched him, they'd find Tara's card. Then it would be over. He turned the computer off and put it away. Nodding to Billy Bob, Ethan walked to his vehicle, waved, and maneuvered his car out of its parking spot, careful not to get stuck in the mud along the shoreline. He drove up the long rough drive, turned south and found a place tucked in the trees to pull off. He didn't know if they'd turn north or south, but from his vantage point, he'd be able to see which way they'd turn.

His stomach growled in protest. He eaten nothing since morning, but he couldn't leave his post. The boys had to come up onto the main road. Or did they? Could Tara and Joe be held in another shed near the shore?

Darn. There wasn't a place for him to hide near the shoreline.

He debated what to do. He didn't know how long they'd plan to stay, and he couldn't drive back down there until they left. Then he'd have to decide whether to follow them, or go back and check out the shoreline. As he debated which way to go, he spotted their mud-splattered pickup with the alt-right flag flying from the tailgate, one more indication of their stupidity.

Ethan started his car and followed.

The pickup truck parked in front of the Bay Deli at the southern end of town. Ethan drove around the block and parked on a side street. The boys came out with Henry James holding a large white paper bag. Ethan figured it would hold enough food for two people. He hoped those two people were the missing agents and not the Brown brothers.

~

The boys drove ten miles west into the countryside. The straight stretches of road made it difficult for Ethan to keep far enough behind so they wouldn't notice him. The truck slowed and turned into a dirt driveway. A large plantation house surrounded by three outbuildings sat in the middle of a large field. The house and buildings were covered with brush and had deteriorated beyond repair. When the boys pulled into the long tree-lined driveway, Ethan continued down the road. He pulled off and waited. He'd taken a quick survey of the property. If he were keeping someone there, in which building would they be?

It was dark when the boys left. He'd have to work fast to explore the outbuildings on the property, and if this is where the agents were being held, he hoped there wasn't someone guarding the place. The other option for their stop here was this was another place where they stored their illegal finds.

He cut his headlights as he cautiously drove down the lane. He approached the house and saw the circular drive. Ethan drove around the circle and parked his car facing down the drive, so if there were a guard or unexpected company arrived, he'd be able to make a quick get-away. He stood by the car to orient himself to the property. The portico columns were rotted, and the few shutters that survived were weathered and hung at odd angles. Part of the roof had caved in. Ethan retrieved his flashlight from the trunk. There was a rustling sound behind him. He tensed, turned and shown the light into the intruder's eyes.

Startled, but recovering quickly, Ethan stated, "We keep running into each other in the most unlikely places."

"I agree," Caitlyn responded, hands on her hips, ready for the lecture she knew was coming.

He let out a sigh of frustration.

"What are you doing here?"

"Dad's in a Richmond hospital. He had surgery and is in ICU. I went home to get my laptop, and now I'm on my way back to pick up Mom. I noticed this place. I wanted to see it up close, and I could ask you the same question."

"I followed the Brown brothers here."

"Was that them?" Caitlyn exclaimed. "When I heard a vehicle drive in I came out of the house and hid. I didn't see who was in the truck, just waited for it to leave. I didn't want to be arrested for trespassing."

"You need to get out of here. It's dangerous."

"So was taking down that drug lord in New York, but I did it anyway."

He let out a long breath. Another debate he had no time for. He had to check the buildings.

"If you won't leave, you have two choices. You can stay hidden or you can come with me and follow *my* directions to the letter. No going off on your own. Agreed?"

She nodded.

He was angry and tense. She had inserted herself into his world where she didn't belong. It was too dangerous.

"You're right. I'll stay back and follow your lead. Let's stop talking and find out why those guys were here."

"Where's your car?"

"On the far side of this building. I didn't want to be caught trespassing, so I found a place to park where no one would notice."

He pulled out his flashlight and proceeded to the first building that had a missing door.

"Wait here," he instructed. Satisfied there was nothing in the that building, they went to the next. That door was solid. Ethan slammed his weight against it several times before it gave way. He walked in, looked around, and returned. Nothing but rotted wood scraps. They walked to the third building, this one built of concrete block.

"This is different," Caitlyn remarked.

"I agree. I wonder what it was used for."

Caitlyn shivered. "Maybe it was where they kept slaves that were being punished."

Ethan shook his head in dismay.

"It isn't much different today. We're still discriminating against people that aren't exactly like us, or of the same mind," Caitlyn said

"You're right, but that conversation is for another time. We need to get into this structure, and if it, too, is empty, we'll explore the main house."

"Did you notice the broken windows at the house? I had just ventured in when the Brown brothers drove in. Some of the flooring is rotted."

"Thanks for the info. We'll be extra careful if we go in there. Follow and stay close. Let's check this last building."

As they approached, they noticed the door had a new padlock.

"That's promising," Ethan whispered. "Something valuable is being stored in this building. Makes sense since it's the most secure of the three. Follow me around back to check the perimeter."

Caitlyn's stomach clenched with anticipation. What if the agents were in there? Would they be alive, or dead? If alive, tortured? She couldn't bear seeing that.

They walked through tall brush to the back of the structure. Ethan stopped and put out his arm to stop Caitlyn.

"Listen."

"Did you hear something?"

"I think so," he responded. He shone the light up the wall until it reached the top where they saw a small window covered with bars and chicken wire.

~

Tara Jones had just finished the soggy egg salad sandwich their captors had dropped off. She, too, heard a noise. She walked to the outer wall and looked up at the window and thought she noticed a light. It was brief, but she was sure it was there.

"Joe," she whispered.

"What? Is your sandwich as pitiful as mine?"

"Did you hear something?" she asked.

"Yeah. Probably an animal."

Tara continued to scan the top of her outside wall.

"I saw a light and it was moving," she said. "It's no animal."

"Help," she called out.

~

At the sound of a female voice, Ethan pointed his flashlight at the window high above.

"I'm Ethan Ewing with the FBI. Who are you?" Ethan asked as he announced himself.

"Tara Jones. Joe's in the next room."

"We have to figure out how to get in. The door is padlocked."

"You might have a difficult time. It gets double locked each time they leave."

"I'll get my tools. Caitlyn Jamison is with me. What's your condition? Will you need immediate medical attention?"

"No. We're okay considering we're trapped in this dark musty place. Food is delivered morning and night, when they remember. Except for the lack of light and sleeping on a damp earth floor, and smelling like, well, we're doing fine," Tara replied. "Joe, you want to add anything?"

"Just get us out of here."

"Does anyone check on you this time of night?" Ethan asked. He needed to know how much time he had to free them. If the door had multiple locks, it'd take him a while.

"Not that we've noticed, and we would have heard something," Joe replied.

"I'm going to get my tools. Hang on. We'll get you out of there. Is Chloe Wright with you?"

"No," Joe replied.

Ethan struggled with the lock. Even his heavy-duty bolt cutters had a difficult time, but he persisted and finally the lock broke apart. He handed Caitlyn a pair of gloves, a pen, and an evidence bag, and then handed her the lock.

"Bag this. Maybe we can get more than the Brown brothers' finger prints from it."

He opened the door and swept his flashlight up and down the walls to locate electrical switches. No such luck. The flashlight lit up a narrow hallway flanked by two doors.

"We're in," Ethan exclaimed.

"We heard you," Joe replied. "I'm in the first room, Tara is in the next one."

Another padlock kept Ethan from easy entry, but this lock wasn't as thick as the one on the outer door, so it broke with little trouble. Ethan pulled another evidence bag from his pocket and they repeated the process.

"Label the bags with place, time, date."

"Will do," Caitlyn responded and then covered her nose. The smell of the old building that had housed two people for several days without bathroom facilities was overwhelming.

At the sound of the lock snapping off, Joe Wheeler pushed open his door. He was young, handsome, fit, and even in these conditions, he gave Ethan a winning smile.

"Thanks," Joe said.

"You're welcome, now let's get Tara out," Ethan said as he focused on placing the bolt cutters in just the right spot to snap them.

Tara Jones bolted out of her confinement and gave Ethan a big hug.

"Please excuse my smell, but I just had to do that. I'd almost given up that anyone would find us."

"We can take them to my parents' house," Caitlyn said. "They can get showers, some clean clothes, and have a safe place to talk."

Ethan nodded. "That sounds like the best plan. Will your parents mind?"

"I'll call Mom, but I know they'll be happy to help." She pulled out her phone and called her mother.

~ THIRTY-ONE ~

Joe rode with Ethan; Tara rode with Caitlyn. The house was empty when they arrived. Caitlyn had called her mother to find out how her father was doing, and was relieved to learn he was resting comfortably.

"There's a guest room and bath down that hall, and one of them can use the master bedroom shower. Show Joe and Tara where they can get cleaned up and I'll find something for us to eat," Caitlyn said as she closed the plantation shutters in the living room and her father's office.

"After they get cleaned up, we'll find another place to stay so we don't intrude," Ethan said.

"Don't be silly. Mom and Dad would want you here. Now, help our guests get settled and I'll make sure they have enough towels. I'll find something for them to wear while I wash and dry their clothes."

While Joe and Tara were showering, Caitlyn was busy in the kitchen warming up a chicken casserole her mother had prepared for tomorrow's dinner. Ethan found the dishes and silverware and was setting the kitchen table.

Tara came into the kitchen wearing Caitlyn's black stretch pants and a long sleeved red tee shirt.

"You look comfortable," Caitlyn commented.

"I am. Thank you. The clothes fit perfectly.

Joe followed, tightening the belt on Herb's pants.

"Thanks," he said. "A little big, but much better."

For the first few minutes all that could be heard was the clanking of utensils. Caitlyn watched as Joe and Tara dug into their food, but then she couldn't contain her curiosity any longer.

"What was it like in there?"

Tara looked at Joe and he nodded for her to share their story.

"We were following a lead on the kidnapping case. We'd worked our way through some thick brush when I heard a noise. I started to turn, and that's the last I remember," Tara said.

"Someone came up on us pretty fast. I was walking ahead of her and didn't hear anything until a thud, and then I was whacked."

"So you didn't get a glimpse of whoever it was that hit you."

"I didn't." Joe said, then stopped and thought. "I was leading the way, and had just dialed my father. I'd told my parents I might be able to get over to the island for a visit after the case finished. The call had just connected when I heard Tara go down. I uttered something, but I don't remember what."

"We woke in separate rooms. At first we didn't know what happened to each other. When I had the strength to make myself heard, I learned that Joe was in the next room," Tara said. "We had major headaches and other injuries. After we'd gotten some rest, we stated brainstorming on how to get out."

"Tell them about the metal box," Joe said.

"Oh yeah," Tara laughed. "When I felt strong enough to walk around the perimeter of the room, I noticed a metal lunch box near the door. I asked Joe if he had one, and he did. I asked him what he thought the box contained." She tipped her head and looked at Joe to finish the story.

"I told her it was probably a bomb. It would be a good way to get rid of us. The culprits would have alibis."

"I decided to look anyway and when I opened it," she hesitated.

"What?" Caitlyn asked, sitting on the edge of her seat.

"It held a sandwich and a bottle of water."

Their laughter was a welcome relief.

When they had polished off the casserole and a green salad, Ethan asked, "Is there somewhere we can talk?"

"Let's use Dad's office. He has a cozy couch and side chair, and a desk where you can sit and take notes. I closed the shutters, so it should be private."

When they were seated, Ethan turned to Tara and Joe.

"I've got a lot of questions and you're exhausted, so we'll discuss a few things now and finish tomorrow. Caitlyn, can Tara and Joe stay for a day or so if needed? We'll debrief and then wait for instructions."

"I'm sure my parents won't mind," she replied.

Ethan turned to Joe. "Tell me what happened."

"As I said at dinner, we'd narrowed our search on the missing girl to a particular area along the shoreline. We'd confirmed Chloe was with the environmental group, but she had wandered off."

"The person who told us he saw her wouldn't identify himself. Said he didn't want trouble," Tara added.

"We were pursuing that lead down through a wooded area toward the bay. Actually," he looked at Tara, "it wasn't too far north of here. We heard a slight rustle, but before we identified who was there, we were knocked out. There must have been at least two of them to get us both at the same time."

"Our phones are gone, but they have such tight security on them, they'll be useless," Tara added.

"How did you get the bruising on your face, Joe?" Ethan asked.

"Twice a day someone delivers food. When the guy comes in, his head is covered with a stocking and we're told to stand facing the far wall while they exchange boxes. One time I tried to grab the arm doing the exchange, not realizing there were at least two people out there. When I got hold of the guy's arm, his buddy sucker punched me in the face. It was pretty swollen for a while. I realized that technique wouldn't work. Tara and I have been trying to figure out another way to escape. We hoped the bureau would get someone to find us. Like you."

"Before you nod off, I have one more question. What did you learn about Chloe Wright?"

"Unfortunately, not much. Senator Wright is chair of the Committee on Energy and Natural Resources and has powerful friends, including the president. We thought the bureau could circumvent his restrictions, but when we left that hadn't happened. Our Airbnb host told us about the protesters that were here last summer, and we talked with a few people around town who thought they'd seen a girl of her description, but then they'd add that there were several girls who looked like Chloe. Tara, do you have anything to add?"

She shook her head. "I think you've covered it."

"I read the file on your flash drive, and it didn't have much. In a kidnapping case, the first few hours are critical, but since she left over nine months ago on her own, that protocol wouldn't work. But after the ransom note arrived, the agents should have been allowed to talk to as many people as they could to figure out her movements," Ethan said.

"So you found the cereal box. Good job. That lead to the bay came in when we were in town, so instead of doing what we planned, we changed course and headed north and towards the water. I didn't have time to update the file."

"That's all for tonight," Ethan said. "You two deserve a good night's rest. We'll talk again in the morning." As he turned to leave he asked, "Do you think Chloe is alive?"

"I don't know," Joe responded.

THIRTY-TWO

Tara was the first one up and she slipped out of Caitlyn's room where her aerobed had been set up. When she walked into the kitchen a woman met her and offered coffee.

"Good morning. I'm Ann Jamison, Caitlyn's mother. Are you Tara?"

"Yes," Tara responded.

"Caitlyn called last night and explained there were a few guests in the house," Ann replied with a smile. "Kind of like old times."

"She and Ethan rescued us yesterday. Caitlyn told us about your husband. How is he?"

"He's doing as well as can be expected. A neighbor brought me home last night so I could get some rest. Help yourself to the coffee. The water in the kettle is hot if you prefer tea."

"Coffee is perfect. Thank you. I've really missed it over the last few days."

"I assume you can't tell me why you're here," Ann said, pouring a coffee. "So I'll ask you a question you can answer. Did you sleep okay?"

"It was wonderful," Tara said as she approached the counter. She poured herself a coffee and sat down at the table with Ann.

"It's generous of Caitlyn and you to house us."

"I'm glad she feels she can offer to help. And Ethan. We've heard about him, and Caitlyn is fond of him more than she wants to admit to us. For some reason they just can't communicate their feelings. I didn't know he was in the area. I wish there weren't so many secrets," Ann said with a sigh.

Tara smiled. "And I wish I could tell you more, but I can't."

"I understand. The last I knew, Ethan was the sheriff of a rural New York town."

"Good morning," Caitlyn said, surprised to see her mother up. "Mom, how are you doing?"

"I'm fine. Just tired."

"How's Dad?"

"Better. I saw him briefly last night. He's sleeping a lot, but if he continues to improve, he might be released in a couple of days."

"And the complications?"

"Those were minor and can be addressed during his next office visit."

"That's a relief. I see you've met Tara. I'm sorry if we've imposed in any way."

"Of course not, Cate. Our home has always been open to your friends."

Caitlyn headed for the coffeepot and said, "Got a text from Chad Owens. The bay authority is closing down fishing and recreational boating on the Chesapeake for the next three days."

"What exactly does that mean?" Ann said. "They can't just shut down an entire body of water."

"It is an extreme measure, and means there's something in the water that's possibly so dangerous they can't take chances. Not sure they've done it before, so whatever is going on is serious. No boating, fishing, swimming. It will create havoc financially for all the businesses that depend on the water," Tara explained.

Ethan came into the room. "Did you hear the news about the bay?"

"We did. Just now. Did you get a text from Dr. Owens?"

Ethan came to an abrupt halt when he saw Ann.

Caitlyn's face turned red.

"Mom, I'd like you to meet Ethan Ewing. Ethan, this is my mom, Ann."

Ethan approached and shook Ann's hand.

"It is very nice to meet you," he said.

"And you, Ethan. I've heard a lot about you," Ann replied with a smile. "Please, help yourself to coffee. Caitlyn, get some breakfast items out for our guests. You must eat before you delve into the next crisis."

Ann rose. "I've got some things to do before I head to Richmond. Make yourselves at home."

"Thanks, Mom," Caitlyn responded, getting up and giving her mother a hug. "I'll get over to the hospital as soon as I can."

Joe walked into the room rubbing the sleep from his eyes.

"What a great night's sleep," he commented, and then noticed Ann.

"You must be Caitlyn's mother. Thank you so much for your hospitality," he said.

"Any time," Ann replied.

Ethan addressed Tara and Joe.

"I've been instructed to transport you to Fredericksburg this morning. Since we don't know where your car is, I'll drive you to the meeting point where you will be picked up and taken to Quantico for a debriefing."

The four sat at the breakfast table sharing information on their backgrounds. They didn't want to discuss the case with Ann in the house. When they were finished and the kitchen cleaned up, Ethan said, "I'll take you to your Airbnb to pick up your things and then we'll drive to Fredericksburg."

"Will you be back this evening?" Caitlyn asked.

"I'll try," Ethan responded.

She turned to Tara and Joe.

"It was nice to meet you and I hope to see you again."

Tara gave Caitlyn a hug and then turned to Ann, who had just come back into the room.

"Thank you for your hospitality."

"That goes for me, too," Joe said, and then turned to Ethan. "We'd better get going."

Caitlyn watched as they drove off, wishing she could be in the car and hear the details of their assignment. It might help her figure out what happened to Cassie White. The similarities between Cassie and Chloe were striking and starting to meld together in her mind.

Could it be?

Caitlyn went to her room, deflated Tara's aerobed, and tidied up. She opened her closet door and looked at the notes on her crime board. An important clue was missing. She needed to find out more about the Labor Day event.

"Mom, I'm going to the restaurant and talk to Joan, the waitress."

The restaurant was busy when she arrived, and conversations were centered on the situation in the bay. Caitlyn looked around for Joan.

Since there was no one to greet her, she picked up a menu and walked to the first empty booth. Caitlyn raised her hand when she spotted Joan rushing towards the kitchen.

"I need to talk with you when you have a minute," Caitlyn said as Joan rushed by.

"About?"

"What you remember about last Labor Day."

"Do you mean the parade and the picnic? We donated a bunch of food they served that day. It was a nice community event. Give me a few minutes. I have two more tables to serve, and then I'll have time before dishes are cleared. In the meantime, I'll think about what I can tell you."

While Caitlyn waited, Joan brought her a cup of coffee. In a few minutes Joan slipped into the booth.

"What kind of information are you looking for?"

Caitlyn placed the newspaper clipping on the table.

"This photo was taken at the Labor Day parade and the girl at the end is identified as Cassie White. I've talked with Lilla Higley and learned that Cassie was one of the environmental protesters in town and stayed a few days with the Higleys. Apparently she was passionate about their mission and aggressive. Do you recognize her?"

Joan studied the photo.

"Can't say I do. There were many people in town that weekend for the end of summer events. The protesters added stress to the parade and picnic planners. There was lots of talk. When you're in a position like mine, you learn to disregard most of it. Gossip thrives in small towns," Joan stated.

"If you can't tell me anything about Cassie, then can you tell me about a company in town called SafeGrid?"

Joan tensed and fiddled with her order pad. She heaved a sigh. Caitlyn watched her struggle with an answer, so she explained.

"I came here to take SafeGrid on as a client. I was told they manufactured electrical transformers, but then I learned about an additional business plan, one that might not be good for the town. You have the opportunity to overhear things while meals are being served and dishes cleared."

"Look, Caitlyn, you mean well, but there are certain people in town that none of us wish to cross. Besides, it isn't my place to share what I've overheard from my customers."

"You didn't answer my question about SafeGrid."

"I just did," Joan said. "If you'll excuse me I have tables to clear and checks to present."

Joan had been evasive in her answers, but maybe she'd think more about the questions over the weekend and decide to share what she knew. Or was she, too, scared to talk?

In the meantime, she'd visit her father and make sure he was okay.

~

Herb was awake when she got to his room. She told him about finding the agents, about Ethan being in town, and about the problem in the bay. She refrained from mentioning her case.

He tired quickly and fell into a peaceful sleep. While he slept, she'd take the opportunity to see if Vince Russell was in the same hospital.

Her luck held. When she inquired about Mr. Russell at the information kiosk, the receptionist gave her his room number.

She entered his room with caution, shocked at the sight of his head wrapped in bandages. Feelings of guilt overcame her. She'd considered him her prime suspect. Did her visit to his office have anything to do with his attack? He faced the window so she couldn't tell if he was awake or not. If not, should she wake him? As she debated, he turned and looked at her.

"Mr. Russell. I'm Caitlyn Jamison. How are you feeling?"

She waited to see if he remembered her. If he had a brain injury, then he might not have recent memory.

"Why are you here?" he asked.

"My father is a patient here. I thought I'd stop in to see how you are doing."

"Is that so, or are you role playing like when you came to my office and posed as a writer. Freelance, isn't that what you said?"

"I apologize. It was the wrong thing to do, but I wasn't sure you'd talk to me if I told the truth."

"Which is?"

"I wanted to learn more about you and what you might have observed last summer and fall. You must have been upset with the protesters that were here. I believe one of them was murdered, and I think that person was a girl named Cassie White."

"Is that the name of the person whose remains were found?"

"I'm not sure," she answered with a deep sigh. "It's what I'm calling her until the remains can be officially identified."

"Who are you, besides the daughter of Herb Jamison?" Vince asked.

"I'm a graphic artist from Arlington. I came to Ingram Bay to meet with a new client. I didn't intend to get involved in a murder investigation. Have the police been here to talk with you?"

Instead of answering her question he asked one of his own.

"Who's your client?"

"SafeGrid," she said, remembering the paperwork she'd seen on his desk.

"Then you need to be careful, and to answer your question, the state police were here yesterday. Asked a few questions and left."

"Has Sheriff Goodall been here?"

"No. The only other visitors were two of my contractors, and they are only worried about getting back to work. Most of the residents of Ingram Bay have no idea or appreciate how much my projects are helping the local economy."

"Do you have any idea who attacked you?" Caitlyn asked.

"No. I was preparing to go on a site inspection. The framing was up and I wanted to check the workmanship. I'm serious about quality."

"You were in your office and unlocked the door when I arrived earlier that morning. Did you leave the door unlocked?"

He stared into space.

"Sorry, trying to remember."

"Take your time. This is important."

"After you left I walked down to the deli for a bagel. I wasn't gone long, so I didn't lock the door."

"Then what happened?" Caitlyn asked.

"I came back to the office, went to my desk and gathered the blueprints. My earbuds were in, listening to music, so I didn't notice anyone until it was too late. The only thing I saw before I blacked out was someone of medium height, and then a sharp pain on the back of my head."

She pulled a small notebook from her purse to jot down notes. "What site were you going to inspect?"

"It's near Sandy Point. There's a new development off the main road. I'm building a house there."

"Did anyone know your schedule?"

"The day before I attended a Chamber of Commerce luncheon at the local restaurant. Twelve attended, and I mentioned that I planned to drive to Sandy Point the next morning to inspect a house. The discussion had been about quality and the fact that I inspect my properties. They all heard, plus anyone sitting nearby, and probably even the wait staff."

"Can you give me a list of who attended?"

"I'll try, but not now," Vince responded, touching his head.

"Do you know why you were attacked?"

He struggled with a response.

"Ingram Bay is a lovely town, but there are strong personalities here. As a business owner, you are expected to be part of the Chamber of Commerce, and join other local organizations. It is part of the plan to control what happens in the community."

"I never thought of it that way," Caitlyn said.

"I thought about packing up and leaving, but by the time I had it figured out, I had already invested in property and had clients eager to move to the area. There's a ready market for this kind of location, a quiet country lifestyle with plenty of boating and fishing opportunities. Hop onto Route 360 and you're in Richmond in no time. And, I've dealt with bullies before.

I suspect the attack was to serve as a warning. Play along or worse things will happen."

Caitlyn shook her head. What did he mean play along. Play along with what?

Before she could form another question, Vince said, "Please go now. I'm very tired. And, Ms. Jamison, I'm sorry someone was murdered and buried in the conservation land. I hope the culprit is found, but you have to believe that it wasn't me."

~ THIRTY-THREE ~

Caitlyn had paced around the house for an hour wondering when Ethan would return. When she heard a car, she ran to the door.

"Where've you been?" she asked.

He gave her a quick peck on the cheek and leaned down to give Summit a pat.

"We had a debriefing at the local police station and then I drove back to the shed where the Brown brothers have me working on their inventory database."

"Do they know their hostages are gone?"

"Oh yeah. They would have found out when they delivered breakfast. They didn't say anything, but acted skittish and angry. There'll be trouble when their boss finds out. I don't think they suspect me, but I'll be extra careful."

"Sounds like things are coming to a head. Did they say anything about the restrictions on the bay?"

"No. Not sure they've heard. They were too wound up about Joe and Tara."

"Dinner's ready. Fill me in on the rest while we eat."

"Ah," Ethan murmured. "Lasagna is my favorite. Did you make it this afternoon?"

She laughed. "I found it in the freezer. Mom always doubles recipes and freezes half. You can compliment her when you next see her, but now tell me what you've learned."

"Several months ago the bureau received word that World War II munitions were making their way into the Chesapeake Bay. The Navy took appropriate action, but no more were found. Then white panel trucks were spotted."

"Which means there's something else going on."

"A ransom note arrived at Senator Wright's home, so Joe and Tara were sent to find Chloe, and also keep an eye out for any other suspicious activity."

"Like munitions."

"Right. Joe and Tara found evidence of munitions being retrieved, and then stumbled on something else."

"What?"

"They located an entrance to a uranium mine."

Caitlyn, her lips tight, nodded, but before she could say anything, he continued.

"Uranium ore is harmless if it stays underground, but exposed to air, it's a different story. The separation process called milling produces yellowcake, and that's what fuels nuclear power plants. You don't look surprised."

"I'm not. My new client, John Graves, asked me to his house the other day and explained SafeGrid's interest in mining the ore. The state has a longstanding moratorium on it, because of the risks, but he explained the company had a plan to deal with those risks."

"According to Joe, the uranium ore under the state of Virginia could be the largest deposit in the U.S., and there are several companies vying for the opportunity to mine it. There's a large deposit in south central Virginia, near the North Carolina border."

"If something went wrong, it could contaminate the water supply of several states."

"Exactly the reason for the moratorium. Before Joe and Tara could report their findings and find out who was behind the operation, they were attacked."

"Why were they kept alive?"

"Ransom, or bargaining power. Whoever is retrieving the munitions and/or opening the mine was keeping them to put pressure on the state's legislators. Tara and Joe were their leverage, or so they thought."

"Wasn't that tricky?"

"These people know which legislators have secrets and will use those secrets to their advantage. Capturing Joe and Tara was a bonus."

"Does this mean my client is part of this? Is John Graves responsible for the attack on Joe and Tara?"

"I can't answer that, but be careful. Don't go to his house alone."

Caitlyn nodded, thinking how she should handle this new situation.

"What if the girl in the photo is Chloe? Maybe she changed her name."

"Anything's possible. We have to wait for the remains to be identified. Joe said the mine appeared to have activity. He knew about the protesters and that they were protesting Vince Russell's developments. Russell was clearing land for houses and another marina, and it would only be a matter of time before the protesters came upon the mine. It's possible the girl wandered off on her own, exploring, and found it. That would have been big news to the environmental protest group. Unfortunately, we think someone noticed her and couldn't take the chance she'd talk."

Caitlyn nodded as the various scenarios played out in her head, and frustrated they were no closer to the girl's identity.

"How could a mine be developed and no one knows about it?"

"Joe thinks it's been there a long time and closed up. Someone must have found it and started the process of reopening it."

"Do you think the girl was killed near the mine or where she was found?" Caitlyn asked and then rubbed her head. "And if near the mine, is the entrance near Forest Green?"

"According to Joe it's a few miles north. It's a fluke Russell's project went over into the exact spot in the conservation land where the girl was buried. Joe and Tara provided me with a lot of information, and will continue to send details as they remember them. I could nab the Brown brothers now with desecration of an Indian burial ground, but I suspect they're working the uranium mine as well as finding munitions when they wash up. One of the boxes I handled at the small warehouse was long and heavy. I suspect it was a piece of the ordnance the boys retrieved. I need to identify the leaders of the operation, and have another conversation with the sheriff."

"Vince Russell is still in the hospital. He claims he doesn't know who attacked him, but I think he does, or at least has an idea. He's frustrated that he isn't appreciated for how he's helping the local economy."

"That sounds about right. People want a healthy economy, but don't want the growth that comes with it. I'll touch base with Dr. Owens to see what he's learned, but now we need to get some rest."

Caitlyn yawned. "It has been a long day."

Ethan cleared his dishes and grabbed his coat.

"Ethan? I'd like to go with you when you talk with the sheriff."

He drew a deep breath.

"Is that smart since he considers you a person of interest in Vince Russell's attack?"

"Probably not, but we're getting close to solving what happened to Cassie and we need to find out if Cassie and Chloe are the same person."

"I have a briefing tomorrow with my boss, and then the first priority is to meet with Chloe's father, Senator Wright on Monday morning. If you want to come along, I'll pick you up at seven. After that we'll visit Sheriff Goodall."

~ THIRTY-FOUR ~

Up at five, showered and dressed by six, she was excited to be helping Ethan on his investigation, which was looking more likely connected to hers.

While she waited for him to arrive, she revised her suspect list.

True to his word, Ethan pulled into the driveway at seven o'clock sharp. She double-checked to make sure she had a steno pad.

"Mom, I'm off," Caitlyn said as she opened the front door.

"Wait," her mother called as she came out of the kitchen.

"What's the matter?"

Her mother hesitated, shook her head. "Nothing. Just be careful."

"Don't worry," Caitlyn replied, and then stopped.

"Will Dad come home today? Should I stay and help?"

"Not today, but if he continues to improve, maybe tomorrow," Ann replied.

~

They arrived in Washington at ten o'clock. Ethan found a parking space close to Capitol Hill.

"Did you hear from your boss whether Chloe's friends were interviewed?"

"Her father requested that no one else be interviewed," he said.

"And the FBI allowed that?"

"Apparently. This guy is powerful in the senate. He must have put pressure on the right person, and the FBI withdrew the agents. I requested permission to talk with him hoping I can convince him to share more information that will help with the search."

"Amazing. You'd think the guy would pull out all the stops to find his daughter."

"Sometimes money and power do strange things to people's priorities."

They found Senator Wright's office and entered. The reception area's carpet was plush, the wood paneling exquisite. Caitlyn admired the artwork while Ethan talked with the secretary, a trim and well-dressed woman in her early fifties.

"Are you Agent Ewing?" the woman asked.

"Yes," Ethan replied and showed her his badge.

The woman eyed Caitlyn.

"This is Caitlyn Jamison. She's here to assist me," he explained.

The secretary gave him a suspicious look, but then announced their arrival over the intercom. She then showed them into the Senator's office. Before shutting the door, she asked the Senator if he needed anything. He shook his head.

Senator Wright was a large man with a commanding presence. Ethan understood how political committees, law enforcement, and even the president would bow to this man's requests.

Senator Wright indicated they take a seat.

"What can I do for you Agent Ewing and, he glanced at the note his receptionist had put before him, Ms Jamison?"

"We appreciate your seeing us, and we don't want to take up too much of your time. The FBI is working hard to find your daughter," Ethan said.

He wanted the senator to know that a missing person, especially a child, should have been reported immediately. The first twenty-four hours were critical. Instead, the senator decided to hire a private investigator.

Senator Wright did not seem ruffled by Ethan's insinuation.

"I was informed by your superiors that you have been assigned to the case. I appreciate all the bureau is doing to find Chloe. We don't understand why a ransom note was sent after so many months," Senator Wright said.

"I'd like more information on Chloe and her interests."

"I gave the bureau all the information I could about her disappearance. I don't think I can add anything else."

"One of my concerns is that you didn't allow agents to do a thorough investigation of your daughter's background. To find a kidnap victim, a thorough search and interview process has to be conducted. Classmates, teachers, neighbors need to be interviewed. Files on her computer showed she was interested in environmental issues. Was she involved in any environmental groups before she disappeared? The reason I ask that particular question is there were environmental protesters in Ingram Bay, Virginia, last summer, close to the location from where the ransom note was mailed. Do you think Chloe was with the protesters?"

Senator Wright cleared his throat.

"We suspected she'd gone off with the environmental group, and that's why we hired a private detective. He traced her to the town of Ingram Bay where she was last seen. We drove to the town to convince her to return home with us, but when we arrived, the group had moved on. Our investigator then traced the group to North Carolina, but by the time they arrived there, most of the group had dispersed. We haven't had any more information on her since. And then the note arrived. I gave the ransom note and its envelope to the FBI. There was no return address and postmarked some small town in southern Virginia. The note was poorly written. I was told the lab couldn't find any identifiable fingerprints on it, which means the kidnapper knew enough to wear gloves."

"Have you received the call for where to drop off the money?" Ethan asked.

"No. Every time the phone rings, we hope, but Agent Ewing, to be honest, my wife and I feel that Chloe won't be coming home."

"I wouldn't give up hope. We will do whatever is needed to find her. Do you know why a ransom note would be sent now since she left last August?"

Senator Wright's face paled. He grew old before their eyes.

"I wish I could answer that. We think it is probably some kind of sick joke. We've tried to keep her absence quiet, but after a while we told people she'd joined an environmental group and was 'traveling'."

"I hate to bring this up, but is there a possibility she's still with this group and is ransoming herself because she needs money?"

"You mean she's alive and trying to get money out of us?" Senator Wright asked.

"Unfortunately, yes. It happens, and it's a scenario we have to consider."

Senator Wright shook his head. He couldn't fathom his daughter would do such a thing.

"Senator, did Chloe know anyone named Cassie White?" Caitlyn asked.

Senator Wright sat back, startled.

"Well, yes. Cassie was her closest friend."

"Where is Cassie now?"

"She died. Last spring. Leukemia, I think. Chloe took her friend's death hard and was sure the toxic environment killed. Our rivers have become more polluted and the kids around here love to frequent their favorite swimming holes. Chloe was convinced it was the polluted water in the river that brought on Cassie's disease. She was also upset about the issues surrounding weed killers. That's what prompted her and her friend, Natalie, to join a group called EnvironmentNow!."

"Did Chloe have any other close friends?" Ethan asked.

"Just Natalie, as I mentioned. But shortly thereafter Natalie moved to Cumberland, Maryland with her family. Natalie is two years older, but the girls were best friends and stayed in close touch. Natalie drove back to Morgantown twice a month for the EnvironmentNow! meetings. They were held Saturday mornings at the local library. We thought it was good for the girls to be involved with an organization like that, but didn't know they'd take it to the extreme. I should have done a better job of investigating the organization, and kept closer tabs on Chloe. But with so much of my time spent here in DC . . ."

"We understand," Ethan stated.

"When we suspected that Chloe and Natalie went off with the group, I checked into the organization and the staff didn't have the girls listed as going. That's when we hired the private detective. I was sure the girls had snuck off and later joined up with that group. We stayed in close touch with Natalie's parents, and in September we received a message from them that Natalie was back at college. We've talked with Natalie, as has the bureau, but she assumed Chloe moved on with the group and hasn't heard anything from her."

Before Ethan could ask another question, the secretary knocked and then opened the door a crack.

"Senator, your meeting starts in five minutes."

"Thanks. I'll be right there," he replied.

Caitlyn opened her purse and pulled out the newspaper clipping and placed it on the desk.

"Senator, do you recognize the girl in this photo?"

He looked at the grainy photo, scanning the women's faces. He pointed to the girl. "That's Chloe. When and where was this taken?"

"At the Ingram Bay Labor Day Parade in September," Caitlyn said. "The caption identifies her as Cassie White."

Senator Wright sighed. "That doesn't surprise me. Chloe and Cassie were so close, and they'd often use each other's names. They thought it was a game. I know it isn't easy being the daughter of a senator, and Chloe struggled with that identity. She wanted to be her own person, and not be just 'the senator's daughter.'"

"Senator, before you go to your meeting, we need Chloe's DNA. Can you provide a hairbrush or anything that might have her DNA on it?" Ethan asked.

"I thought we had provided that, but I'll call my wife and we'll get it sent to the bureau immediately. Now, if you'll excuse me, I'm late for an important meeting."

Senator Wright rose and shook Ethan's hand, then turned to Caitlyn and offered her his hand.

The girl in the photo was Chloe Wright, but was she the girl in the shallow grave? They'd know as soon as the DNA was run.

~

They were well down I-95 before either of them spoke, both deep in their thoughts.

"Do you think Chloe is the girl buried in the shallow grave?" Caitlyn asked.

"I think Chloe chose to honor her friend by using her name when she joined the environmental group. It would also make it difficult for her parents to track her. Assuming Chloe/Cassie is the girl who was murdered, my gut says yes, but we can't be certain until the DNA results are in," he responded. "It is also curious why Natalie didn't think it odd that she hadn't heard from Chloe."

"Sometimes girls have disagreements. It sounds like Chloe was pretty strong-minded, and maybe difficult to get along with. How long will the DNA results take?"

"Depends on how soon a sample is sent. I'll contact the bureau and alert the lab that an item is coming. They can pressure the parents if the item doesn't arrive soon."

"What about the bracelet with the initials CW?"

"I've sent that to the lab and it will be compared to Chloe's DNA. Let's stay the course and get more information on what was going on in Ingram Bay late summer and early fall."

"If the victim is Chloe, who sent the ransom note and why?"

"I can't answer that yet, but I have a suspicion."

Caitlyn picked up her phone, touched a search engine and typed in a term.

"What are you doing?"

"I'm finding the contact information for EnvironmentNow!" she responded. "If Chloe and Natalie are members of this group, they might have their contact info."

"Don't you think her parents and the FBI have already tried that?" Ethan stated, pulling out into the passing lane.

"It doesn't hurt for us to try," she responded, and then turned back to her phone.

"Hello," she answered, and eyed Ethan. Someone had actually answered the phone.

"I'm looking for information on one of your groups that was in the Northern Neck late last summer. We're trying to get in touch with one of the girls that traveled with the group. The name is Chloe Wright, though she could have been going under the name of Cassie White," she explained. "Yes, I can hold."

Caitlyn put the phone on speaker and waited for the information.

"Ma'am?" the young man came back on the line.

"Yes, I'm here."

"We have a Cassie White and Natalie Connor in our contact list, but only their emails. They are not listed with the group that went to Virginia, but they could have joined the group after it left Morgantown. Our organization holds meetings and provides educational information. We only sponsor small groups for peaceful demonstrations."

"Can you give me the girls' email addresses?" Caitlyn asked.

"I'm sorry, but that information is private."

"What about the name of the group leader?"

"Sorry, ma'am, but I can't give you that either. Is there anything else I can help you with?"

"Not at the moment. Thank you."

"That guy wasn't very helpful. EnvironmentNow! only organizes *peaceful* demonstrations. Either the group that descended on Ingram Bay last August was unsupervised, badly supervised or it was a fringe group."

"They might have been a subgroup of kids that got together and decided to apply what they'd learned," Ethan said. "We're almost to Ingram Bay. Are you ready to visit Sheriff Goodall?"

When they pulled into the sheriff's office parking lot they noticed a familiar vehicle parked near the door.

"That's Bud Higley's truck," she said.

"I see that," Ethan replied.

"What do you think he is doing here?"

"Let's find out. Bud Higley was here when I came to talk with the sheriff a few days ago. We'll talk with him later, but right now, let's see what the sheriff can tell us," Ethan said.

Conversation stopped when they entered the office. Bud Higley jumped back from the counter, surprised by their entrance.

"Can I help you folks?" Sheriff Goodall asked. He nodded to Bud, indicating he should leave.

"Don't let us interrupt," Ethan stated. "We're happy to wait until you finish your business with Mr. Higley."

"We're done," Sheriff Goodall stated. "Nice to see you again, Bud. Give my best to the bride, won't ya?"

Bud scurried from the room.

Sheriff Goodall turned to Ethan and Caitlyn.

"What do you two want?"

"You might remember me, sheriff. I was here a few days ago asking about employment opportunities," Ethan stated.

The sheriff looked at Ethan, then recognition dawned. "Well, you've cleaned yourself up a bit now, haven't ya?"

"I have. And I'm no longer looking for a job."

Ethan pulled out his identification.

"I'm a federal agent investigating a kidnapping case."

"Kidnapping?" Sheriff Goodall exclaimed. "I haven't been told about a kidnapping."

Ethan leaned his six foot two inch 175-pound frame against the counter.

"I've got several questions."

"Ask them," Sheriff Goodall stated, standing tall to assert his authority.

"First, I want to know about the protesters that were here last summer. They caused a stir, we're told, and we've learned that a number of them didn't make it to their next site."

"That's not my concern. They were a bunch of troublemakers. Glad they're gone. If they lost some, it meant those kids had enough sense to go back to where they came from."

"I'm particularly interested in one of them. She went by the name of Cassie White. Did you have any contact with her?"

"No. I didn't catch any of their names. I couldn't even find out the leader's name. It was a busy time. End of summer, water people in town, and the Labor Day celebration."

"Okay. We'll revisit that question after you've had time to think about it. Give me your opinion on the skeletal remains uncovered in the conservation land. Were any missing persons reported?"

"No," Sheriff Goodall said, wiping a drop of sweat from his brow.

"The medical examiner reported the approximate date of death as during that timeframe, and damage to the skull indicated foul play," Ethan said.

"If you know so much, why are you here?"

"Because I think you know more about what happened during that time. I also think you suspect what and who is behind the contamination of the bay."

Sheriff Goodall turned red and stated, "Is that an accusation? If so, maybe you should talk to the town's attorney. Now, if you don't mind, I have other matters that need my attention."

"Here's my card. Call me when you have information to share, and it's better to do it sooner rather than later," Ethan stated and slid his business card across the counter.

Sheriff Goodall walked back to the counter, glanced at the card, and then looked at Ethan.

"I won't be needing this," he said as he tossed the card into the wastebasket.

"It's up to you, sheriff," Ethan said. He turned and escorted Caitlyn from the room.

When they got into the car, Caitlyn fastened her seat belt.

"That went well," she said.

Ethan clicked his seatbelt into place, turned and explained, "He's scared and in over his head. He's only a pawn. We have to figure out the head of the organization. Let's see what Mr. Russell has to say. Hopefully he'll talk. Whoever tried to kill him was sending a strong message. We need to find out who that is."

~ THIRTY-FIVE ~

Ethan followed her into Vince Russell's hospital room. Bandages still covered his head, but the IV line was gone. He was on the mend.

Vince eyed Caitlyn, then Ethan. His attention came back to her.

"You again. What do you want?"

"We want the truth, Mr. Russell," she replied.

Ethan stepped around her.

"Mr. Russell, I'm Ethan Ewing." He produced his ID.

"A fed. I told her I didn't do anything," Vince Russell stated.

"We believe you, but you know more than you admit. I've been sent here to investigate a suspected kidnapping, and I think the attack on you might be connected."

"What are you talking about? First, I'm blamed for the skeletal remains that I had nothing to do with and now you are accusing me of kidnapping?"

"We aren't accusing you of anything," Ethan stated.

"Calm down, Mr. Russell. We're on your side," Caitlyn stated, touching his arm.

That had its effect. He placed his head back on his pillow and let out a sigh.

"Okay, maybe I suspect who attacked me. It's a small town, and people like John Graves and William Webber have an agenda. They also have a number of people working for them."

"What are they into?" Ethan asked.

"They want to overturn the moratorium on uranium mining. They're lobbying the state's legislators. When a new business starts in Ingram Bay, like mine, Graves and Webber invite the new business owner to join the Chamber of Commerce. I had a lot to do to get started and didn't have time for meetings. When I declined the offer, I learned it wasn't an invitation, but a command. Membership required political action, with the agenda set by Graves and Webber. I've been distancing myself from them and at a recent meeting objected to their plan to open a mine in this area. It would kill my housing and recreation plans. In fact, it would destroy the entire area."

He turned to Caitlyn. "Do you realize this mine isn't far from where your parents live?"

Caitlyn felt Ethan's eyes on her, but she didn't look his way.

"I do now, Mr. Russell."

"Do you think Graves and Webber had any kind of confrontation with the protesters here last summer?" Ethan asked.

"I wouldn't put it past them. They'll stop at nothing to get what they want. I suspect it was one of their men who attacked me. It's a warning."

Ethan and Caitlyn left the hospital and drove back to Ingram Bay. They'd get a bite to eat before talking with the Higleys, assuming they could catch them at home.

They parked in the public lot on one of the side streets, close to the family restaurant and when they walked in, Joan greeted them and showed them to a booth.

"Have you seen Lilla recently?" Caitlyn asked.

"She was in yesterday and asked about you," Joan replied.

"Do you have any idea what it was about?" Caitlyn asked as she removed her coat and slipped into the booth.

"No, and I didn't have time to ask," Joan replied as she placed two menus down in front of them. It's been crazy busy the last few days. It's spring and the 'water people' have arrived all anxious to ready their boats for the season. We're also getting business from the conference attendees at the hotel who want to get away from the others and have private conversations. Have a seat and I'll be back to take your order."

While they ate, Caitlyn went over the notes she'd taken during the interview with Sheriff Goodall and Vince Russell.

"I think we can rule Mr. Russell out," Ethan stated.

"I agree," Caitlyn said. "Although I had him pegged as our murderer."

"You mentioned you had a suspect board set up?"

"Let's go back to the house and rearrange the notes with what we've learned? It'll give me a chance to add information to the SafeGrid website. I should have done it before now."

"Let's go," Ethan said as he picked up the check.

~

"The board is set up, and the notes rearranged," Ethan stated. He turned to Caitlyn, who was at the kitchen table busy on her laptop. She had paid no attention to what he was doing, and he was getting frustrated.

"One more minute," she said. "I'm almost done."

Ethan turned back to the board and studied the names and dates. He glanced back to see if she was through working. He wasn't used to waiting. When she showed no sign of stopping, he walked over to see what was so important that she was holding up their investigation. Had she forgotten the critical time element involved?

Caitlyn swayed back and forth to the rhythm of her fingers as they danced over the keyboard. He watched as she viewed the various pages coming up on her computer screen.

"Why do you have to do that now?"

"I made the changes and now I have to make sure they uploaded appropriately. After I make the updates I have to check for typos, and that the pages can be viewed on various mobile devices. I'll just be a few seconds more."

Ethan looked over her shoulder at the screen.

"Stop," he shouted.

Caitlyn lifted her hand from the mouse, frightened at his tone.

"What are you working on?"

"I just told you. I'm reviewing the work I did on the SafeGrid site. I'll need to edit this one picture. What's the matter?"

Ethan pointed at the computer screen. "Who's that?"

Caitlyn looked at Ethan and then back at the screen.

"That's the president, John Graves, why?"

"Not him. The guy standing back in the corner."

She leaned in to see whom he was pointing at.

"Oh, that's William Webber. He's the CFO. I'm going to cut him out of the picture and only show Mr. Graves signing their first transformer contract."

Ethan studied the two men, pointed at William Webber and said, "He's the guy who hired me. That's JR."

Caitlyn's mouth dropped.

Ethan sat down beside her.

"You just blew our case wide open."

~

"I don't know what to say," Caitlyn whispered, stunned.

She went to her purse and pulled out John Graves's business card. "John R. Graves, President and CEO, SafeGrid. If you say William Webber is JR, then it appears Mr. Webber used Mr. Graves's initials. Does this mean . . . ?"

Ethan put his hand on her shoulder to calm her.

"It means William Webber is involved in some shady, and probably illegal activity. It doesn't mean that John Graves is also involved. We have no proof that William Webber had anything to do with the body buried in the conservation land. Now, tell me your impressions of William Webber, what you observed and your feelings about him. You're good at catching details."

They sat quietly for a few minutes while Caitlyn thought about how best to describe William Webber.

"He comes on tough, but Mr. Graves said Mr. Webber was the one who convinced the board to hire me. But as more information on what they were doing came out, I had reservations about things he said. When I found an account discrepancy, he took the papers from my hands. He insinuated I couldn't read a budget."

"I'll talk with both him and Mr. Graves to find out how deep each is into this additional business plan. It's getting late, so tomorrow, I'll talk with the Higleys," Ethan said.

"They are in a position to know what's going on in the town, though I understand their reluctance to talk. He depends on these businessmen for jobs. I have a relationship with Lilla, and she was looking for me at the diner, so I need to go with you," Caitlyn said, her voice shaking from the shock.

A call on Ethan's cell interrupted their discussion.

"I'll be right back."

He returned to the kitchen, placed the phone on the table, and sat back with hands clasped behind his head.

"Who was that?" Caitlyn asked, knowing it'd be information on the case.

"That was Joe. They've been released. Their biggest issue was dehydration, but they're fine. He was checking in to see if I needed any more information from them."

"And you said?"

"I told him what we just discovered. Joe and Tara will catch up on their reports, and run a check on SafeGrid and its board members."

THIRTY-SIX

Caitlyn directed Ethan to the Higleys. As they drove down the country roads, she pointed out where she had found Bud working.

"I stopped to talk with him. He was grading that parcel, which is another one of Vince Russell's housing projects."

They pulled into the driveway that led to the Higley's mobile home.

"We're in luck," Caitlyn said. "Bud's truck is here."

Bud Higley came to the door.

"What do ya want?"

Before Caitlyn could respond, Ethan stepped forward to take the lead on the conversation.

"Mr. Higley, I'm FBI Agent Ethan Ewing," he said as he presented his badge.

"So what are doin' here?"

"We need to talk with you about John Graves and William Webber," Ethan stated.

Bud's expression turned grim, he glanced back into his home, and then quickly recovered.

"Let's sit out here. Lilla isn't doing well today."

Two wicker rocking chairs were on the narrow porch. Ethan motioned for Caitlyn and Bud to sit. He stood and leaned against the railing.

"Bud, tell us about William Webber and John Graves," Ethan said.

Bud fidgeted in his seat. Caitlyn put a hand on his arm.

"Tell Agent Ewing what's going on. If they're doing something illegal, it has to stop. Do the right thing."

They waited for Bud to collect his thoughts and weigh his options.

Bud spoke softly. Ethan leaned in to hear.

"It started innocently enough, and then one thing led to another. Mr. Webber asked me to do a job for him and for decent pay. All I had to do was clear a path to the bay. I thought he was going to build a small dock. I'd just put the finishing touches on that when the Brown brothers showed up."

"And?" Ethan said.

"A few months later I saw the dock from the water and it was bigger than I thought necessary. I talked with Mr. Webber and he said not to worry. He had the Brown brothers working on some odds and ends type jobs. Nothing important, but I knew better. I mentioned my concern to the sheriff, and he promised to check it out, but nothing happened."

"Mr. Higley, you saw me working at the storage shed, loading boxes into a white panel truck. What is stored there?" Ethan was pretty sure of the answer, but he wanted to hear it from Bud.

Bud shifted his weight, hesitant with his response.

"Mr. Higley?" Ethan coaxed.

"I think firearms of some kind are being shipped in and out of this area. I've noticed trucks unloading, and then the Brown brothers are sent to reload the boxes into other trucks with license plates from various states."

"How can you be certain? The boxes could hold drugs, or even machine parts," Ethan countered.

Bud's weight shifted again. He looked scared, but Ethan wasn't going to give up.

"One day one of the larger boxes broke open. It was full of assault rifles. I pretended I didn't see. I don't want the Brown brothers coming after me."

"Tell me about your work with Vince Russell."

"When Mr. Russell arrived in the area, he bought a lot of property and hired me and some other contractors to clear land for houses and a new marina. I tried to keep an eye on what was happening at the storage shed and down by the bay, but with the new projects, I couldn't keep up. But one day I saw what looked like mining equipment being delivered."

"What kind of mining did you think they were planning?"

"Wasn't sure at first. Mr. Webber assured me everything they were doing was for the good of the country. He can be very persuasive. Talks to you like you're his best friend, but I know better. There was too much secrecy around the project, and that told me they were up to no good."

"But he didn't say exactly what they were planning to mine?"

"No, but Lilla went down there one day. She thought I was working there, and since I had forgotten my lunchbox, she wanted to surprise me with a special lunch. She didn't see my truck, but she's a curious one. She walked in and poked around. We think she went into an area where the ore was exposed. With her compromised immune system, that was all she needed. Within a few months her cancer came back."

"Joan, the waitress at the restaurant, said Lilla was asking for me. Is that what she wanted to talk about?" Caitlyn asked.

"I suspect it is. It's been bothering her recently. Ever since you came around asking about Cassie," he said, looking at Caitlyn.

"The path behind Mr. Russell's construction site. Is that where the mine is located?"

"No. Plans changed and the property was sold to Vince Russell. The larger dock that I'm talking about is six or seven miles north of the retirement community. Woodlands surround the site, and the narrow drive off the main road is barely visible."

Ethan nodded. The drive down to the Brown brothers shed was in similar condition, and apparently close by the mineshaft.

"Does Vince Russell have a part of the mining operation?"

"Oh, no. In fact, if mining is allowed, Mr. Russell's business will crash. I think he's doing whatever he can, quietly, to stop the mining. What I don't understand is why he altered the plans for the condo units from what he submitted to the county. That's not like him. He's a perfectionist, knows what he wants, and if it isn't done right, you do it over. If it's not right the second time, you're taken off his contractor list."

"Have many been taken off the list?" Ethan asked.

"A few," Bud responded.

"Would those contractors be angry enough to jeopardize his construction projects?"

"Maybe," Bud replied.

"Tell me about the condo job."

"I was upset the driveway plans went over onto the conservation land. No excuse for that," Bud stated emphatically. He sat back and crossed his arms.

"You haven't mentioned John Graves."

"That's because I don't know much about him. Don't see him around town, and never had any dealings with him," Bud replied. "I've answered your questions, now I need to get back inside to see if Lilla needs anything."

"Of course," Ethan said. "Thanks for talking with us."

~

Back at the house, Caitlyn waited while Ethan reported to his contact at the bureau. Although she heard only his side of the conversation, she knew backup was being sent. As soon as he disconnected, she asked, "Are Joe and Tara coming back?"

"Yes," he replied, putting his phone away and preparing to leave.

"What else?" she asked following him to the door.

Ethan stopped and said, "I can't tell you any more about this operation. I suggest you stay here." He hesitated. "Have you decided whether to continue with your SafeGrid contract?"

"That's the question," she responded, shifting her weight from one foot to the other. "I believe in their transformer replacement business, but if they're involved in something illegal . . ."

"We don't know that for sure. Webber is involved in the mine operation and the shipments, the content of which we have to verify, but his activities might be separate from the transformer business and John Graves. It's possible that John Graves and the SafeGrid board know nothing about Webber's activities."

"I agree. The board members are all local businessmen. I can't believe they are involved, except possibly Jack, the president of the local bank."

"I've got to meet up with Joe and Tara. I'll call you tomorrow," he said and gave her a peck on the cheek.

She watched him drive off, thinking about their conversation. And they definitely had to do something about their relationship. If she moved away from DC, how many clients would she lose? Would The Bay Foundation keep her on? Now that Ethan worked for the FBI, would he work out of Quantico or off on assignments around the country?

The house was quiet, but she couldn't concentrate on work. There was nothing for her to do but walk around and deal with her feelings. She stopped pacing and stood by the French doors that led out onto her parents' patio. White caps indicated the bay was angry. It was saying that pollution of the waterways had to stop.

Dark clouds on the horizon and a stiff breeze meant a storm was coming. The rumble of thunder in the distance prompted her to think about what she'd learned and a pattern evolved.

She went to the closet, pulled out her crime board, added notes with the new information, stepped back, rubbed her chin, and knew what she had to do. She took Summit for a quick walk, and when they got back to the house she said, "I'm not sitting around here doing nothing."

The dog tilted his head in understanding.

She grabbed her purse and headed out the door. It had just started to rain.

~

Caitlyn drove to the home of John Graves where the same young woman as before met her at the door.

"Is Mr. Graves available? Tell him Caitlyn Jamison is here to see him."

She'd driven by the SafeGrid office and noted his car wasn't in the parking lot, so she hoped she'd catch him at home.

She was led into the foyer, her sharp no nonsense tone duly noted.

Caitlyn slipped her phone and keys into her coat pocket and handed it to the housekeeper, making a further statement that she was not going to be put off.

"I'll see if he is available," the woman replied, as she hung up the coat.

Caitlyn walked into the great room and noted the dark brown soft leather sofas and chairs that made a nice contrast with the lighter shades of brown and cream of the fieldstone fireplace. She noticed details she'd missed the first time, which brought a question. Did John have a wife? He never mentioned one, and she didn't appear during their first meeting. Who decorated this place?

"Caitlyn. What can I do for you?" John Graves said as he walked towards her.

"John. I thought we should have another talk."

He cocked his head in question. "Is it about your assignment for SafeGrid?"

"In a way."

"Come, sit down, and I'll try to answer your concerns," he replied.

Caitlyn settled into one of the side chairs that faced the fireplace. She concentrated on the symmetry of the stones and prepared what to say.

"I interviewed for your marketing position because I thought SafeGrid only made replacement transformers, but when I got here I noticed anomalies in what was discussed at the meetings. I asked questions and received no satisfactory answers. I then learned that SafeGrid is lobbying the state to change their legislation on mining uranium ore. When I questioned line items that turned out to be offshore accounts, your response was to protect your investors."

John Graves sat back in his chair.

"I'm sorry, Caitlyn, if you are uncomfortable with our expanded business plan. We hired you to develop a marketing strategy for the transformer project, and if things worked out, we'd have you continue to work on the mining piece of the business. There are several companies vying for a mining permit. We are not the only ones lobbying the state. To be considered a frontrunner, we have to show we are ready and have all safeguards in place."

"Are you mining that ore now?" When he didn't respond, she said, "If so, it's illegal. You can't market it in the U.S., so if you are, who are you selling to?"

John Graves let out a sigh.

"You don't have the full picture. We are raising money for both entities. What we're doing is preparation, so when the moratorium is lifted, we'll be ready to operate. But that's not your concern. You should concentrate on SafeGrid," he replied.

"You're right, but what is my concern is a young girl was murdered and buried in conservation land, and I can't help but wonder if she found out about your mining operation and threatened to tell?"

John Graves stiffened. "I don't know what you're talking about and I don't appreciate the accusation. Of course we didn't murder anyone."

He took a deep breath and then he leaned towards her.

"You are making a lot of assumptions and accusations. I'm sorry you feel that way about mining uranium. I thought you understood that uranium ore is vital to our country's power usage. It's estimated that 119 million tons of ore are underground in Virginia just *waiting* to be mined. Without more nuclear power plants, the country will run out of available and affordable power. Blackouts will occur, and eventually the entire electrical grid will be in danger. Getting this ore out of the ground is critical to national security."

"Many feel the environmental risks are too great," Caitlyn countered.

"We've had this discussion. The risks result when the ore is separated from rock. When the moratorium is lifted, we'll either set up a safe and highly regulated milling operation, or we'll send the ore offsite for milling."

"I'm still concerned about the risks, about the radiation when the ore is exposed to air or water. One of the reasons for the moratorium is because Virginia has plenty of rain and can be hurricane prone. There are health impacts for those living near where the ore is mined and milled. And what will it do to the Northern Neck? It will ruin this entire bucolic area."

"Everything beneficial to society has its risks, and I suspect you are only thinking about where your parents live and not seeing the big picture. If you aren't comfortable with our mission—providing a sustainable power source, then we can void your contract. I'm sorry to lose you, because I'm impressed with your work. I'd hate to see you go."

Caitlyn tensed, her hands gripped tightly together to keep them from shaking. She was being fired. This was not how she wanted the discussion to play out, but then she hadn't thought it through. Instead, she'd rushed off to slay the dragon. She turned when she heard the front door open. The housekeeper said something, and then William Webber entered the room, his coat dripping over the polished wood floor. He peeled off his wet coat and threw it across one of the leather chairs.

John Graves turned his attention to welcome his chief financial officer, disregarding the rude behavior.

"Bill. I lost track of the time. I've been preoccupied with calls to our state senators and then Caitlyn stopped by. Why don't you join us? I'm afraid I have some bad news. She has reservations about the mining aspect of the business."

"That's a shame," William Webber stated as he walked into the room. He did not take a seat, but stood, his presence menacing.

She would not let him intimidate her.

"I told John that if SafeGrid has started to mine the ore, it's illegal and the operation should be shut down."

"Why would we do that and who would make us?" William Webber asked sarcastically. "We pretty much run this town. Finding a rich source of uranium right under our feet is a gift. We purchased the property and can do with it what we want."

"You aren't above the law, and I'll make sure law enforcement knows about what you're doing," Caitlyn stated, her arms crossed.

"I doubt you will get very far, and I don't like to be threatened," William Webber said, moving closer to her.

Where is Ethan when I need him? To save her dignity, she lifted her chin and stated, "It's the right thing to do. There are too many environmental and health risks involved, and it's the reason the moratorium is still in place."

William Webber laughed as he walked to the fireplace. He rested his arm on the mantel and said, "Your empty threats don't concern me. We're successful in dealing with situations as they are presented, and so far we're making progress with our legislators."

Dealing with situations.

She thought about Ethan identifying William Webber as JR.

A loud crash of thunder overhead, followed by a lightning strike nearby, was her prompt to force his hand. If he weren't guilty of murder, she'd find out soon enough.

"Is that what a sixteen year old girl was, a 'situation to be dealt with?'"

John Graves looked from Caitlyn to William Webber.

"What is she talking about, Bill?"

~ THIRTY-SEVEN ~

Henry James was tired of being bossed around by his brother; tired of diving for old junk. Who cares about Indian bones and artifacts, anyway? Except that it brought in good money. He'd figured out they were getting a pretty small return on the items they worked so hard to find. The boss was taking the biggest share and wasn't doing the hard and dangerous work. Not fair. That's why he'd come up with an alternate plan to raise money. The problem was, he didn't know how to follow through. Maybe he could bring the new guy into his confidence.

He wouldn't show up to dive today. His brother would be furious and there would be repercussions, but he'd deal with that later. He'd borrow his mother's car and go visit Uncle Chuck.

While Billy Bob was getting ready for their dive, Henry James drove into town. Their uncle tried to be a good sheriff, and he cared about the town, but Henry James had learned that sometimes events take over one's life. And that's what happened to their family. They fell under the influence of people who had money and power.

His uncle was sitting at his desk, staring at his computer screen when Henry James entered.

"Hi," Henry James said as he walked in, not knowing how his uncle would react at seeing him.

Sheriff Goodall looked up. "What do you want and where's your brother?"

"He's down at the shed. He wants to work today. I don't," Henry James responded. They'd never told their uncle all of what they were into. He hadn't asked and they didn't tell.

"So what do you want?" Sheriff Goodall said as he continued to sort through the papers on his desk.

"I want to do something different," Henry James said. That was lame, but he didn't know how to explain that he was tired of Billy Bob putting him down, always deciding what they would do and when. How could he express his frustration without giving his uncle the details? Would his uncle take action, and continue to cover for them? Henry James didn't want to think about what would happen when the boss found out.

~

Sheriff Goodall didn't have time for his nephew's whining. The feds had contacted him for information on those damn human remains. Like he had any information. He should have, but he didn't have the help nor did he have the computer skills he needed to do what they asked. Up to this point he'd been able to fake it, but time was running out, and that made him anxious.

"Listen up, Henry James, my job is to keep this town a safe place to live. I'm not proud of how you boys have turned out, and I hope you haven't gotten yourselves into serious trouble."

Henry James hung his head.

"You're here because you and Billy Bob aren't getting along. Right?"

Henry James nodded.

"I'll have another talk with him and set things straight. Maybe I can find something for you to do around the office. You need time away from each other."

~ THIRTY-EIGHT ~

Joe Wheeler and Tara Jones arrived at Ethan's apartment and developed a plan of attack on the Brown brothers' operation. They would shut them down, document their violation of the Indian burial grounds, and gather evidence of the munitions retrieval.

Ethan had taken photos of the building where the suspected boxes of arms had been stored and then shipped.

After the boys were arrested and presented with all the information they had gathered, they'd be pressured to name the others. Although Ethan had identified William Webber as JR and the one involved in shipping out the items, he didn't know to what extent others were involved.

The agents drove their vehicles down the rutted drive to where the Brown brothers had their operation. Ethan pulled in first, placing his vehicle across the back of the Brown's pickup truck. Joe and Tara parked crosswise in the drive blocking the escape route.

"Ready?" Ethan asked.

Joe and Tara nodded as they tightened their bulletproof vests.

The three walked over to the shed where Billy Bob was putting on his dive gear.

"Getting ready for a dive?" Ethan asked.

Billy Bob jumped at the sound. He looked up at Ethan, then to Joe and Tara.

"What the hell're you doing bringing folks down here?" Billy Bob asked, his face red with anger.

"These folks are here to arrest you and Henry James," Ethan stated calmly. "Where's Henry?"

Billy Bob smiled. "He ain't here."

Joe put handcuffs on Billy Bob and read him his rights. In the meantime, he and Tara documented the contents of the shed.

Ethan confiscated the computer and pointed to a cabinet against the wall. "That's where I found your ID."

When Billy Bob was handcuffed to a support inside the shed, Ethan said, "You'll be comfortable here until we return."

In the meantime, Joe had checked out the boat. "Nothing of interest," he said as he turned to survey the shoreline.

"This way, I think," Ethan said. He walked north along the shore, Joe and Tara behind, one after the other, on the narrow path. Their arms down with hands near their weapons. It was a half-mile over rough terrain before they came upon a small opening in the cliff. They stopped when they came upon another shed, tucked into the brush, so it wouldn't be seen from the water, and listened. Ethan approached it and opened the door. Protective gear, masks, and other paraphernalia hung from hooks.

"It's unlocked. Someone must be here," Tara added.

Ethan looked at the bay, and then the treed hillside. "If the moratorium is lifted, and this mine becomes operational, the Northern Neck will change, and not in a good way."

"That's right," Joe stated. "Besides the mining, they'll set up a milling facility nearby. I don't know how they plan to dispose of the toxic waste, but it will impact the entire state."

Ethan walked over to the opening and noticed a door several yards in.

"Should we go in?" he asked.

"No," stated Joe. "Someone's inside. Let's wait and see who comes out."

They didn't have to wait long. The mine door opened, clanged shut, and then someone shuffled towards the shed. In a carefully chosen moment Ethan, followed by Joe and Tara, walked to the front of the shed.

Henry James, partly undressed, turned around, his face registering shock.

"What the . . . ?"

"Hello, Henry James," Ethan said. "Please, finish changing and then we'll join your brother. He's waiting for us at the other shed."

~

Ethan, Joe and Tara marched the handcuffed Brown brothers into the sheriff's office, much to the sheriff's dismay.

Billy Bob held his head high in a look of defiance; Henry James's eyes were downcast, his expression one of defeat.

"Good afternoon, sheriff," Ethan said. "Meet FBI Special Agents Joe Wheeler and Tara Jones. I hope you have room in your facility to lock up these two until transport can be arranged."

Sheriff Goodall rose, shook his head, and asked, "What have they done now? Illegal fishing? I told you boys there was to be no more fishing until that dead zone issue was solved."

Ethan led the boys to chairs up against the wall. He turned to the sheriff and stated, "We've charged them with desecration of an Indian burial ground, retrieval of munitions, illegal mining, and involvement with the kidnapping of federal officers. I read them their rights. We may add additional charges depending on how the government wants to handle the situation. We want your help to get them to talk, because they aren't the brains behind these operations."

Billy Bob gave Ethan a nasty look. He didn't like anyone talking down to him.

Ethan knew exactly what he was doing.

~

Sheriff Goodall pulled up a chair and stared at his nephews. Joe and Tara occupied chairs along the opposite wall and let Ethan pace back and forth in front of the boys, stopping occasionally to provide more information about their activities.

The silence went on for five minutes before Henry James blurted out, "I can't stand this. I'm sorry Uncle. We've . . ."

"Shut up you numbskull," Billy Bob snarled.

Henry James turned on his brother. "You think you're so smart. You're always the boss. I'm done with you and I'll be out of here when the money arrives."

"Henry James, apparently you don't realize how serious these charges are," their uncle stated softly. He sensed Billy Bob was ready to blow and using a softer tone had worked in the past.

"You've done bad things, but it isn't all your fault now, is it?" Sheriff Goodall said to Henry James, and then turned to Billy Bob.

"You stay quiet. I don't want to hear any more comments unless you're willing to provide the information that these officers need."

He turned back to Henry James.

"Now, tell us who you work for, and what money are you expecting?"

~ THIRTY-NINE ~

"Don't be naïve, John," William Webber snarled. "I told you I'd take care of the details. It was your job to keep the businesses running, and find buyers for our merchandise."

"What about the girl?" John asked. He stood and faced William Webber. John's fists, shaking, hung at his sides.

"It was just some kid snooping around the mine entrance—one of those protesters in town last summer. She found the mine, and then started asking a lot of questions. It was obvious she understood what she'd seen. She threatened to report us. I'd had a difficult day and didn't have the patience to put up with some smart ass kid."

"So you killed her?" Caitlyn interjected. She couldn't believe what she was hearing. She, too, stood to present a united front against his actions. She reached into her pocket for her phone, and then realized it was in her coat pocket that hung in the hall closet. She didn't dare move.

William Webber looked from John to Caitlyn and stated in a measured tone, "It was an accident. She mouthed off; I got angry, and before I knew what I was doing, I picked up a shovel and swung at her. I thought she'd run, but instead she stood her ground. It all happened before I knew what I had done. Her head hit a rock. I tried to revive her, but she was gone. I didn't mean any harm."

"And then you buried her in a shallow grave." Caitlyn said.

"Bill, say you didn't do that," John pleaded.

"I panicked. I had to do something. I put her and the shovel in my car and drove her to the pathway we had cleared earlier in the year. I found a spot in the conservation land, but the shovel broke. I did the best I could and planned to return to do a better job, but Vince Russell had purchased the property and his crew started clearing for his condo units. Workmen were there from early morning to dusk. One evening I went and ran into hikers. After that I didn't dare go near the place. Never thought the body would be found."

"If it was an accident, why didn't you report it to the sheriff?" John asked, his face pale, sweat dripping off his forehead.

"Yeah, right. What was I going to say? 'Oh, sheriff, we are illegally starting a uranium mine, and a kid found out and I killed her.'"

John Graves paced the room, shaking his head. He looked at Caitlyn, then at William Webber. "I can't believe this."

"Don't get all moral on me, John. You're as guilty as I," William stated.

"What do you mean?"

"You're the one who's finding buyers for our shipments of the firearms."

"But that's funding SafeGrid. Don't you understand? We're trying to save the country's electrical grid, saving lives and providing nuclear power."

"The law won't see it that way," William replied with a smirk.

"What do we do now?" John asked.

"Since we lost our hostages, we now have a replacement," he responded, looking at Caitlyn.

That's why Joe and Tara were kept alive, to pressure the government to lift the moratorium on uranium mining, Caitlyn thought. *And now I'm the hostage.*

The look on John Graves face told Caitlyn he was shocked at William's plan. It was clear he did not understand the lengths William Webber would take to fund their operations. They both were culpable, but William Webber was in control. He instructed John to gather bottled water and snack items from the kitchen.

"But she's seen us," John stated, and then the reality of the situation sunk in. "No, we can't."

"Let me worry about that," William said. "Now move."

I've got to figure a way out of here. They are going to kill me.

John walked out of the room, his head down in defeat.

"Leave your purse," William instructed and then poked her in the back indicating she should follow John into the kitchen.

"Where's that girl of yours?" William asked.

"I'll look for her," John replied, his voice shaking.

"If you're sure she didn't hear us, give her the rest of the day off."

In the kitchen, John handed William a bag with bottled water, banana and a small bag of potato chips.

Carrying the bag of snacks, William forced her up two flights of stairs to the attic. He pushed her inside the room and threw the bag onto the floor.

"Make yourself comfortable," he stated as he closed the door. She heard the click of the lock and then his footsteps returning down the stairs.

The unfinished space was just beams and subflooring. There were no windows, only small air vents on either side. The one light fixture was missing a bulb. Dead flies her only company. The storm raged outside with more thunder and lightning close by.

She walked around the space, looking for something she could use to free herself. She sat down with her back to a support beam. Who'd find her in this isolated location? Ethan thought she was with her parents and her parents would assume she was with Ethan. If Ethan tried to communicate with her he'd assume she was busy. Thoughts swirled through her head, each one bringing a heightened sense of anxiety. She got up and paced. She had to get out of here.

The storm brought total darkness earlier than normal, and the only other sound was from a few peepers as they called to attract their mates. She'd lost track of time. Caitlyn walked in a small circle so she wouldn't trip over anything, her arms wrapped around her for warmth. She tried to see out the vents, but with the awkward angle, she had no success. She gave up, sat down, and let thoughts of her rescue swirl through her mind. She tensed when she noticed a shuffling sound. She sat up. Bats? This is the time of night that they'd wake and slip out to feed.

Or had William Webber decided he didn't need her after all? Would she join Cassie White as one of his victims, not found until . . . what had she'd seen in the attic she could use as a weapon? A trunk, a broken chair, and a three-drawer dresser.

A broken chair. That could be a weapon. When he opened the door she'd catch him by surprise, whack him, and hopefully slow him down enough to allow her to escape. She made her way carefully around the attic, trying to locate the chair.

Ouch. She literally ran into it. She held onto the chair's arms and quietly walked over to the door.

Her assailant was on the last flight of stairs. She raised the chair up over her head to give her the most momentum for when the door opened. Caitlyn held her breath, every muscle on alert. The door opened a crack. She was ready.

~ FORTY ~

Billy Bob was stubborn and Henry James took his cue from his older brother, but after several more minutes of questioning, and viewing photos of William Webber and John Graves, the brothers finally pointed to William Webber as the person to whom they reported. They then provided information on how they retrieved the munitions and how shipments came and went out of the storage shed.

"What's in those boxes?" Ethan asked, needing to confirm what Bud Higley had told him.

Billy Bob hung his head.

Ethan approached and Billy Bob sat back to avoid a possible blow.

Instead, Ethan stood within inches of Billy Bob, waiting.

"Arms," Billy Bob whispered.

"Louder," Ethan demanded.

"Illegal firearms. Mr. Webber was buying them cheap, having them shipped here. We'd unload the boxes, keep them in storage for a while, and then reload them when another truck arrives. We don't know where the boxes were going," Billy Bob stated, looking Ethan in the eye.

Ethan stepped back. "Now tell us about who was buying the Indian artifacts."

"His card is in the shed. When we get enough, we contact him and he arranges the shipment. Lately, we haven't been able to do much diving. Our boat is giving us trouble."

Agent Joe Wheeler transmitted this information to the bureau and requested transport for the brothers. They didn't trust the sheriff to keep his nephews locked up overnight.

By the time the transport arrived, it was after nine.

Ethan, Joe and Tara watched as the suspects were driven away. Sheriff Goodall stayed in his office to call his sister and tell her about the boys' arrest.

"Should we find Mr. Webber this evening?" Joe asked.

"No," Ethan said. "He's not working alone. If we question him tonight, he could alert his partner. Let's get a good night's sleep and visit him early tomorrow. I don't want to scare these guys off, and we don't know how deep this operation goes. I'll check with Caitlyn to see if she can give me any more details on the SafeGrid board."

"Sounds like a plan. We'll check into a motel and start fresh in the morning," Joe said.

As they walked towards their vehicles, Ethan pulled out his cell and called Caitlyn. The call went straight to voicemail. *Darn.* She probably turned her phone off if she was working or visiting with her parents. He dialed her parents' home phone.

"Hello," Ann Jamison answered.

Ethan asked to speak with Caitlyn.

"She's not here. I thought she was with you."

Ethan motioned to Joe and Tara to stop.

"What's the matter?" asked Joe.

"I think Caitlyn's gone to confront her boss."

~ FORTY-ONE ~

"Anyone here?" a female voice whispered through the crack in the door.

With the chair in attack mode, Caitlyn stopped mid-swing. What should she do? Did William Webber suspect she would try to attack him and sent a woman instead? She pulled the chair up over her head and held tight. She waited to see if she could identify any more sounds, but the house was quiet. She took a chance.

"Who are you?"

The door opened wider. "I'm the housekeeper."

"Why are you here?" Caitlyn held the chair high, not sure she could trust this woman.

"I left my phone and came back to get it. The house was dark, so I assumed no one was home. I have a key to the back door, but when I entered, the light switches didn't work. The power is out. I checked the garage to see if Mr. Graves's car was gone, and noticed your car in there. After what I overheard this afternoon, I became concerned."

"What did you hear?" She wanted to keep the woman talking.

"I heard loud voices when the three of you were in the great room, and later Mr. Graves and Mr. Webber arguing, though I couldn't make out what they were saying. When I heard them coming towards the kitchen, I picked up a broom and went to the back porch and pretended I'd been cleaning out there. Mr. Graves found me. His face was ashen and his voice shook. He said the three of you were going to the office, and I could leave for the day. He waited for me to put my broom away. When I got home, I realized I'd left my phone on the kitchen counter. With the storm, I debated whether I should come back, but I needed my phone. I was also worried about what happened to you. I sensed something was wrong. I just didn't know what, but when I saw your car was still here, I wondered. I went around the house checking every room."

The door opened wider. Caitlyn placed the chair down on the floor. The women stared at each other.

"It's good you decided to check the attic. Let's go," Caitlyn said as she followed the woman down the stairs, holding the handrail, taking one step at a time in the dark.

When they got to the kitchen, Caitlyn said, "Thank you for coming back and then looking for me. I don't even know your name."

"Donna," the woman replied. "And you are Caitlyn. I've heard Mr. Graves talk about you. He appreciates your work. What happened here today?"

"We'll talk about that later. Right now I need to find my coat, because that's where I left my phone."

"You can use mine," Donna responded, but as she turned it on, she said, "oh."

"What's the matter?"

"My battery is dead. I forgot to charge it today."

"Is there a house phone?"

"Over there."

Caitlyn picked up the phone.

"It's dead. I'll get my phone. Are there any flashlights or candles?"

Donna retrieved a flashlight from one of the kitchen drawers and gave it to Caitlyn. Her coat was not in the closet, so they searched the great room.

"My purse is missing, too. Where would they put my things?" Caitlyn asked.

"How about your car?"

"Where's the door to the garage?"

~

"Do you think she's in trouble?" Joe asked.

"She's not home, and she hasn't contacted her parents or me. Her mother thought she was with me, and I thought she was home. That's where I left her."

"I bet she's gone after whoever she thinks killed Cassie White," Tara said.

"I bet you're right. That's just like her."

"And you think she suspects her boss is in on it?" Joe asked.

"We'd identified his chief financial officer as the person orchestrating the shipments of goods from a small storage facility. Mr. Webber isn't working on his own, and she needs to find out if John Graves is involved."

"Then let's go," Joe said, starting his car. "Do you know where he lives?"

"Yes," Ethan responded. "I made sure I did."

"Lead the way."

Ethan found the road that led to John Graves's house. The driveway was more difficult to find, especially in the rain. He drove past, realized his mistake, and turned around. He'd turned his headlights off and cursed the weather. Joe Wheeler followed and they coasted down the drive. When halfway there, they made a K turn and parked off the pavement, with the cars facing back down the drive. The house was dark. They approached slowly and tried to identify security cameras.

Joe put his arm out to stop them and pointed to an older model Chevy parked near the garage.

"Not a car John Graves would drive," Ethan said.

"Does he have a housekeeper?" Tara asked.

"I suspect he would, but where is she? The house is dark and it's late," Ethan said.

"There doesn't appear to be a personnel door to the garage," Joe said. "Let's walk around the house."

"Nothing." Ethan said, frustrated, as they checked the bay side of the property. "And there aren't any lights. Power must be out."

"If he had security lights, they'd run on batteries," Joe pointed out.

"Maybe he felt safe enough here that he didn't have outside lights installed," Ethan countered.

They walked back to the front of the house and stood by the garage.

~

Caitlyn and Donna were in the third bay of the garage when they heard a noise.

"Did you hear that?" Caitlyn asked.

"Yes, sounds like a car, maybe two, coming down the drive. They're back. What are we going to do?" Donna said, her voice shaking.

Caitlyn put a hand on the woman's shoulder. "Don't panic. I have a plan. We'll hide on the other side of my car. If my phone is there, I'll call for help. Either way, if we can get the garage door opened, we'll pick the right moment, sneak out and run to your car. Do you have your keys ready?"

"Yes," Donna said.

"Good. If we can't get to your car in time or it's blocked, follow me through the woods."

The women crouched down alongside Caitlyn's car. When they heard nothing more, she quickly shone the flashlight into her car and saw her coat and purse.

"Are they there?" Donna whispered.

"Yes. I'll have to figure out how to open the door without the dome light coming on. Wish these garage doors didn't have the windows at the top. If we hear them in the house, I'll open the garage door and we'll run."

It sounded so easy, but Caitlyn knew it would be difficult to escape from a house this far from the road and any neighbors. With the power out, did she have enough strength to pull on the manual garage door release? Could they reach Donna's car in time? Would it be blocked? Whoever was out there would see Donna's car. A search would begin. Time was running out.

Caitlyn slid closer to the door.

"Why did they come back?" Donna asked.

"They must have forgotten something, or maybe it's the electric company come to restore power. Listen."

The snapping of twigs told them someone was walking around the house. Donna clutched Caitlyn's arm and whispered, "What's going on?"

"I'm not sure. Just be ready to move when I give the signal."

Caitlyn pushed her ear against the garage door. A voice sounded like Joe Wheeler, but she wasn't sure. If she made a mistake, and it was one of William Webber's men, she and Donna would be in a worse situation.

What if it's the Brown brothers?

She had to take the chance. She stood and pounded on the door.

"Help," she yelled.

"What are you doing?" Donna asked, pulling on Caitlyn's arm.

Caitlyn turned to Donna. "I think I know them."

"You think?" Donna exclaimed. "And if you're wrong?"

~

"That's Caitlyn," Ethan said. He put his ear to the garage door. "Are you okay?"

"Yes. The housekeeper, Donna, is with me. My car is in here. The power is out so we'll try to manually open the garage door."

"Pull the cord down with a sharp movement to unlatch the door and we'll lift it up. Which bay is your car in?" Ethan asked.

"The farthest from the house," Caitlyn stated.

It took a few minutes and several tries, but Caitlyn's adrenalin kicked in and she tugged the cord hard enough for it to unlatch. When it clicked, she and Donna breathed a sigh of relief.

It took both Ethan and Joe to lift the heavy reinforced door high enough to slide it open. Caitlyn got in her car, and the group stepped aside so she could back out.

"You must be Donna," Ethan said.

"Yes," Donna responded, her mouth dry.

"She found me locked in the attic," Caitlyn explained.

"I came back to get my phone and when I looked to see if Mr. Graves's car was in the garage, I noticed hers there instead. After hearing Mr. Webber giving orders, I wondered, could she still be in the house?"

"And I'm glad you wondered," Caitlyn said, giving Donna a hug.

"Go home, but watch for any strange vehicles. I'll contact the state police and ask them to keep an eye on your place until we can capture Mr. Webber and Mr. Graves," Ethan instructed.

Donna shook her head. "I don't believe Mr. Graves would do anything bad. He's been good to me."

Donna jotted down her address and phone number and gave it to Ethan.

Ethan handed her his card. "Call if you see anything out of the ordinary."

"I will," Donna replied. "Can I go now?"

"Yes," Ethan said. "I'll walk you to your car."

~

After Donna left, the four sat in Ethan's car and discussed the next steps. Caitlyn told them everything she'd learned earlier in the day. That William Webber was the major player and was feeding on John Graves's desire for his company to succeed, at any cost. And that it was William Webber who murdered and buried the girl.

"John Graves is so passionate about protecting and supplying the country's energy needs that he was blind to what Mr. Webber was doing," Caitlyn said.

"Where do you think they'd go?" Ethan asked.

"If they realized the power was out here, maybe to Mr. Webber's house?"

"Do you know where that is?" Ethan asked.

"No. Or they might have gone to the office to get rid of any damaging evidence," she said.

Joe leaned forward between the seats and said, "Caitlyn, you realize that since you could recognize them and know what they've done, they wouldn't be able to let you live."

She shivered.

"Yes. That was implied."

"I think they're at the office, as Caitlyn mentioned, and figuring out how to get rid of her body," Tara added. "Sorry to be blunt, Caitlyn, but those are the facts."

"Let's head over to the SafeGrid office and if they're not there, we'll find out where Webber lives. Tara, drive Caitlyn's car into town and leave it in the sheriff's parking lot. We'll meet you there," Ethan instructed.

"Will do," Tara said.

Caitlyn handed Tara her keys.

~

They met up in the sheriff's parking lot and the two vehicles headed to the SafeGrid building.

"This is it," Caitlyn said. "Drive around back."

When Joe and Tara pulled in next to them, they surveyed the parking lot. Three cars were parked close together at the far end of the lot.

"What's the layout?" Ethan asked.

Caitlyn explained how the building was laid out.

"I recognize those two cars," she said as she pointed to William Webber's black Maserati and John Graves's silver Lexus. "The other car, a light-colored Toyota Camry, looks familiar, but I can't place it."

"If someone else is with them it could complicate matters," Ethan said. "Tara, check the front entrance."

Tara came back and reported the front entrance was blocked.

They were not surprised that the back door was locked. Caitlyn reached into her pocket and pulled out a key ring.

"Try one of these," she said as she handed him the ring.

"Where did you get that?" Ethan asked.

"When we searched the house for my purse and coat, I came upon this bunch of keys and thought if they had taken my car, maybe there would be a car in the garage I could use."

Ethan took the ring, checked the keys against the size of the lock, chose one that might work and inserted it. The key fit; the lock turned. He handed the ring back to Caitlyn.

They entered the reception area; he motioned for her to stay put. She walked over to the corner of the room, alert to escape routes. John Graves's office was dark, but a light was visible under the boardroom door.

Joe and Tara entered the room with weapons in hand. Ethan followed and identified himself.

Caitlyn couldn't stand to be left out, so she followed, and when she entered the room she was shocked by what she saw. The table was strewn with papers and money. Three people, two men and a woman, were stuffing briefcases. William Webber's eyes resembled those of a caged animal. He reached into his briefcase, but Ethan caught his arm and pulled it back, stating, "I wouldn't do that if I were you."

Recognizing the third person, Caitlyn asked in disbelief, "Tricia, what are you doing here?"

Tricia stopped, a look of resignation on her face.

"I'm sorry, Caitlyn. I didn't want you to find out. Bill's my brother. I suspected he was into something, and when he came to the house tonight and told me what he'd done, I *had* to help him. I thought if I helped him through this, we'd have time to work out a plea bargain. He's the only family I have."

"Do you know what kind of operation they were running? Do you know that he killed an innocent sixteen-year-old girl?" Caitlyn asked, voice rising to near hysteria.

"I did not. Not until tonight. He said if I'd help clean out the office, he'd turn himself in."

"And you believed him?" Caitlyn stated with disgust. "I hope you all go to jail."

She walked out of the room.

~ FORTY-TWO~

"Thanks for coming," Caitlyn said. "Why do you think Dr. Anderson wants to see me?"

"I guess we'll find out when we get there," Ethan replied.

Caitlyn was silent as she thought about the scenarios.

"Dr. Anderson wouldn't have asked me to come to Richmond if it wasn't important. I'm afraid there's some bad news. Maybe she wants to explain why there's no hope of identifying the remains."

Caitlyn helped Ethan navigate the streets of Richmond and showed him where to park. With a comforting arm around her shoulder they walked towards the medical examiner's office where they signed in and waited for the receptionist to give them guest lanyards.

"Dr. Anderson will be with you shortly," the receptionist said with a smile. "You can have a seat over there."

Caitlyn thought about her first visit to this building and how the smell of death had permeated the air. It was an odor she'd never get used to. It seemed a lifetime ago when she sat in this same spot with adrenalin pumping through her system as she developed marketing ideas for the SafeGrid account and the anticipation of solving a cold case. Neither had turned out as she'd hoped. While she sat, hands clasped on her lap, Ethan walked around, noting the exits and entrances—always a policeman.

"Caitlyn?" Dr. Anderson's voice brought her out of her reverie.

"Yes," she responded. "I hope you don't mind if my friend Ethan accompanies me."

"Not at all," Dr. Anderson replied.

"We're wondering why you wanted to see me. Is there a problem?" Caitlyn asked, twisting her hands.

"There's no problem. Come to my office. There's someone who wants to see you."

Caitlyn was confused. She didn't know of anyone who would want to see her.

Dr. Anderson reached her office and held the door so Caitlyn and Ethan could enter. A couple sat on the couch, but the man rose as they entered. Caitlyn recognized him. Senator Herbert Wright. Her stomach tensed. She knew what his presence meant. They'd identified the remains. Her suspicions about Cassie and Chloe were correct.

"Caitlyn, this is Senator Wright and his wife Cora."

Caitlyn stepped forward.

"It's nice to see you again Senator Wright, and nice to meet you, Mrs. Wright."

Ethan did the same and turned to Dr. Anderson.

"I didn't tell her. I thought it would be better coming from you."

Caitlyn looked from Ethan to Dr. Anderson, then at the Wrights.

"What's going on?" she asked, confused.

"Please sit and I'll explain," Dr. Anderson said. "Mrs. Wright sent her daughter's hairbrush to the FBI lab in Quantico. The DNA was run and was compared to the bone fragments. It was a match. The victim is Chloe Wright, aka Cassie White. The facial reconstruction confirmed the findings. The Wrights are here today to claim her remains. I told them of your interest in her case, and how you worked to identify her and catch the killer . . ." she hesitated, and then yielded the floor to Senator Wright.

Caitlyn approached the Wrights. "I'm so sorry for your loss. I didn't know who the girl was, and whoever she turned out to be I knew she was someone's daughter. After meeting you, Senator Wright, and learning about her passion for saving the environment, I didn't want it to be Chloe. We wanted to find her. Alive."

"We know," Senator Wright replied, a tear forming in the corner of his eye. "Dr. Anderson told us how concerned you were and how hard you worked to identify her. Cora and I thank you for your caring and diligence in finding Chloe. It was not the outcome any of us wanted. And although we'd encouraged her interest in saving the environment, we didn't realize the depth of her passion and to where that passion would lead."

"I'll never forgive myself for not stopping her," Cora stated.

"What do you mean?" Caitlyn asked.

"The day she left, her backpack was unusually full. I started to say something, and then the phone rang. I got involved in a conversation and Chloe waved goodbye. I didn't know that she'd planned to leave with the environmental group, but I should have expected something was up. Instead I got involved in planning a luncheon."

"As you know, we hired a private investigator," Senator Wright said, "Deep in our hearts we knew she was gone, but there's always a ray of hope and that hope was reignited when the ransom note arrived."

With tears in her eyes, Caitlyn sat next to Cora Wright.

"Chloe sounds like she was a wonderful girl and passionate about life. I wish I could have known her, but there are people in Ingram Bay who did get to know her. Their names are Bud and Lilla Higley. They took her in, fed her, and tried to keep her safe."

"Thank you," Senator Wright said. "We'll contact them, but now it's time to take Chloe's remains back to West Virginia. We have a funeral to plan."

"Before you go, Senator, we have something to give you," Ethan said. He walked over to Caitlyn and put something in her hand.

She smiled, closed her eyes, and held onto it a minute before giving it to Chloe's mother.

"My dog, Summit, found this bracelet. I admit I didn't want to let it go to be tested. It was my special connection to her."

Cora Wright held the bracelet and said, "Thank you."

The senator reached into his pocket and pulled out an envelope. "You cared about our girl and identified her killer. Dr. Anderson mentioned you have your own business. Cora and I hope this will help."

Caitlyn opened the envelope and pulled out a check.

"I can't take this," she said

Cora raised her hand. "Please. It will help us heal knowing that we've helped someone who cared about our precious daughter."

With that said, the senator and Mrs. Wright rose, nodded to Caitlyn and Ethan, and left the office with Dr. Anderson.

Caitlyn remained on the couch, stunned. Ethan joined her and placed his head next to hers, holding her tight as she broke down in sobs. The stress of the last week was finding a release.

She took the handkerchief he offered, wiped her eyes and then blew her nose.

"I can't accept this," she stated. "Twenty thousand dollars. It's crazy."

"If you don't, they'll be hurt," Ethan said, rubbing her back. "I've seen these types of situations before. The victim's parents feel helpless. Helping someone else is an important part of the healing process. The senator can afford it. Now, it's time we head back to Ingram Bay."

~

Four blocks away, Bud and Lilla Higley sat in the oncologist's office. Lilla fiddled with her cane while Bud walked around the waiting room and tried not to look at the other patients, also waiting to learn their fate. Lilla had finished her course of chemo, had had blood tests, and now the doctor would tell them whether all that she'd gone through had done its job. Or not. Memories of their life together flooded through his mind—the good times and the bad. They had weathered them all, because they were a team. Had been since high school. He couldn't imagine life without her, and this office, with its medicinal smells, brought that image way too clear. He looked over at his wife. She was still as pretty as the day they met, and still sharp. She was his best friend.

A nurse opened the door to the hallway that held the exam rooms and called Lilla's name. Bud's stomach tensed. This was it. Would they get a reprieve or was more treatment needed that would further weaken her immune system?

Lilla got up and motioned for him to follow.

~ FORTY-THREE ~

Ethan sat in the same conference room where he'd sat less than two weeks ago. He'd met the challenge and successfully completed the job. He'd proved himself. What now? Had he kidded himself thinking he'd work out of Quantico? Rod said the bureau needed experienced *field* agents. His goal of developing a closer relationship with Caitlyn dissipated.

Chin up. I have a report to give.

Special Agent Jensen entered the room. He placed a folder on the table.

Ethan waited in silence.

"I've read through the reports. The ones that Joe Wheeler and Tara Jones provided, and the report you filed."

Ethan's stomach clenched.

Did I leave something out?

"I have a few questions. Just for clarification," Special Agent Jensen stated.

"Yes, sir. Happy to answer anything I can."

"How did you figure out the ransom note?"

"That stymied us for a while. When we arrested the Brown brothers, the younger one, Henry, mentioned something about money. Working with them I'd noticed Henry wasn't as mentally slow as he appeared. He resented being under his brother's control and I noticed his temper was coming to a boil. At some point he'd have to find a release, and when he mentioned 'money,' I figured that would be a way for him to get free of his brother. When the environmental protesters were in town, we learned the brothers taunted them. Henry got into the habit of following them, and the day Chloe explored on her own he followed her. Unfortunately, she discovered the mine when William Webber was doing an inspection. According to Henry, Chloe and Webber had a heated discussion and then he witnessed Webber lose his temper and hit Chloe. When he couldn't revive her, he removed the body. Henry found Chloe's bag and took the money, but he didn't look at her ID until recently. I'm sure he didn't know her father was a senator. No one inquired about a missing person, so he thought he was in the clear. Then Henry got fed up with his brother, so he had the idea of sending a ransom note, but he didn't know how to follow up. If Henry hadn't sent the ransom note, and Caitlyn Jamison hadn't become involved in solving the cold case, the missing girl, the munitions and firearm sales, desecration of an Indian burial site, and the uranium mine wouldn't have come out. The ransom note and the discovery of the remains started a series of investigations, which then solved the murder of Chloe Wright. The brothers have been charged accordingly."

"The mine. How did they get that done without drawing attention?"

"They didn't. When Vince Russell explored property to purchase, he came upon an abandoned mine shaft. He mentioned it to William Webber, who told John Graves. John knew about the amount of uranium in Virginia and the legislative battles over mining rights through the years. Because of his concern about protecting U.S. energy sources into the future, this was great news. They purchased the property and hired the Brown brothers to start shoring up the mineshaft. In the meantime, Webber and Graves would lobby the legislature to lift the moratorium. When the moratorium was lifted, they'd be in a position to start production. A clever plan if it wasn't so risky," Ethan explained.

Special Agent Jensen nodded. "Clever indeed. I'm glad we were able to shut it down before it became operational, though I doubt the state would have lifted the moratorium. It's unfortunate that it cost Chloe Wright her life in order to bring these illegal activities out in the open."

"Caitlyn Jamison played a pivotal role in that investigation," Ethan said. "Her perseverance in solving the cold case was instrumental in our realizing that the body buried in the conservation easement was Chloe Wright. She also suspected that the Brown brothers were behind much of what was going on in the area."

"Your friend does good detective work," Special Agent Jensen said.

"The other vital piece of information that came from our interviews with the Brown brothers is that William Webber had several financial deals going. One of those was shipping illegal firearms to various locations around the country. That charge has been added. He'll be in prison for a very long time. As for John Graves, along with the mining violation, he's been charged with illegal shipment of firearms. His mistake was giving too much control of the company to William Webber."

Special Agent Jensen closed the file and cleared his throat.

"Ethan, we're impressed. You solved the kidnapping case, though it was not the outcome any of us desired. You found the missing agents, and shut down the illegal activity the bureau had been tracking."

"Sir," Ethan said. "What about Joe and Tara?"

Special Agent Jensen smiled. "We've given them a week's vacation. Joe's on Tangier Island with his parents, and Tara has gone home to Michigan."

"I'm glad to hear that. According to marine biologist Chad Owens, Mr. Wheeler was very concerned about his son."

Special Agent Jensen cleared his throat.

"There's another reason I asked you here today."

"Yes?" Ethan responded, sitting up and ready for whatever was to come.

"We want to offer you a job."

Ethan sat back, confused.

"I thought I had a job."

Special Agent Jensen laughed.

"This is a different job. We've created a new position, Law Enforcement Liaison Officer for the State of Virginia."

Ethan nodded, waiting to learn more.

"That officer will serve as an information conduit between local, state, federal, and military police in the state and work special assignments, like cold cases, large theft cases, and terrorist threats. The office will be based at Quantico, but will require travel to various locations within the state depending on the need. We hope you will accept this position."

Stunned, Ethan was at a loss for words.

"It sounds like an amazing opportunity."

"It is," Special Agent Jensen stated. "The position requires exceptional skill, determination and drive. You have those qualities."

"Then I accept."

Special Agent Jensen stood, as did Ethan. They shook hands sealing the deal.

"I'll call you later and tell you when to report. You didn't think you'd get time off, did you?"

Ethan laughed.

"No sir. I did not."

~ FORTY-FOUR ~

The Chesapeake's waters were calm; the town of Ingram Bay was at peace. At least that is how Caitlyn viewed it as she sat on her parents' patio on this warm April evening. She'd just received a call from Lilla Higley saying she'd been cleared by the doctor and didn't need another checkup for six months. The Wrights had contacted the Higley's and had invited them to dinner in Washington.

Chad Owens reported the mysterious dead zone resulted from a leak in a World War II ordnance the Brown brothers had tried, but failed, to dredge up. The scientists at Stony Brook University had made the determination and contacted the Navy.

At the same time Caitlyn received an email from The Bay Foundation announcing the new date for its annual meeting, and that she'd receive revised data soon. The foundation had additional work if she had the time. She readily accepted.

William Webber was arrested for Chloe's murder, the sale of illegal firearms, and other charges. He and John Graves were under indictment for mining uranium without a permit as well as their involvement with shipping of firearms. Tricia Reilly was keeping a low profile in the community.

Before being taken into custody by the state police for accepting bribes, Sheriff Goodall had assisted Ethan in pressing charges against his nephews—retrieving World War II ordnance, and disturbing an Indian burial ground. Henry James's role in sending a ransom note was one of the reasons the brothers were in the hands of the federal government.

Caitlyn's thoughts went to her relationship with Ethan. Her father's declining health made it important that she stay in Virginia. She couldn't ask her parents to move again. The muscle around her heart tightened making it hard to breathe. Plans of starting a life together now seemed impossible. If the FBI needed field agents, Ethan could be sent anywhere. He'd probably be assigned to a regional office in Manhattan or San Francisco. A tear formed at the corner of her eye. She discretely wiped it away.

~

Ethan stepped out onto the patio. She hadn't heard him arrive.

"What's the matter?" he asked, noting her sad expression. "Are you having closed case syndrome?"

"Maybe. What's closed case syndrome?" she asked, wiping away another tear.

"It's when your body doesn't know what to do with the adrenalin it produced while working a case. When the case is solved, the body can't adjust to the feeling of relief and get back to normalcy fast enough. Creates an emotional imbalance," he explained. "At least that's my interpretation."

She didn't know how to explain her tears. Instead she asked, "Has Vince Russell named his assailant? I'm sure he knew, but feared retaliation."

"He finally admitted to the state police it was the Brown brothers who attacked him, on William Webber's instructions. As he mentioned to us, it was a warning. Since Vince was already on the outs with his friend William Webber, he didn't want to burn more bridges by accusing the sheriff's nephews."

"That's no surprise," she stated, and hesitated, reluctant to ask the next question.

"How did your meeting at Quantico go?"

"It went well. The agent in charge asked several questions that I successfully answered. I think they like me," he chuckled.

She turned to him.

"I've been trying to figure out how we can live closer, but with Dad's health, I can't move away, and you'll probably be assigned to one of the large regional offices."

There. She said it. He had to respond. She braced herself. She wanted their relationship to be more, but their jobs and her family responsibilities now made it impossible. She took a deep breath, afraid to look at Ethan because he would see her anxiety.

~

"Are you two enjoying this beautiful evening?" Herb Jamison said as he came through the French doors onto the patio. He approached Caitlyn, leaned down and gave her a hug, oblivious to the tension.

"Cate, why don't you move down here? It's more peaceful than the DC metropolitan area. How can you stand all that traffic? You have clients all over the U.S.; you can work from anywhere."

"I know, Dad, but a majority of my clients are in DC."

Ann joined them and asked, "What's going on?"

Caitlyn tried to smile, but her stomach was in knots. The all-important question was still on the table. Ethan had not responded, and wouldn't with her parents' there.

Ann broke the ice. "I have a surprise."

"Tell us," Caitlyn said.

Ann went into the house and returned holding a black cat.

"Mom, she's beautiful," Caitlyn exclaimed. "It is a 'she,' right?"

"Right. She's been hanging around the museum for several months. The volunteers have taken turns feeding her, and when it was my turn, she'd come right up and purr. I just couldn't stand it any longer. She needs a home. And now she has one," Ann said, giving Herb an appealing look.

Caitlyn rushed over and took the cat from her mother. The cat snuggled into Caitlyn's neck and purred even louder than before.

"For a feral she is awfully friendly."

"I don't think she's feral. I think someone dropped her off, which is a crime."

"I agree, it is, or should be," Caitlyn stated, and handed the cat back to her mother.

Ann turned to her husband.

"Can I keep her?"

"It appears I'm outvoted," he replied with a smile.

"What will you do with the reward money?" Ann asked.

"A bigger office?" her father suggested.

"A new car?" her mother asked.

"I've talked with the Ingram Bay school system superintendent and we are setting up the Chloe Wright Scholarship fund. The scholarships will be for students pursuing science careers. An additional stipend will go to those going into the environmental sciences. I learned a lot from Chloe. She wanted to make the world a better place and she did what she thought was right. We all should."

She glanced at Ethan, and then her parents.

"Excellent idea," he said as he gave her a big hug. "I'm very proud of you."

Her parents nodded their approval.

With the big announcement over, Ann turned to her husband.

"Herb, will you help me get some food out? We're hungry, and I want to get the cat settled in."

"Yeah, sure," Herb replied, though he didn't understand why she needed his help.

Caitlyn and Ethan laughed. Her dad didn't have a clue, but her mom understood.

"Before we were interrupted," Caitlyn began.

"I agree. You asked a question and I want to answer it."

At that moment Ethan's cell phone rang. He glanced at the number displayed.

"Sorry, have to take this," he said and headed into the house.

~

When Ethan returned to the patio, he found Caitlyn had moved and now sat in one of the lounge chairs. A sliver of moon had appeared. She looked so peaceful.

"Another crisis?" she asked.

Ethan pulled a chair over and sat down next to her.

"No. It was a call from my boss at the bureau."

Caitlyn sat up. This meant his job here was done and he'd be sent . . . to where?

"When do you leave?" she asked, her heart hurting.

"Soon."

Her face fell. This was it. This was the answer.

"They offered me a new position. Law Enforcement Liaison Officer for the State of Virginia. I'll work out of Quantico."

All the anxiety she had tortured herself with, thinking about how their relationship could continue, suddenly dissipated. Her emotions were in turmoil at the sudden turn of events.

"I want to be closer to you. What do you say? Can we make this work?" he asked.

She turned to Ethan and gave him a hug.

"And that's not all," he said.

She sat back, tipped her head, and waited for the next surprise.

"The call was about my first assignment. It sounds like a challenging investigation. Are you up for it?"

Caitlyn grinned, "You bet!"

Author's Note and Acknowledgements

A neighbor once asked, "Is the next book always easier?" The answer was, "no." I like to tackle a new challenge with each book, and *The Death of Cassie White* was particularly challenging. There were so many things going on with so many details to keep straight. I hope I got it right.

When the characters are developed, they want a say in how the plot progresses. Inevitably, the characters will change what the author originally intended, and that has happened with each of the Caitlyn Jamison mysteries. It is not always the main character that alters the story, but a minor one who demands a bigger role. The author's job is to manage the characters and come up with a compromise.

In *The Death of Cassie White*, I wanted Caitlyn to solve a cold case. The story began with the uncovering of skeletal remains, but I hadn't thought that through any further. As the story progressed, the skeletal remains became a character and the story turned into one of passion for a cause and trying to bring about change.

With characters vying for control, and the author striving to hold the story together, there is vital need for other eyes on the text. Consequently I can't thank enough my friends who offered to be first readers: Mike Hammer, Ray Maki, Elizabeth Spragins, Cheryl Wicks, and Andrea Zimmermann. I also appreciate the encouragement and helpful suggestions that the Central Rappahannock Regional Library's Fiction Critique Group and Fredericksburg's Old Town Sleuths provided.

I am indebted to the Rappahannock Art League in Kilmarnock, Virginia, for connecting me with their talented photographers. Finding the right photo for my cover was the most difficult choice, because of all the wonderful photos that were shared. I chose Laura Dent's photo of the *Elva C.,* a restored boat now residing at the Reedville Fisherman's Museum in Reedville, Virginia. I thank Laura for her patience while I decided on just the right photo. The photo of *Elva C* is also available in note cards. When the photo needed pixel adjustment, Laura introduced me to Charles Lawson who then worked his magic, enlarging the pixels to make a perfect book cover.

Readers often ask where I get my ideas. The answer is from everywhere. When one of my high school classmates, Bill Meeker, read *Fatal Dose*, he wrote and told me about the large uranium deposit under the Coles Hill Farm in Pittsylvania County, Virginia. In 1982 the Virginia legislature enacted a statewide ban on uranium mining. This ban has been challenged several times since, and again recently. I filed his comment away, and as I got into the story, I remembered it, and the issue seemed to fit.

I am blessed with a loving and supportive family. Through their *Gratitude for Wellness Center* in Willsboro, New York, Melissa and Rebecca make sure my books are available to my Adirondack readers. Brennen and Jessica keep me supplied with my favorite Glastonbury, Connecticut, *Daybreak Coffee.* And I couldn't accomplish this work without the support of my husband, Ray. He helps keep the house running, is my IT support, and at the end of a long writing/editing day, has a glass of wine ready.

Made in the USA
Middletown, DE
18 June 2022